POLICE
UNDERCOVER

POLICE UNDERCOVER

The True Story of The Biker, The Mafia & The Mountie

by Mark G. Murphy
RCMP (Ret.)

distributed to the book trade by
Hushion House, Toronto

Avalon House Publishing Ltd.

Printed in Canada

Cataloguing in Publication Data

Murphy, Mark G., 1943–
        Police undercover: the true story of the biker, the mafia & the mountie

        ISBN 0-9627562-6-1

        1. Murphy, Mark G., 1943– 2. Undercover operations--Canada. Mafia--Canada. 4. Organized crime--Canada. 5. Royal Canadian Mounted Police--Biography. 5. Kirby, Cecil. 6. Volpe, Paul, 1927-1983.

HV7911.M86A3 1998   363.2'32'092   C98-900775-8

distributed by:
Hushion House Publishing Ltd.
36 Northline Rd.
Toronto, ON M4B 3E2
Orders:
        1-800-387-0141 ON & QC
        1-800-387-0172 Canada
        1-800-805-1083 US
Fax:
        1-416-285-1777

This book is dedicated to those in the RCMP who are honest, hard-working members, to those who answer the gun calls, family disputes, mental patients, and major criminal offences. I have, and I'm certain the general public has, the utmost respect and admiration for a job well done. You have earned the right to be considered part of one of the finest police forces in the world.

"The galleries are full of critics. They play no ball. They fight no fights. They make no mistakes because they attempt nothing. Down in the arena are the doers. They make many mistakes because they attempt many things."

"Ford forgot to put a reverse gear on his first automobile, and then went on to revolutionize the automobile industry with his model T."

"The man who makes no mistakes lacks boldness and the spirit of adventure. He never tries anything new. He is a brake on the wheels of progress."

- Graham, Texas, Rotary

Contents

Author's Note

I wrote this book out of dedication and respect for the RCMP. No serving member ever loved the Force more than I did. Although at times this may seem a contradiction to the reader, my main motive in writing about these events is to point out some of the inequities that exist within the Force. If this book serves to improve the support given to investigating officers, and by some small measure the quality of police work performed within the RCMP, then it was not written in vain.

1

Meeting A Hit Man

S itting in my surveillance vehicle, a loaded shotgun across my lap and a bullet-proof vest hugging my chest, I watched as a blue sedan circled the parking lot and slowly approached our undercover agent. There were four men in the car—three more than expected.

It began to look as though the Mafia was doing a take-down of their own. I had told our agent to drop to the deck if anything went wrong. Reaching for the door handle, ready to hit the pavement, I couldn't believe how a simple phone-call had led to these increasingly dangerous encounters between the biker, the Mafia, and the Mountie.

The 10th of November, 1980, began as a regular day. The shrill sound of the phone at 12:55 PM was to change all that. The NCIS (National Crime Intelligence Section) of the RCMP (Royal Canadian Mounted Police), located on the 8th floor of the RCMP Headquarters at 225 Jarvis Street in Toronto, routinely receives calls and visits from citizens feeling that organized crime somehow plays an important part in their lives. Most of the callers and walk-in visitors are referred to the RCMP by their professional counterparts, either Metro (Metro Toronto Police; recently changed to Toronto Police) or the OPP (Ontario Provincial Police). To be charitable, let's just say the NCIS has a wide variety of calls and visitors of questionable nature, whom they, by reciprocal agreement, refer back to Metro or the OPP. This call was different.

Over the lunch hour the phone rang. There were only a couple of people in the office and I answered the phone. The conversation went as follows:

(M.M.: Cpl. Mark Murphy; U.M.: unknown male, later identified as Cecil Kirby)

M.M.:   NCIS, Murphy.

U.M.:   Yeah, is the Staff Sergeant in charge there, please?

M.M.:   No, I'm sorry, not at the moment. Can I help you?

U.M.:   Well, I want to speak to the man in charge.

M.M.:   He's out of the office at the moment. (Recognizing a tone of urgency, I suspected this guy had something to offer.) If there is something you wish to discuss, I'd be happy to help you. In all probability, the boss would ask me to speak to you anyway.

U.M.:   Yeah, O.K. Well, I'm not going to tell you my name, but I'd like to meet you.

M.M.:   Well, I'd like to have some idea of what you want to talk about.

U.M.:   Yeah, O.K. Well, myself, my girlfriend and a friend of mine are charged with a break, entry and theft into my friend's neighbour's house. Now, we were caught cold turkey because York Regional had us under surveillance at the time. I'm looking to work a deal and I was wondering if you could help me.

M.M.:   If there were exceptional circumstances and you had something really worthwhile to offer, maybe I could speak to the coppers involved and to the Crown and go from there. What are we talking about here?

U.M.:   Well, I'm charged with robbery, extortion, mischief and assault causing bodily harm, but they're all bullshit charges. What happened on that was, me and my girlfriend were living common-law and we got into a fight and decided to split up. So, I took some of the furniture, which I bought to begin with, and she called the police and the bastards charged me on a bullshit charge. My girlfriend and I are back together again so she'll be dropping the charges. It's the break, entry and theft that I'm worried about. They want to get me really bad and they are looking for two years.

M.M.:   O.K., what kind of information are we looking at? Do you have any ties or connection to organized crime, because that's our main interest?

U.M.:   Well, to be honest with you, I'm an ex-Satan's Choice biker. I was a biker for seven years, but I got out. I can get you some guns.

M.M.:   Well, to be up front with you, I can get all the guns I want. In fact, I can have a Sherman Tank on your front lawn tomorrow morning if you want it. Guns aren't of too much interest to me.

U.M.:   I have some information on some old murders. In fact, do you know Terry Hall from OPP and Ron Tavenor, Metro Police, that work on the bike gangs?

M.M.:   Yes, I do.

U.M.:   Well, I went to them to try and work a deal and they really tried to jerk me around. I gave them some information on a murder. I told them who did it and that the guy who did it was shot and still had a bullet inside him. They picked the guy up and got him for the murder. I gave them that information because I was in court for an assault charge. They said they would help me, but they went and told the Crown I was a biker, and that they were asking for heavy time. They even testified against me. When I saw I'd been double-crossed I changed my plea to not guilty, beat the charge, and walked away. I can't trust them, and that's why I'm coming to you.

M.M.:   O.K. Well, listen, I'm very interested in talking to you, but you understand we have to be a little bit careful. You don't want to tell me your name?

U.M.:   No, I won't tell you my name, but you got nothing to worry about. I want you to come alone and don't be wired (no hidden tape recorder).

M.M.:   I'll take the chance. Where do you want to meet?

U.M.:   How about the Casa Loma? (An old castle and well-known Toronto landmark)

M.M.:   O.K., I'll meet you there at 1:30 PM.

U.M.:   O.K., come alone and no wires.

M.M.:   What are you driving?

U.M.:   A green Chev. I'll watch for you.

M.M.:   O.K., 1:30 PM at the Casa Loma.

By the time the conversation was finished, my remaining fellow officers had left the office. I tried in vain to raise another member for back-up. The only other person in the office was the secretary, Marlene Jones, whom I held in very high esteem. I gave her the details of the planned meeting and asked that she stand by the radio. I said I would call back a licence plate number of the unknown male's vehicle before we conversed.

It was exactly 1:30 PM when I pulled into the parking lot at the Casa Loma. The unknown male was circling the lot looking for the person he had arranged to meet. When we saw each other, there was only a slight nod of acknowledgement. We went to a remote area of the parking lot to find a place to talk. In the meantime, I held the police microphone on the seat of the police car, to prevent being seen, and called in Ontario licence plate number PKK-109 to Marlene Jones, my only conceivable back-up.

When the unknown male stepped out of the 1973 green Chevrolet, he didn't give the appearance of being a biker. What's more, he didn't even look like the stereotypical criminal. He stood 5'-10" tall, had light blond hair and a moustache, and was clean-cut, dressed in a dress shirt, brown corduroy jacket and blue jeans. Extremely well-built, with arms like tree stumps, he presented an extraordinarily clean appearance, like an applicant for a new job. Little did I realize at that point in time that he was to be an applicant for a very dangerous and special job, that of an undercover agent for the RCMP.

Dealing with people over the course of many years in situations such as this, one develops a sort of a sixth sense, an ability to read personalities and intentions quickly. Body language speaks volumes if one knows what to look for. Despite the casual appearance of a law-abiding citizen, I noticed he was always glancing around, surveying his surroundings. This is a classic trait of a criminal, particularly one involved in organized crime. But I also detected an element of sincerity and good faith, and began to feel a little more comfortable about the lack of back-up support.

When this unknown male sat in the police car, he looked at me with piercing blue eyes and stated that his name was Cecil Kirby. He grinned, and we carried on with small talk for a few moments. Let me say that no matter what you read in the pages that follow, Cecil Kirby is a very personable and likeable man. I later learned the details of his youth that led him into crime—a broken home, the lack of education and opportunity, the usual conditions that cause young people like Cecil Kirby to fall through the tears in our social fabric. Cecil left school at an early age to work with his father. Although not formally educated, he was intelligent, street-wise, and had a phenomenal memory which was later demonstrated by his ability to recall in detail something that had taken place years before. He was also generous, the kind of person who would literally give you the shirt off his back if he liked you. I would later see his other side: the fierce and intense violence of a temper that was, although never directed at me, uncontrollable at times; the egotism and love of attention that drove him to finish first, no matter what the challenge.

At our initial meeting I discovered that Kirby might be an experienced criminal with a great potential as an informant, although I had no idea at the time how valuable he would become. Yet during his time as an informer, he would also prove to be quite unpredictable, and at times very difficult to control. In spite of Kirby's volatile personality, he would end up providing the police with phenomenal amounts of information on organized crime, and investigators have yet to find errors in the details he has supplied. It was not Kirby's nature to be a trusting soul, yet from the moment we shook hands on that fateful day a trust and friendship were initiated that would stand the tests of time and play an integral part in the events that followed.

During our first conversation in person, Kirby explained the circumstances of the break, entry and theft charges. He stated that he did not expect to walk on the charge, and was willing to plead guilty. The only problem was that Hall and Tavenor had earlier approached the Crown and were insisting on a two-year sentence; Kirby was looking for a two-year suspended sentence for himself and his two associates. Kirby pointed out that the Crown Attorney handling the case was Steven Leggett, and that Sergeant Robert Silverton, 31 Metro Police Division, was the police officer in charge. Kirby reiterated that if we could help him he would be willing to hand over some stolen guns, maybe a few machine guns, and provide information regarding old, unsolved murders. I again told him I had little interest in stolen guns (this being a common bargaining tool among criminals and police when the criminals are looking for help), since I could easily obtain stolen guns, machine guns, AR-15's, and any other type of weapon. I told Kirby I was interested in the information on old murders, but my main focus and that of the NCIS was organized crime. I mentioned that if Metro Police were handling the charges, they would be interested in crimes such as armed robberies, murders, major break-and-entries, and other criminal code offenses. I told Kirby I would find out the circumstances of his charges. We arranged to meet again on November 13, 1980.

There was something about Kirby that made me eager to pursue his case. When I arrived back at my office on Jarvis Street, I spoke with Constables Mike Atkinson and Paul

Lennerton, two members of NCIS assigned to liaison with
Metro and the OPP. Metro and the OPP had formed a JFO
(Joint Forces Organization) to gather intelligence on biker
gangs operating in Ontario. Atkinson quickly produced a
large binder containing a dossier on known bikers. Listed
under the caption "Satan's Choice", along with a photograph,
was the individual that I had just met, one Cecil Murray Kirby.

A quick check also revealed that Kirby was well known to
the police in a wide variety of circumstances. Kirby was
known as Cecil Murray Archie Kirby, fingerprint section
#35B777A, born on August 17, 1951. The following is a run-
down of his criminal record from 1969 to 1980. It also includes
charges that were eventually withdrawn:

DATE	PLACE	CHARGE	DISPOSITION
09 Dec. 69	Toronto	Unlawfully in dwelling house	30 days
		Assault causing bodily harm	$50/10 days
10 Oct. 70	Toronto	Illegal poss. of narcotics	$250/30 days
31 May 70	Toronto	Break, entry & theft	All withdrawn
		Possn. stolen property	
		Possession of weapon	
		Dangerous to public peace	
		Indecent assault on female	
04 Jun. 71	Toronto	Possession of weapon	No disposition
23 Sep. 71	Toronto	Wounding	Withdrawn
17 Nov. 71	Mississauga	Dangerous driving	Withdrawn
21 Dec. 71	Collingw'd	Break, entry, & theft	Withdrawn
		Mischief	Sentence suspended

30 Dec. 71	Toronto	Possession of stolen property	Dismissed
		Break, entry & theft	6 months on theft charge
23 Nov. 72	Richm'dhill	Break, entry & theft	Withdrawn
15 Dec. 73	Toronto	Assault causing bodily harm	50 days
22 Jun. 76	Toronto	Wounding	Withdrawn
15 May 78	Toronto	Assault causing bodily harm	Withdrawn
03 Jan. 79	Toronto	Threatening (3 charges) Assault (4 charges)	Withdrawn
22 May 80	Toronto	Attempt to obstruct justice	Acquitted
23 Sep. 79	Toronto	Break, entry & theft	Withdrawn
29 Oct. 80	Newmarket	Robbery, extortion, mischief, Assault causing bodily harm	Withdrawn

Given this history, it wasn't difficult to imagine the kind of individual Cecil Kirby was; nor was it difficult to comprehend his potential as an informant. I could appreciate why Hall and Tavenor wanted him so badly. Now I was interested.

At our next meeting just 3 days later, I was far better prepared to deal with Kirby. Now that we were able to establish that he was not just a kook, but was heavily involved in crime and tied in with the notorious Satan's Choice Motorcycle Gang. Our second meeting took place at Casa Loma, under much the same conditions as the first. Kirby was driving a different vehicle, a new Chevrolet Caprice Classic .

During this meeting Kirby supplied information about a murder in Newmarket; the news that a prominent Toronto lawyer (who had recently been appointed a judge) and his wife were cocaine freaks; and information on a bombing involving an individual who owned a prominent disco on Bloor Street and wanted it bombed for insurance purposes (Kirby told me this individual stated he could do the bombing himself, because he had experience with the Palestine Liberation Army as a mercenary and knew how to make bombs).

Kirby's next statement was of particular interest. He said that his information was that Chuck Yanover, known enforcer for Toronto Mob Boss Paul Volpe, had someone come from Europe to kill Ian Rosenberg. Rosenberg, also an enforcer for the Volpe Mob, was killed on April 22, 1977.

The execution of Ian Rosenberg and his common-law wife, Joan Lipson, was of utmost significance in affecting the direction of the investigation that was to follow. The moment Kirby mentioned the name Rosenberg, I reinforced his belief that Rosenberg probably knew too much, was in jail and the Mob was afraid he would talk. I told Kirby that I felt it was the Volpe organization that bailed Rosenberg out of jail for $50,000 one day and arranged his execution the next. The death of Rosenberg, and more significantly that of Joan Lipson, had a tremendous effect on Kirby's way of thinking. Rosenberg and Lipson were both shot in the head by an unknown assassin while sleeping in their newly acquired apartment in Toronto. Their five-year-old child had the horrifying task of finding the bodies and calling for help. Kirby, facing a term in jail while living in commonlaw with a woman, Linda Caldwell, and her young daughter, drew an uneasy parallel between his own situation and that of Rosenberg.

During our conversation Kirby mentioned that his main occupation was armed robbery. In fact two years earlier he had travelled to Vancouver to rob a guy involved in the fish industry who reportedly would be carrying $300,000 in cash on his person. Fortunately for this individual, Kirby had arrived one day too late. He intended to return in the fall and try again.

Kirby mentioned another name of particular interest. He stated that while in Vancouver he was met by Carlo Gallo, well known underling of the late mobster Joseph Gentile. Gallo took Kirby to his restaurant in Vancouver and told Kirby if he was successful in grabbing the $300,000, he would have to give Gallo two-thirds of the grab; Kirby could keep only one-third for himself.

Carlo Gallo was of extreme interest to me. I explained to Kirby that I knew Gallo. In fact about five years earlier, Gallo and Joe Gentile had arrived in Toronto to visit some heavy people connected with the Mob. While in Toronto, they stayed at the Holiday Inn on Dufferin Street, where Toronto RCMP Intelligence Squad kept them under surveillance. As it turned out, it was fortunate that I mentioned to Kirby that while in Toronto, Gallo and Gentile had visited the Commisso brothers at the Casa Commisso, 1275 Lawrence Avenue West, Toronto. Kirby looked at me with his unique kind of grin.

"Yeah, I know the Commisso brothers," he said. "In fact, I've done some work for them. It was Cosimo Commisso who had asked me to go to Vancouver."

I asked Kirby if it was the same Cosimo Commisso who owned the Casa Commisso on Lawrence Avenue.

"Yeah," Kirby replied, "I have his phone numbers for the Casa and his home."

Kirby supplied the phone numbers, and I told him I would check them out. If what he said was true, we were really in business.

This meeting had taken place in Kirby's Chevrolet. After some small talk I got out of the vehicle and prepared to leave. We had already arranged to meet at the Holiday Inn next to the City Hall in downtown Toronto on Monday, the 17th of November, for a proper debriefing. It was going to be difficult to meet and talk freely, with Kirby's fear of police surveillance and both of our fears of being seen by other criminals. I was standing outside the vehicle on the passenger side when I mentioned to Kirby that I would call him and make some final arrangements for the meeting on the 17th.

I was about to close the door when, as an afterthought, I leaned in the door and said to Kirby, "By the way, if you call me at the office and I'm not there, don't leave your own name. You never know who might be around the office. How about leaving another name. . . how about Jack Ryan?"

Kirby looked at me like a man who had just seen a ghost. His eyes were popping and his face went completely white. I knew I had touched a sensitive nerve, but I had no idea why. Talk about body language—in a few seconds he had told a whole story. He was visibly upset, so I got back in the vehicle and tried as delicately as I could to have Kirby explain his extraordinary reaction to the name of Jack Ryan. He was reluctant to elaborate. The only thing he did say was, "You people know quite a bit about me, don't you?" Not wanting him to think any differently at this point in time, I bluffed and said, "Yeah, I guess so." We shook hands and parted company. It was to be several months later at a Holiday Inn in Darien, Connecticut, just outside New York, at approximately 2:00 in the morning, that I was to learn the true reason why Kirby recoiled from the name Jack Ryan.

Policeman are trained to be composed, but when I arrived back at RCMP Headquarters in Toronto and confirmed that the phone numbers Kirby had in his possession were indeed those of Cosimo Commisso and the Casa Commisso, a huge banquet hall operated by the Commisso Family, I must be honest, I was excited. Since my arrival in Toronto in 1973, most of my efforts dealing with organized crime were concentrated on the Paul Volpe Group. As of then I had had little to do with the Commisso Family, nor did I know much about them.

2

Getting Acquainted With The Mob

The Metro Police Intelligence Unit was mostly responsible for investigating the Commisso Family. The Commissos were inevitably mentioned at every gathering of Intelligence Officers in the city of Toronto. It was obvious that a great deal of time and money was spent on the Commisso Organization, but little progress had been made in apprehending any of the family members who were strongly suspected of being involved in various criminal activities. Several Joint Forces Operations involving Metro Toronto Police Intelligence, Ontario Provincial Police, and the Royal Canadian Mounted Police Intelligence Unit had been launched against the Commissos, but with little or no success. At the time I wondered why.

It was generally felt among the rank-and-file officers involved in major investigations against organized crime families such as the Commissos that the police themselves were partly to blame. Politics, narrow-mindedness, and petty jealousies sometimes got in the way of good police work. On several occasions the investigations had been compromised by police officers "on the take" and by other police officers who just talked too much. Over the years there have been a number of officers dismissed from their various forces on charges of divulging information to criminals. When conducting a major operation against a target, there can be up to one hundred people involved directly or indirectly as support units. These people include transcribers, physical surveillance team members, technical surveillance team members, computer processors, analysts, senior police management, rookie police officers, Crown attorneys and judges. It is very difficult to convey the importance of security to such a large and diversified group. Many investigations have been compromised by honest coppers who perhaps have had too much to drink or who bragged to a girlfriend.

Over the years the Commisso Family and their activities have been highly publicized in newspapers, periodicals, and books such as *Mob Rule* and *Mafia Assassin*. My intention with this brief chapter is not to rehash this information, but to introduce the reader to the Commisso brothers most directly involved with this story, and relate my first encounter with one of them.

In 1980 three brothers comprised the leadership of the body of suspected criminals known to the police as the Commisso Family. The eldest of the three brothers was Cosimo Elia Commisso (Born: 2 Feb. 45) who lived at 477 Ellersie Avenue, North York, Toronto. The second oldest brother was Rocco Remo Commisso, (Born: 21 Jun. 46) who lived at 484 Ellerslie Avenue, North York, Toronto. The third brother was Michael Jimino Commisso, (Born: 2 Feb. 48) who also lived at 484 Ellerslie Avenue with his brother Remo and their mother. Although Cosimo was the oldest brother, there was a difference of opinion, especially among police circles, whether Cosimo or the second oldest brother, Remo, was the actual leader of the Family. That question has remained unanswered. The Commissos were considered members of a larger entity known as the Siderno Group, Italian criminals whose ancestors, or they themselves, directly immigrated to Canada in the 1950s from Siderno Marina in Calabria, Italy.

In the years that I had spent in Toronto, I had never had an opportunity to work directly on cases involving the Commisso

Family. I had often seen photographs of the Commissos, but had never seen them in person.

I believe it was May of 1979 that I was walking up the steps of the Court House at the Old City Hall, at Queen and Bay Streets in Toronto, when the huge oak doors swung open and an equally huge man of Italian descent emerged. He had large shoulders, like those of a professional boxer, and an enormous scar on his right cheek. His dark eyes darted about. There was no mistaking the identity of Rocco Remo Commisso. He was accompanied by Mr. Edward Greenspan, famous Toronto Criminal Defense lawyer.

Eddie Greenspan is one of the most talented defence lawyers in the country. Whenever a case was prepared against a suspected criminal, there would inevitably be some small crack in the prosecution's armour. Greenspan was always able to spot that crack and exploit it to his client's utmost advantage. On the other hand, Greenspan commanded respect, not only from his clients but from the prosecution and the police community as well. Greenspan had a touch of class as a defence lawyer—he pressed his advantage whenever possible, but he always acted as a professional and a gentleman. He didn't resort to underhanded tactics, nor did he try to embarrass the witness. In the months to follow, Greenspan would be instrumental as Defence Council for the Commissos, forcing the police and the prosecution to make certain that their case was air-tight.

Although the police community was aware that the Commisso Family was part of the organized crime scene in Toronto, they had no idea how extensive their criminal activities were. They were soon to find out.

3

The Politics Of
Negotiating A Deal

S gt. Norm Ross and I had arranged to meet Kirby
on November 17, 1980, at 2:00 PM at the Holiday
Inn on Elizabeth St., just behind the City Hall in downtown
Toronto. What we hadn't bargained for was that Kirby would
be under surveillance by Metro Police and the OPP on this
particular day. Ross and I had reserved room 1630 at the
Holiday Inn which, of course, was located on the 16th floor. I
had arranged with Kirby prior to the meeting that we would
meet on the fifth floor for his protection, and to make sure he
was not being followed.

While Norm Ross waited in the room upstairs, I hustled
down to the 5th floor at approximately five minutes before
two. It seemed like a long five minutes and it gave me more
time to think than I really needed. Here I was, standing in the
hallway of a downtown hotel waiting for an ex-Satan's Choice
biker with Mob connections, and I had no way of knowing
whether or not he could be trusted. What if he stepped off the
elevator with a gun? I decided to make the odds a little more
even, so I stepped over by a doorway, removed my snubnose
.38 from my belt and placed it in my coat pocket.

Several elevators stopped on the 5th floor prior to our
appointed time, but at precisely 2:00 PM the elevator doors
opened and out walked Cecil Kirby. There were several other

people on the elevator, but Kirby was the only one who got off on the 5th. I was to learn later that a member of the surveillance team was on the elevator but stayed on so he wouldn't get burned. Kirby and I got the next elevator and went to room 1630 where we met Norm Ross. Unknown to us, the surveillance team sat outside watching Kirby's vehicle for the next two hours and forty-one minutes. During our debriefing with Kirby, Ross and I were impressed with the knowledge this young man possessed. He talked about four murders that had taken place nine years earlier, large drug-dealing operations, and a stabbing. We recorded this information and after the meeting, forwarded the details of the homicides and stabbing to Metro Police, while the drug information was passed along to the RCMP Drug Section. Since our mission was to learn about organized crime, we had to be patient until Kirby started to mention things of real interest to us. He spoke of a $58,000 extortion in which Cosimo Commisso was involved; of a robbery set up by Cosimo Commisso, in which an individual was shot in the leg; of an intended hit of an individual in Vancouver, requested by Vancouver mobsters and to be organized by Cosimo Commisso; and finally of more details of the intended $300,000 robbery of the Herring Fishing Industry in Vancouver that was mentioned earlier.

The next meeting took place on November 26, 1980 at Casa Loma. While talking to Kirby, I noticed some vehicles go by that looked all too familiar. I suspected they were police surveillance vehicles, and was suspicious enough to record several licence plates. I could only hope that if we were under police surveillance and Kirby realized it, he didn't think I had double-crossed him. For whatever reason, Kirby became agitated as if suffering from acute paranoia. I began to feel most uncomfortable and terminated the meeting as soon as I could.

When I arrived back at our offices at 225 Jarvis St., Cst. Mike Atkinson was talking on the phone to Ron Tavenor from Project Rontario, the unit set up by Metro Toronto Police and the OPP to investigate bikers. This was the same Tavenor who had, according to Kirby, double-crossed him earlier on the assault charge. Tavenor was asking what member of NCIS had met with Kirby. Since Atkinson was acting as my backup at the office that day, he was compelled to tell Tavenor that it was Murphy. Tavenor wanted a meeting.

Atkinson, Cst. Paul Lennerton, his partner, and I made an immediate patrol to the Rontario office where we met Tavenor and four or five of his fellow officers. Although Kirby had specifically asked that I not tell Tavenor and Terry Hall that he was talking to me, and in fact had made an unveiled threat to come after me if I did, I really had no other choice after being spotted by Tavenor's surveillance. I briefed Tavenor and his associates on the information Kirby had supplied to date. I pointed out to Tavenor that I wouldn't interfere in any way with their project on Kirby, and emphatically requested that they not mention to Kirby that I had told them he was talking to the RCMP. Hall was not actually at the meeting, but Tavenor assured me that no mention would be made to Kirby and my safety would certainly not be jeopardized.

On the 28th of November Kirby called me to advise that there was a large quantity of drugs at an address in the East end of Toronto. That information was immediately passed on to Staff Sergeant Wayne Horrocks, RCMP Drug Section, Toronto. Horrocks and several Drug Section members conducted a raid on the address supplied, and came up with 40 pounds of Hash, 900 hits of LSD, some pornographic films, and a stolen stereo. Three persons were arrested and charged with trafficking in narcotics and various other crimes.

Over the next couple of weeks, Kirby continued to call and supply invaluable information on current things that were happening in Toronto. Under normal circumstances any one incident that Kirby had relayed to the police would have been more than sufficient to solidify a deal on a rather insignificant break, entry and theft, to which he was willing to plead guilty in return for a probation. I began to realize that the politics, narrow-mindedness, and petty jealousies mentioned earlier, and so prevalent in the OPP, Metro Police, and the RCMP, were quickly coming into play. These had affected major operations in the past, and it looked as though my dealings with Kirby were no exception. Unfortunately, when the police fight their petty battles on the inside, the criminal elements flourish and prosper on the outside. And the sad part of it is nobody seems to give a damn.

It was 11:00 PM on December 10, 1980, when Kirby called me at home and relayed information about two guys at the Conroy Hotel, 3080 Dufferin St., Toronto, who had just committed an armed hold-up at the IDA Drug Store, 2558 Danforth Ave., Toronto. Kirby stated that they were carrying guns, high on drugs, and should be considered dangerous. The information was immediately passed on by phone to Sgt. Lamont, Metro Toronto Police Hold-up Squad. I also told Lamont that the informant was trying to get some help on a break, entry and theft charge, and I would appreciate if he could intercede in any way possible if the information turned out to be accurate. Lamont had considerable interest in the information because at that time there had been a large number of armed hold-ups of drug stores in the Toronto area, where the bandits were looking for the drug Percodan. In fact, the drug stores were so concerned that they offered a $1,000 reward for the arrest of the "Percodan Bandits" as they were called. Lamont sounded reluctant when he said he would get back to me.

Five days passed with no word from Lamont. I called Staff Sgt. Scoular, Metro Police Hold-up Squad. He told me that, as a result of the information, two people had been arrested and charged with two counts of armed robbery in relation to drugstores, and eighteen charges of break, entry and theft with another eleven charges for the same offence still pending. There were also numerous frauds, false pretenses, mischief in relation to private property, the possession of stolen property, the use of stolen credit cards and the possession of dangerous weapons. Although he couldn't have been more pleased with the outcome, he said he would not be able to help in my efforts to cut a deal with Kirby. At this time, I couldn't understand why. I was becoming rather frustrated, and began to realize from the tone of Scoular's comments that something wasn't right. Even at this point, the information supplied to date by Kirby was more than sufficient to bring about a deal. I had also recently had a call from S/Sgt. Roy Herder who said that he was unable to help with Kirby. What I didn't realize at the time was that Herder was in charge of Project Rontario, which included Sgt. Tavenor and Cst. Hall. In fact, Herder had attended the very first meeting, but I had not recorded his name at the time.

Meanwhile, Kirby continued to serve as an ideal informant. He told me of a recent contract killing, and of a large jewelry robbery at the Italian Gift Store, Bloor St., Toronto. That information was passed on to Metro Police, and was readily accepted and acted upon with tangible results. I was beginning to feel awkward and compromised, since I still had no deal to offer Kirby.

Just fourteen days after our meeting with Tavenor and his associates at OPP Headquarters, I had a meeting with Kirby at the Casa Loma. Kirby was noticeably upset. I could see the anger in his eyes as he approached me. He was intensely excited and seemed ready to pounce. I recalled vividly that he had promised to come after me if I told anyone he was talking to the police. Without preliminaries, he burst out, "What the fuck is going down here?"

I tried to diffuse his anger the only way I knew how—I leveled with him about my conversation with Tavenor. Thank God I chose this course. I told him about being spotted by police surveillance at the last meeting, and of the subsequent meeting with Tavenor at the OPP. Kirby asked what I had told them about him. Again, I did the thing that was to carry us through some difficult times in the future—I told Kirby the truth. He soon realized that I had no choice, and he began to regain his composure. Kirby appreciated how I handled the situation and went on to relate an incredible story.

The previous week, he had had to appear in Court in Markham, Ontario, on charges pertaining to the break, entry and theft. He noticed that the Crown had gone to great lengths to delay his normally brief appearance before the court for a remand on his charges. The reason for the delay became quite apparent when Sgt. Ron Tavenor and his partner Terry Hall appeared on the scene and told Kirby they wanted to talk to him. Hall took Kirby to a nearby interview room and confronted him. "We know you were talking to the Horsemen (the RCMP)," Hall told Kirby.

Hall went on to say that the Horsemen couldn't help Kirby with his charges, that he and his partner were the only ones with the right connections, and no matter what the Horsemen did they would not be able to help him. Hall again insisted that there would be no deal unless Kirby dealt with him. Kirby finished the interview by telling Hall that he had put his trust in him in the past, and Hall had double-crossed him. Kirby made it clear he did not trust Hall, and refused to have anything more to do with him. Hall was furious.

It's difficult to imagine what motivates policemen to do what Hall and Tavenor had just done. The information from Kirby on criminal activities was coming through, and I had continued to keep Tavenor's group apprised of everything I received as I had promised in our initial meeting. Yet they apparently had decided to confront Kirby in an effort to cut the RCMP out. I wouldn't be critical if they knew that vital information was being withheld, or if their actions were necessary to further some investigation, but as far as I knew that was not the case. Were they motivated by petty jealousy, or the need to make themselves look good in the eyes of their superiors? Whatever the motivation, I found it hard to accept that two fellow policemen would potentially jeopardize on-going investigations and the safety of a fellow police officer, and perhaps cause the loss of the best informant the Toronto area had seen. Cecil Kirby remained an undercover agent for the RCMP, but in my view what Hall and Tavenor did manage to lose by this indiscretion, at least temporarily, was their credibility.

On January 5, 1981, Sgt. Norm Ross and I met with Sgt. Bob Silverton and his partner at the RCMP Headquarters, 225 Jarvis St., Toronto. Silverton was actually the Metro policeman in charge of the Kirby break, entry and theft charges. After outlining the information and intelligence which Kirby had supplied to date, we asked Silverton if it was possible for him to speak to the Crown Attorney and consider looking for a probation for Kirby. Silverton had been well versed by his Metro and OPP cohorts and when he checked inside his mitten, the answer was still no deal.

As discouraged and frustrated as we may have been at this point in time, there were two very positive underlying aspects of the situation which Metro and OPP, by their narrow-mindedness and stubbornness, had unintentionally kindled. Kirby knew that we were doing our best to assist him, which made him draw closer to his RCMP contact, and Kirby was being forced to dig deeper for information that would be required to consummate a deal. Only Kirby knew at that particular juncture just how deep he could really go.

On January 7, 1981, I met Kirby at the Casa Loma and explained our frustration resulting from the meeting that

Norm Ross and I had just had with Sgt. Silverton. I told Kirby, as I had told Silverton, that if we could not come to some agreement, I would have to speak to his superiors. I could not let stupidity stand in the way of progress. I would have to speak to my Inspector, who, in turn, so I thought, would speak to Sgt. Silverton's Inspector to see what arrangements could be made. Kirby knew we were doing everything within our power to help. We were totally convinced that Tavenor and Hall were behind the "no deal" stance that Silverton had projected, and it was necessary to bypass this obstacle.

Kirby was having second thoughts concerning whether his efforts would ever pay off. He wondered if he should throw in the towel, forget the whole deal, and take his chances in court. I didn't panic because I knew Kirby was a fighter. He had fought all his life and that's exactly why we were sitting together at this point in time. I looked at him and said, "You Irish son-of-a-bitch, we're not quitting now." This particular meeting was to last three hours and thirty-eight minutes and cover a lot of territory. We both recognized the value of the information he had supplied, but of greater significance, although neither of us mentioned it, was the feeling that things of much more importance lay ahead.

Kirby went back through his childhood years and his time with the bikers. We recognized the dangers we faced from his vast knowledge of organized crime figures and the fact they owed him a lot of money. And there was always the unspoken reminder that once Kirby was behind bars, he would be an easy target for anyone who felt he might talk too much. The recent Rosenberg-Lipson murders were no source of comfort. Despite our fears and the odds we faced, we knew we must continue.

Before we parted, Kirby gave me information which he felt would turn the tables. Kirby knew that if there was any hope to strike a deal, he would have to supply something of real interest to Metro Police. There had been an attempted murder a short time earlier on an individual by the name of Allen Dubie, a well-known biker associate. Kirby stated that Dubie was shot with a .38 caliber snub-nose American model gun that had been purchased in Florida by an individual who was also heavily involved in a drug lab. I told him I would call Sgt. Silverton and get back to him if they were interested.

The following day I called Silverton and passed on the information about the attempted murder of Dubie. I advised him that Kirby was in a position to supply the names of persons responsible and further details if Metro was interested. After checking with the investigator of that case, Sgt. King of 11 Division Metro Toronto Police, Silverton came back and advised that King was not interested since Dubie was just another biker and they fully intended to write it off. Silverton and his Metro cohorts had their backs up on this one and it appeared that there would be no giving in. I tried to convince them they were dealing in lives here, to no avail. Kirby eventually passed the name to me and I passed it on to Metro; to the best of my knowledge, nothing was ever done.

Around 1:30 AM on January 20, 1981, Kirby called me at home as he did so many other times in the middle of the night. Apologetic and polite, he said he was calling from the Beverly Hills Hotel in the north end of Toronto, and he was with two guys who had done an armed robbery at Dolly's Credit Jewellers at 1971 Weston Road, Toronto. On January 15, 1981, the robbers had stolen an estimated $50,000 in jewelry. The following day I contacted Staff Sergeant Douglas, Metro Toronto Police, who was in charge of the investigation, and Staff Sergeant Scoular, Metro Toronto Hold-up Squad, and explained Kirby's situation to both of them. They wanted the information desperately, but Scoular said he and Douglas did not want to get involved. Tavenor and Hall had obviously covered a lot of territory, blocking all avenues to ensure Kirby would have no deal unless he talked to them. Kirby and I were convinced that there would be no deal even if he did talk to them.

It was at this juncture in the investigation that I felt that justice was being obstructed. It was time to go beyond Tavenor, Hall, and Silverton since I had told them I would if necessary. I had a meeting with my immediate bosses, Sgt. Norm Ross and the Staff Sergeant in charge of the National Crime Intelligence Section. They were already well aware of the problem and told me to go to Inspector Jack Wylie, Division Intelligence Officer (DIO), RCMP for Southern Ontario. For the purpose of clarification and in fairness to another individual who would be known by many members of the RCMP, this was not the same Jack Wylie for whom I had worked years earlier, who was in charge of General Investigations at Corner Brook, Newfoundland. That Jack Wylie later became Assistant Commissioner of the RCMP in Ottawa, since retired.

At any rate, I went to see the DIO Jack Wylie to outline the problems we were facing. In appearance, Jack Wylie fitted the mold for an RCMP officer. He was tall and thin, with reddish hair and, as they say in the RCMP, "presented a neat, well-groomed appearance in uniform and mufti." He was very soft spoken and mild mannered. One would readily call him a gentleman, though in my opinion he could not so readily be viewed as a policeman. Not that a policeman can't also be a gentleman, but to me he was a product of the Old Boy network, which is how so many commissioned officers are appointed. He was stereotypical of those who were considered for promotion because they never were in trouble, never made mistakes. But if you don't make decisions and don't take action, it's all too easy to avoid making mistakes. It's sad, but in general the rank-and-file of the RCMP don't have as much respect for the officers as they should. Nor do I see signs of it changing, to the detriment of the Force and the public welfare and to the advantage of criminals.

At the time Insp. Wylie must have had approximately 25 years of service with the RCMP, but in my view he was purely an administrator, a man with little real operational experience. It seemed odd to me that this man was charged with directing the entire Southern Ontario area for the RCMP in the fight against organized crime. It has always been discomforting for me to think we were representing Canada's national police force, with the availability and the resources to make inroads into organized crime, and yet we were so desperately lacking in leadership and direction. In the ten years I spent investigating organized crime in Toronto, I never received one ounce of direction from a superior on how to best focus and execute our efforts. I think it's fair to say that over the years our group had a great deal of success, but mostly as the result of self-generated work from the rank-and-file as opposed to upper management direction. I still ask why.

The meeting on the 20th of January, 1981, with Insp. Wylie was to be no different. I painstakingly outlined the difficulties with Tavenor and Hall, the phenomenal amount of information that Kirby had supplied to date, and the fact that Kirby knew the Commisso family and could undoubtedly supply valuable Intelligence on the bikers and organized crime in the Toronto area. I stressed that lives were at stake. I used all my powers of persuasion. Inspector Wylie's answer was a severe blow, but not totally surprising. He said he knew that Kirby was a hot item, and that if I was to continue to be involved with him there would have to be some hard-nosed decisions reached. I read between the lines—decisions might mean mistakes, which could jeopardize a career. Insp. Wylie's advice to me, though I had explained that Kirby did not trust nor want to deal with anyone from Metro or OPP, was to turn him over to Metro Police. Then came the quote I'll never forget.

"We are not investigators and we have no jurisdiction to do anything."

I could feel the hair bristle on the back of my neck.
Intelligence gathering was indeed NCIS's mandate, but it had
been realized years earlier that intelligence had to lead
somewhere; what was the point if bad guys didn't end up in
jail? The staffing officer told me when I was hired that one of
the reasons I and others were being transferred to NCIS at that
time was to give them a greater ability to investigate, to make
things happen. Inspector Wylie's statement was a direct
contradiction to what we believed to be a new direction and
opportunity for NCIS.

Bordering on insubordination, I blatantly asked, "Would
you tell me what those 26 men next door in NCIS are
supposedly doing, along with the other six or eight NCIS units
in southern Ontario you're supposed to be running?"

I was dismissed without an answer. Kirby had already
proven himself as one of the best informants in Toronto, but it
looked as though Wylie was determined to let him go to jail
and forget the whole deal. He would not intercede on Kirby's
behalf.

My options were running out. In desperation I sought
another commissioned officer just across the hall from my
office. His name was Inspector Jim McIlvenna, the officer in
charge of the SEU (Special Enforcement Unit). The SEU was a
joint forces operation consisting of supposedly experienced
investigators from the three police forces in the Metro Toronto
area: Metro Police, OPP, and the RCMP. The SEU supposedly
had the mandate and the ability to follow through on the work
that NCIS initiated. McIlvenna was in command of this
outwardly impressive group.

To me Jim McIlvenna didn't fit the mold of an RCMP
officer. He was small in stature and unkempt, and his
personality was abrasive. I had had few dealings with him
prior to this; I found him loud and uncouth. He was known to
his co-workers simply as "The Bear." He would sometimes
pull rank or make derogatory comments at someone's expense

in front of a group of people, then walk away as if nothing happened. If you were able to refute the statement quickly, proving him wrong, he would force a grin and let on it was all just a joke. I remember one such moment when he entered our office uninvited and began a verbal assault on Sgt. Robin Ward. Although junior in rank, the Staff Sergeant in charge threw him out of the office.

It seemed to me that McIlvenna liked to share in the success of others in his department. I remember one case that was the result of a project called Oblong. Corporal John Beer, an honest, intelligent and determined young investigator working for McIlvenna on Commercial Crime at the time, was instrumental in putting the case together. The case charged and convicted Vincent Cotroni and Paul Violi, two well-known mobsters from Montreal, Hamilton mobster John Papalia, and Sonny Swartz, a small Toronto rounder (repeat criminal) with conspiracy to possess stolen goods as the result of their extortion on a Toronto contractor. Although Cpl. Beer put the investigation together for a successful prosecution, Jim McIlvenna had his chest stuck out for the medal when the credit was given. I happened to know the inside details of that investigation, and from that day forward my respect for McIlvenna was diminished.

McIlvenna had been one of the more vocal skeptics who felt the authorization for Project Oblong would not stand up in court, rendering the tapes useless. But the authorization did stand up and the convictions held, even though it was appealed to the Supreme Court of Canada. Ironically, the SEU section was created as the result of Project Oblong, a project I conceived in 1975 (so many people have taken credit for this successful operation, I welcome the opportunity to set the record straight).

In 1965 I joined the RCMP in Charlottetown, Prince Edward Island, then travelled to Regina, Saskatchewan for basic training. After training I went to Corner Brook, Newfoundland, where I worked for one year in uniform duties, followed by seven years on General Investigations (plain clothes criminal investigations). One afternoon the Officer Commanding asked me if I was interested in going to Toronto on NCIS. The only thing I'd heard about NCIS regarded their mandate to gather intelligence on organized crime. That peaked my interest; after a short conversation with my wife I said I would go. Within a few days I heard they had interviewed two or three other investigators from across Canada and had filled the position with someone else. Since I was due for a transfer, I was sent to Stephenville, Newfoundland, still in plain clothes. They told me if anything came open at a later date I would be considered, but I thought there was little hope. After seven months in Stephenville, and having recently built a new house, I received word that there was another opening in Toronto NCIS if I was still interested. I answered in the affirmative on Friday; on Monday I was on my way to Toronto to fill the position.

When I arrived in Toronto in 1973, I was fairly naive about organized crime. After asking a lot of questions and reading numerous files, I realized that simply gathering information on a subject associated with organized crime—such things as where he lived, what cars he drove, and with whom he associated—was not to my liking and, in my mind, not why I was brought to Toronto. My belief was that criminals belonged in jail, and we had to do more than just gather intelligence; we had to gather evidence. I soon learned that this division had gathered intelligence for twenty years on some individuals while they remained untouched.

After three months of research and pleading with my sergeant, unsuccessfully, to go out and do some field work, I started to investigate the activities of the best known organized crime boss in the city of Toronto. His name was Paul Volpe. Within a month or two Metro Police, OPP, and the RCMP set up a Joint Forces Operation out of a privately owned building at the corner of Wilson Ave. and Yonge St. in the north end of Toronto. After several months of physical and technical surveillance (wire-taps, which at that time did not require a court order or authorization), the information pipeline went completely dead. A couple of years later a young Metro copper who worked on our project was convicted of feeding information to the Mob. He was an habitual gambler and was heavily indebted to Mob loansharks. Indirectly, we managed to secure information that Paul Volpe and his associates were responsible for acts of violence and extortion in the construction industry. That information produced a gun used to shoot up Acme Lathing, a Drywall Construction firm in Toronto. We passed this on to the Waisburg Commission on organized crime in the construction industry.

Since there was no steady supply of information forthcoming—and there was no doubt in my mind that we were compromised by a crooked copper, though we had no evidence of this at the time—it was decided to shut down the investigation. But before doing so, someone came up with the idea of offering Nathan Klegerman, Paul Volpe's closest criminal associate, $200,000 if he was willing to testify against Volpe and put him in jail. The money was to be raised from the Attorney General's office and the three major police forces coffers. I didn't express my feelings at the time, but I was against this proposal for two reasons. First, if Klegerman did testify he was a dead man, since we didn't have such a thing as a witness protection program. Second, those guys could make $200,000 in an hour with some of the scams they were pulling. At any rate Cpl. Leo Debon, an excellent, honest and dedicated OPP officer, and myself were asked to approach Klegerman and make the offer.

We decided to try to isolate Klegerman and speak to him without anyone's knowledge. Through surveillance we knew he would be dropping his daughter off at a north end Toronto school on a given morning. Debon and I discreetly followed Klegerman to the school. Instead of dropping his daughter off and proceeding down Avenue Rd., as was his custom, he went into the school to talk to the teacher about some problem. Our intention was to stop him on the road with the police red light in our unmarked car. We moved to within a few yards of his vehicle and waited for him to return. In a few minutes Klegerman emerged from the school and walked to his car. Debon and I got out of our unmarked car and approached him. Debon went to the driver's side and I went to the passenger side. I now know more about the expression on a person's face when he feels he is going to be executed gangland style. When Debon put his hand inside his overcoat pocket to reach for his badge, Klegerman turned white, probably thinking it was his last day on earth. His fear turned to visible relief when we identified ourselves as police officers. Klegerman, a personable enough fellow, went with us to a local restaurant to hear what we had to say. Both Debon and I were somewhat embarrassed in making the proposal, but we had no choice. I remember Klegerman's answer to this day. "Do you see this body you're talking to? Well, it's all I have to walk around in." There was no need to say any more. We expected to hear from Mr. Volpe.

We had just arrived in the office the following morning when the phone rang. It was Nate Klegerman on the other end. He said he had told Paul Volpe about our proposal and that Volpe wanted to talk to us. Debon and I agreed to meet Klegerman and Volpe at the Zumberger Restaurant at Yonge and Walton at 10 am that morning. I threw on a body pack (hidden audio tape recorder) and we headed for our meeting. We really expected Volpe to be outraged at us, but when we explained that it wasn't our idea he accepted us on a more friendly basis. That meeting lasted for two and a half hours and we covered a lot of ground. We talked about organized crime and many other topics. One thing that Volpe unknowingly did was supply valuable information about his friendship with those in the "ice cream business" (organized crime), close pals such as Paul Violi (Montreal mobster) and Jimmy Luppino (Hamilton mobster). That information was instrumental in later obtaining authorizations to investigate further Volpe and his organization.

I found Volpe a fascinating character. He came across as congenial, highly intelligent, and streetwise. Out of that meeting—and I know this is sure to shock some of my former superiors—even though I knew he was heavily involved in organized crime, I developed a liking and a friendship for Paul Volpe that I will always cherish. I make no apologies; to me he was just that kind of guy.

One thing more of significance was that Volpe respected Debon and me for coming to meet him face to face as no other coppers had done. He told us two things. If we caught him fair and square without framing him, he would shake our hands before he went to jail. Secondly, if we ever needed anything to come and talk to him. We all shook hands and parted company. Volpe asked one small favor from me before I left. He wanted to know if he could travel stateside (to the US) without being arrested. I checked it out and found he could not. I passed on that information with the approval of my supervisor, and then, shortly thereafter, I was ordered to have no further contact with Paul Volpe.

Some time passed and I had a chance to reflect on the previous project conducted on Paul Volpe. I thought that a clever criminal like Volpe was not likely to say something during a phone conversation that would put him at risk of going to jail. The Criminal Code, containing a new act called Protection of Privacy, had just been introduced into law by Parliament. The new act specifically pointed out "named offences" or sections of the Criminal Code under which an authorization would be legally granted by a judge, offences such as extortion, murder, and traffic in narcotics. I felt there was no point in asking for an authorization under an offence such as extortion, since there would undoubtedly be no conversation to support the charge. We also wanted to have an in-depth look at the Volpe Organization, and an authorization at that time was valid for only thirty days. After that you had to get a renewal for another thirty days based on evidence obtained. It would be useless to start a project for such a short period of time.

Parliament had seen fit to add an additional rider to the named offence section; at that time it read: "or any other indictable offence in respect of which there are reasonable and probable grounds to believe that it forms a pattern of similar or related offences by two or more persons acting in concert, and that such a pattern is part of the activities of organized crime." That little rider opened up an avenue of investigation unheard of in the police community. Since it had to be an indictable offence, I did my homework and discovered a little-used section of the Income Tax Act – Sec. 239(2) which said, "Every person who is charged with an offence described by sub-section 1 (and in this case, we used willful evasion of payment of taxes; conspiracy to evade the payment of taxes; making false or deceptive statements in returns; and conspiracy to make false or deceptive statements in returns) may, at the election of the Attorney General of Canada, be prosecuted upon indictment and, if convicted, in addition to any penalty otherwise provided, is liable to imprisonment for a term not exceeding 5 years and not less than 2 months."

Combining these two elements gave us a tremendous advantage. Now, for an extended authorization and an in-depth look at the Volpe Organization, we had to establish only two basic facts. One was that Paul Volpe and his associates were involved in activities of organized crime. Photographs, years of intelligence-gathering and the interview with Debon and me established Volpe's association to organized crime. The other was that they were deriving income on which they were not complying with the provisions of the Income Tax Act. Volpe hadn't paid taxes for 15 years. I felt certain this tactic would work, but I had to get it approved.

I had a meeting with the five other members of the NCIS that formed our particular unit. They all agreed to fully support the project. We approached the Sergeant, Staff/ Sergeant and the Division Intelligence Officer, and obtained their approval. The next step was to approach the Federal Justice Department to see if the idea was feasible and whether or not an authorization might be granted under this new approach. I had a meeting in November of 1975 with Mr. Julius Isaacs, who was in charge of Federal Crown Attorneys. I can still picture him, sitting back in his chair, reviewing the idea and thinking about it for a few short minutes, then leaning forward and saying, "Yes, I think it will work." I was elated because I thought it was going to be much tougher to win an ally. Mr. Isaacs assigned Mr. Ari M. Coomaraswamy, Federal Crown Attorney, to draw up and make an application on our behalf before a Supreme Court Justice to obtain "an Order Authorizing Interception Of Private Communications" of Paul Volpe and his named associates. That was the beginning of Project Oblong.

Over the years I've held Mr. Isaacs and Mr. Coomaraswamy in great esteem. They laboured with integrity, devotion and untiring effort over the next fifteen months so that we could continue with our investigation and gather evidence against the Volpe Family. I would be negligent if I failed to mention the support given to the police by the Supreme Court Justices who granted the authorization and the renewals. It was Justice S. G. MacDonald Grange who granted the first of fifteen orders which ran from the 29th of December, 1975, to the 28th of March, 1977. I well remember the off-the-cuff verbal support we received from the Supreme

Court Justices to pursue and prosecute organized crime. It was a welcome boost to the men involved in the project, as compared to the support—usually negative criticism—we received from the upper echelon of the RCMP.

I affectionately called Project Oblong "The little project that grew." When we started there was only myself and the five other men from NCIS involved. When the project got off the ground and things started to look promising, I was told one day that Sgt. Robin Ward would be taking over. As the project developed further, S/Sgt. Phil Yackovovich took control. Eventually, the Inspector took charge. As the months rolled by and interest began to wane, control was passed back to the Staff/Sergeant and finally back to the Sergeant. Up to 125 men were involved in the project. It was the largest project ever conducted on organized crime in Canada, and it was the first time we used a computer to record our information. In total, the investigation lasted approximately six years.

Project Oblong focused on income derived from illegal activities by the Volpe Family. Examples of that illegal activity included loansharking. Nate Klegerman and his associates operated Flight Investments, Spadina Ave., where we identified well over 100 loanshark victims who paid hundreds of thousands of dollars in interest, for which several Volpe associates were convicted under the Income Tax Act. I knew of one dentist who paid Paul Volpe $35,000 in interest over a five- year period on a $70,000 investment in the stock market. The stock deal went sour because it was controlled by organized crime. The dentist lost his $70,000 to the Mob and then they collected $35,000 in interest. They may be collecting interest from that dentist to this day. Other scams involved diamond thefts from New York, extortion, other thefts, frauds and just about every other crime in the book. One of the scams involved a homosexual bank manager at a Bank of Montreal in the west end of Toronto. Because they had filmed the bank manager in a homosexual act, they bribed him into supplying loans of several thousand dollars to street people with criminal records, which were never repaid. It amounted to well over $200,000, and the total cost was written off unknowingly by the bank.

In total, there were several successful prosecutions for income tax evasion and literally hundreds of other criminal charges. Ironically, because of the tremendous amount of intelligence and evidence gathered and recorded on computer, it became necessary to form a criminal investigation body to do the follow-up investigation on that information. That resulting body was called the Special Enforcement Unit, with Insp. Jim McIlvenna in charge.

Considering the fact that the SEU was now in place, it's important that I convey to the reader what, in my mind, should have been the logical procedure for dealing with Cecil Kirby at this point in time. My efforts with Kirby should have been fully supported by NCIS because of the obvious potential inroads we could make against organized crime. As intelligence and evidence were gathered, they would then be passed on to the SEU. My relationship with the informant would make it necessary for me to continue to work closely with the SEU during the follow-up investigations. In an ideal world, SEU would welcome the opportunity to work together.

Logic, however, did not prevail as I envisaged. As mentioned earlier, I was running out of options to make a deal on the Kirby affair. My next move was to approach Jim McIlvenna, although from what I knew of him I didn't expect much support. After describing Kirby's plight in detail and the ramifications of what could follow, and pointing out that McIlvenna was in the ideal position to intercede, his answer was simple. Without elaborating, he said, "I wouldn't touch that with a 100 foot pole." He then turned and walked away. It looked as though my options had run out.

On January 18, 1981, I called Silverton, the Metro copper heading up Kirby's charges. He had read the reports containing the information Kirby had supplied to date and considered relenting on the request for a heavy sentence for Kirby. There was still a problem, though. Frank Armstrong, the Crown Attorney in charge of the case, was still insisting on a heavy sentence.

On February 5th I had another meeting with Kirby and he supplied the names of the two persons responsible for an armed robbery at Dolly's Credit Jewellers. The two were Nick Polada and Rick Cucoman. I told Kirby that I would contact Metro Hold-Up Squad and do some negotiating on his behalf. At this same meeting Kirby told me something that would change the whole situation. Cosimo Commisso wanted some unknown person killed, with $5,000 up front and the rest to follow. Kirby would be meeting Commisso the next week.

On February 16th I called Sgt. Bob Cowan, Metro Hold-Up Squad and told him that Kirby could supply the names of those people involved in the hold-up at Dolly's Credit Jewellers. I didn't bother to tell him I already knew the names. Kirby would be coming up for sentencing on February 26th and we needed to make some arrangements rather quickly. Cowan stated that he would arrange a meeting with the Crown, Hold-Up, and myself to discuss sentencing. There was some light at the end of the tunnel, but still no deal.

4

The Murder Contract
On A Beautiful Lady

At 10:00 AM on February 17, 1981, Cecil Kirby called me at the office. He was onto something and you could sense the excitement in his voice. Kirby said, "I met with that guy (Cosimo Commisso) and they want someone hit outside the country." I thought that this might just be what we've been waiting for. We arranged to meet at 1:00 PM at the Casa Loma.

I had asked Sgt. Norm Ross, Toronto NCIS, and my immediate supervisor to come along with me to the meeting. Kirby was on time as usual. While we talked Kirby relayed that he was supposed to meet Cosimo Commisso at 3:15 PM that same day at Faces Disco in the Howard Johnson Hotel on Dixon Road. Commisso would be bringing an unknown male, supposedly from New York, to meet Kirby. Commisso wanted Kirby to go to New York with this unknown male, and there meet two other friends. They wanted a hit done on "some broad that was causing a problem." Kirby wondered what he should do. We concluded that this unknown female must have incriminating evidence about the Mob and some reason to use it for them to put out a contract on her life. I told Kirby to go to the meeting with Commisso and the unknown male and accept the offer to do the hit. Our game plan was to have Kirby travel to New York, identify the girl, then return to

Canada with the story that, with police everywhere, there was too much heat to do the hit. I had a friend in the New York Police Department, Peter Miceli. Peter could be trusted to approach the girl and tell her about the intended hit. We reasoned that she would most likely be willing to pass on her information about the Mob.

Kirby told me he was flat broke. I took it personally that this guy had supplied information to me from November 1980 to February 1981, yet I had been unable to get any money for him from the coffers of the RCMP. God knows I had tried. I had approached Inspector Wylie, Division Intelligence Officer, many times requesting money for Kirby to no avail. In fairness to the RCMP, at that time they had a policy which stated that an RCMP informant would not be paid monies while under charge, unless there were exceptional circumstances. The reasoning, of course, was to prevent an informant from using the excuse that he committed the illegal act while under the direction and payment of the RCMP, thus raising an alibi for committing the offence. One can appreciate that policy, but there were provisions for exceptional circumstances. Kirby had already pleaded guilty to the break, entry and theft; it was only a matter of sentencing. There was nothing to jeopardize. I ended up giving Kirby my last $10 so he could buy Commisso and his friend a round of drinks at the meeting. I could hardly believe that in a situation dealing with top Mafia people and a contract killing, I had to supply money from my own pocket for informant expenses.

Sgt. Ross and I hurriedly nabbed a few Special "O" (members of RCMP Surveillance) from another job and rushed to the Howard Johnson to cover the meeting. Commisso and his friend were late in arriving; we appreciated the few extra minutes to get organized. It was 4:35 PM when a black Matador AMC pulled onto the lot. The licence plate number was HHH-835; the registered owner was Antonio Romeo (Born 28 Mar. 49), 19 Gravenhurst Avenue, Toronto. Romeo was the driver and Cosimo Commisso was the passenger. I had never seen either one before and I desperately tried to get a look at both men because I knew I would have to pick one of them out in New York later. The Special "O" guys covered the meeting inside the hotel. Working with limited manpower, they did an excellent job. At 5:01 PM Special "O" indicated the meeting had finished and Romeo and Commiso returned to their car. I followed them out of the parking lot. As they waited for a traffic light at the intersection of Dixon Road and Eglinton Avenue, I drove up beside them and was able to sneak a quick look at their faces. Special "O" let me know they were headed for a club on Eglinton Avenue called the Las Vegas. I followed them there and waited. At 5:40 PM both men came out of the club and returned to their car. I was able to get a better look at Mr. Romeo as they crossed the street. The next time I would see him would be four days later at LaGuardia Airport in New York.

The following day I called New York City detective Peter Miceli and briefed him on what had transpired to date. Miceli was with the NYPD Intelligence Division, whose responsibility it was to work on organized crime. I had worked with Miceli in New York some years earlier in relation to Paul Volpe and Project Oblong. Miceli, who is quite small in stature, was a well-respected, tenacious investigator. He had proved to be a valuable asset to Cst. Mike Croucher, an investigator with SEU, who performed some excellent follow-up work on Project Oblong regarding a huge diamond fraud out of New York involving Paul Volpe, Nate Klegerman and a local Toronto diamond merchant. It was Croucher who had introduced me to Miceli.

To digress for a moment, I want to relay two coincidences that occurred in New York which to this day make me shake my head. In March 1977, we had finished the actual wiretap work on Project Oblong. Several months later I was reas-

signed to work temporarily with Toronto Commercial Crime
Tax Unit on a follow-up with Sgt. Ron Hartlen, whose responsibility it was to analyze the intelligence we had gathered and
put together a package for the prosecution with respect to
charges under the Income Tax Act. Several agents from the
Federal Income Tax Office were also assigned to the project
and, jointly, they put together several very successful prosecutions against the Volpe Organization.

While I was employed with Hartlen's crew we noticed that
Lisa Volpe, Paul's wife, made numerous visits to New York
City. Lisa was employed by Creed's, a large, exclusive furrier
with a huge store located at Bloor and Yonge Streets in
Toronto. Personally, I always believed she was a buyer for the
company and was required to travel extensively on legitimate
business. Nonetheless, we felt she could be conveying money
or messages on behalf of Paul to the New York Mob. We had
learned that Lisa Volpe and Jack Creed, listed with his brother
Eddie as the owner of Creed's, were scheduled to travel to
New York in two weeks time. Sgt. Hartlen asked me to
arrange for a surveillance in New York to determine their
activities and to try to alleviate or substantiate the suspicion
that arose each time Lisa travelled to New York.

Cst. Mike Croucher recommended we get help from Det.
Peter Miceli of the NYPD, so I called him and briefly explained
our situation. I arranged to meet Miceli in New York a week
prior to the actual visit by Lisa Volpe and Jack Creed. Miceli
would then know what I looked like and would have no
trouble picking up the targets when we all arrived the following week. I also wanted to fully brief Miceli on our
investigation so he would know exactly what we wanted to
accomplish.

On Monday morning, a week prior to the actual visit, I
was at Toronto International Airport waiting for the 9:50 AM
departure of my American Airlines flight to New York. I
called Miceli and told him I should be there in an hour. Miceli

was very apologetic, and stated something had come up and he would not be able to meet me at the airport. I told him I would grab a limo and meet him at his office. The short flight to New York was uneventful. After landing at LaGuardia, I grabbed my luggage and went outside to find a limo. I walked across the roadway to where the limos were parked, converging on the first limo along with four other people. LaGuardia is a bustling spot on Monday mornings, so I wasted little time in throwing my luggage in the back and securing a spot in the right rear seat of the limo. Fred, the good-humored driver, asked our destinations. When my turn rolled around I stated I wanted to go to 25 Hudson Street, which on the outside gave no indication that it was a police station. Seated next to the driver was a well-dressed lady with blond hair, probably in her late forties, wearing an expensive fur coat. She was quite friendly and outgoing, and had just arrived on a flight from Houston, Texas. Next to her was a businessman from Buffalo. In the back were two men from Chicago, in the computer business, and myself. The twenty-minute ride downtown was quite enjoyable with small talk and good humor. As we arrived in the downtown area, Fred asked the lady about her destination again, since she would be the first to be dropped off, and she stated she was staying at the Park Lane Hotel, Park Avenue. One of the computer businessmen made the comment that the Park Lane was a pretty ritzy place to be staying. The lady answered with a touch of humility that the hotel might look ritzy, but the rooms weren't all that great. I commented that it was probably much like the Royal York Hotel in Toronto, which at that time looked elegant on the outside, but the rooms needed to be upgraded. With that the lady wheeled around in her seat and asked if I was from Toronto, to which I replied, "Yes."

She said, "I'm in the fur business, and I have two great friends in Toronto, Jack and Eddie Creed. Do you know them?"

Here I was trying to discreetly arrange for police surveillance on Lisa Volpe and Jack Creed. A cold chill ran up my spine and I replied, "Not personally, but I know of their business at Yonge and Bloor in Toronto."

She said, "Well, if you do run across them, say hello from Helen Ryder for me."

"Sure, I'd be happy to do that." I wondered if organized crime could be this well informed, and thought perhaps I should catch the next flight back to Toronto and forget about this business.

Now for the second coincidence. The meeting with Miceli went well, and I returned to Toronto to await the departure of the two targets the following week. Monday morning arrived and I was again at the Toronto International Airport clearing US Customs. After Customs I passed through the security area and entered the holding area for passengers. Lisa Volpe and Jack Creed were already in the secure area. I walked over and sat nearby hoping to overhear some conversation of interest, but no luck. They announced the flight and we all boarded for another uneventful trip to LaGuardia. We deplaned in New York and at 6'-5" tall I never had a problem seeing in crowds. I followed my two targets at a safe distance. It wasn't long before I spotted Det. Miceli. He in turn pointed out the targets to his counterparts and we were on our way. If you've ever been to New York, you can appreciate the large number of yellow cabs in the city. Just outside the door at LaGuardia there must have been fifty yellow cabs waiting for fares. Lisa Volpe and Jack Creed went to the first cab in line and got in. The cab's license plate number was 5E-294. Miceli and his partner did a phenomenal job, following the targets in and out of businesses and warehouses all day long. His partner, Tony, was also small in stature and walked near the targets virtually unnoticed. He had more change of clothes than a New York department store. After seven hours of surveillance (and I mention now for later reference that I even drove the NYPD vehicles in assisting Miceli and his partner) the two targets headed out to the Avenue of the Americas—an eight lane, one-way northbound street literally filled with yellow cabs and regular traffic—to hail a cab for the return trip to LaGuardia. After dozens of cabs passed them without stopping, they were able to catch the eye of the driver of an empty cab. He pulled to the curb and picked up his fare. Believe it or not, it was cab number 5E-294, the same cab they had taken in the morning at LaGuardia. In fairness to Lisa Volpe and Jack Creed, we did not learn anything to suggest this trip was anything other than legitimate business.

Returning to the story, on February 18, 1981, at 11:10 AM, I met with Kirby for a debriefing with respect to the meeting with Cosimo Commisso and Antonio Romeo the previous day. Kirby stated Commisso asked him to do a hit on an unknown female in Stamford, Connecticut. Commisso instructed Kirby to go to the Marriott Hotel in Stamford where he would meet Antonio Romeo, who in turn would introduce him to "some of my people." Romeo was to introduce Kirby to a friend of Commisso by the name of Vince. Kirby was told to go to the lobby at the Marriott Hotel at 10:00 PM, where Romeo would meet him and introduce him to Vince. Kirby was also told Vince would arrange to get him the keys to the female's apartment and vehicle. He would be given $5,000 up front from Vince and another $5,000 later. Kirby had arranged to meet Commisso at the Howard Johnson Hotel that day at 3:00 pm, where Cosimo would give him $400 to $500 in expense money to get him to New York. Kirby was not the type of guy to procrastinate. I told him I was really pleased with the way things were taking shape, but he didn't realize the bureaucratic workload he had created for me. This was going to be a very busy day.

On the way back to 225 Jarvis Street, Toronto, I radioed ahead to my office and requested an emergency meeting with

Sgt. Ross, Staff Sgt. Don Kennedy, my immediate bosses and Inspector Wylie so I could bring them up to date on the new developments. I had been able to contact them the previous evening and give them a small indication of what we anticipated might happen—we just hadn't expected it to happen this quickly. The meeting went well. Inspector Wylie had already touched base with the Criminal Investigations branch officer and they had agreed to allow me to accompany Kirby to the US for the purpose of identifying the unknown female and removing her from danger.

The next step was to send an urgent telex to the Commissioner, RCMP Headquarters, Ottawa, for approval to travel to the US. The telex read as follows:

"Commissioner, Ottawa – from Commanding Officer "O" Division: On 17 Feb. 81, confidential source 0-1901 attended meeting in Toronto with Organized crime subject Cosimo Commisso and unknown male believed to be Antonio Romeo, possibly from New York. Purpose of meeting was to arrange contract murder of as yet unidentified female in New York area. Confidential source 0-1901 asked to do hit and offered $15,000. Source scheduled to travel New York this date, departing flight 501, American Airlines at 7:00 PM. Source to meet Romeo, for further instructions at 10:00 pm this date Marriott Hotel, Stamford, Connecticut, at which time he will receive intended victim's name, $5,000 cash and suitable weapon. Contact already established with Det. Peter Miceli, NYPD, and circumstances outlined. Can expect full cooperation with NYPD; FBI may also be involved as intended hit to take place outside New York City. Source requested Cpl. M.G. Murphy, his contact, be allowed to accompany him to New York for purpose of liaison with US Police Forces. Purpose is to identify target, secure her safety and approach her pertaining to her knowledge of organized crime activity in New York area. Request permission for Cpl. Murphy to travel to US this date."

At 1:30 PM that same day, a return telex was received:

"From the Commissioner, Ottawa: Permission granted to travel to New York for the reasons indicated. Please keep us apprised of any further developments."

When time permitted some reflection on what was transpiring, new ideas started to enter my mind. Realizing that Project Oblong had had such a devastating effect on the Volpe Organization, and that my name had been front and center on the wiretap authorization for approximately fourteen months, I knew the danger of retribution was always present. Now I was making arrangements to travel to New York City with an ex-Satan's Choice biker who had been hired to do a contract murder for the Mob. Two thoughts crossed my mind. What if they were setting Kirby himself up for a hit, or what if they were more interested in repaying me on Volpe's behalf? With this in mind, I approached Inspector Wylie and asked if Sgt. Don Pospiech, a hard-nosed copper and close personal friend with whom I had worked on several projects, could accompany me to the US. The answer was no; it would cost too much money. As it turned out, an intensive internal investigation, which would have been averted had Pospiech accompanied me, cost many thousands of dollars more.

I didn't realize it at the time, but I was also supposed to ask permission to take my service revolver to the US. Although US criminal laws make provisions for a peace officer from any friendly foreign country to bring their weapons into the US, RCMP policy states you must request permission from the Force. I had carried my service revolver to the US on business several times prior to this without asking permission, as many other RCMP members had done, and there had never been a problem. I simply didn't realize policy existed on the subject. On this occasion I checked my gun through American Airlines Security and US Customs at Toronto International, but that would not adhere sufficiently to correct procedure; the internal investigation, mentioned earlier, would want their pound of flesh. Regardless of correct procedure, it would be unthinkable to be travelling under these circumstances without my snubnose.

I spent the rest of the day arranging financing and flight reservations for 7:00 PM that evening. I made a quick call to Det. Miceli to keep him abreast of events. He told me he had contacted the FBI and the man that would be coordinating the investigation outside the New York City area was agent John Schiman from Connecticut.

Kirby called at 2:35 PM and stated he had his reservations confirmed for the flight. When he arrived in New York he was to take a limo to the Marriott Hotel, Stamford, Connecticut. Det. Miceli had advised earlier that Kirby should stay at the Holiday Inn, just across the street from LaGuardia Airport in New York and Kirby agreed.

At 3:30 PM Kirby called. His intended contact, Antonio Romeo, had been involved in a minor car accident and would not be able to make the meeting. This was on Wednesday, so the trip was postponed until Thursday or Friday. Kirby would keep me advised. After all the hustle and bustle of making arrangements for the flight, I appreciated the time to become better prepared, although I had to cancel all the current arrangements. Kirby said he had gleaned some information as to why they wanted the unknown female murdered. Apparently Vince, the man who wanted the hit done, had a brother who was going out with the intended victim and Vince felt she had given the police some information on him.

On Thursday, February 19th, Kirby called and said he would now be going on Friday, February 20th, on American Airlines Flight 351, departing at 11:40 AM and arriving in New York at 12:50 PM. The meeting at the Marriott Hotel was set for 9:00 PM Friday evening in the hotel lobby. Kirby had arranged a meeting with Cosimo Commisso at 6:00 PM Thursday night, at which time he was to get his expense money. I said I'd call him at 9:00 PM to confirm he had received the money.

Det. Miceli, NYPD, and agent John Schiman, FBI, were kept informed of events. We arranged for Kirby to stay at the Holiday Inn, Ditmars Blvd., East Elmhurst, New York, directly across from LaGuardia Airport. We arranged to set up a surveillance on Kirby and a counter-surveillance to make sure we were not being followed.

At 9:00 PM Thursday evening I called Kirby. He was upset because "the cheap bastard, as usual" only gave him $300. I told him not to worry; if necessary I would loan him some money. We arranged to meet near the American Airlines counter at Toronto International at 10:00 AM the following day. Commisso had reneged on payment many times and owed Kirby a great deal of money (Kirby estimated approximately $100,000). This played an important role in later convincing Kirby he was becoming more of a liability and potentially expendable.

So much was happening on this case, it seemed like no time at all before Sgt. Pospiech was driving me to Toronto International Airport. I was apprehensive and would have appreciated Pospiech's company on the trip. Kirby and I had already drawn a comparison between the Commissos being so cheap with Kirby and the RCMP being just as cheap for not allowing two officers to make the trip, even though it could well mean someone's life.

When I approached the American Airlines counter, I noticed Kirby standing off to one side. We made eye contact but neither dared to acknowledge each other's presence in case Kirby was being watched. It was exactly 10:00 AM when I obtained my ticket and boarding pass. When that was completed I mentioned I was a member of the RCMP, on my way to New York on an investigation, and it was necessary to take my snubnose revolver with me. I was then introduced to a Mrs. Murphy and a Mrs. Hillier, American Airlines Security. After a short, courteous discussion and the display of proper

identification, I filled out and signed a special form clearing
me for boarding the aircraft and notifying the captain of the
aircraft that I was on board and where I was sitting. Sometimes a captain will take custody of the weapon and store it in
the cockpit, though generally it is left with the police officer. I
then cleared US Customs and, since I was armed, was escorted
to the plane. This caused a slight inconvenience because I
could tell by Kirby's expression there was a problem. I told
my escort I wanted to catch the washroom before getting
inside the secured area and he agreed to wait.

Kirby walked to a secluded area near some lockers and I
followed, with both of us checking for surveillance. When we
felt it was safe, Kirby mentioned again that they had only
given him $300 and the airfare alone cost him $264. He said he
didn't have enough money for a hotel and taxi. I reached in
my pocket and gave him $50. Kirby grinned when I said,
"We're both working for cheap bastards." I quickly mentioned to Kirby that when he arrived in New York he should
grab a cab and go to the Holiday Inn, across the Blvd. from
LaGuardia. I would meet him in the lobby. I returned and
joined my US Customs escort. With his kind assistance I
entered the secured area without further incidents.

While inside the secured area I made two quick calls. One
was to S/Sgt. Don Kennedy at my office to see if expense
money I had requested for Kirby had been approved. I
received the normal reply of negative. I then called Det. Miceli
and advised him we were about to board the flight and
everything was a go.

We boarded the flight at 11:40 AM. Shortly thereafter the
captain announced that due to a build-up of air traffic at La
Guardia, the flight would not be leaving Toronto International
until 12:20 PM. I had no way of letting Miceli know and I was
hoping the delay would not cause a problem for the surveillance. I didn't want to deplane because Kirby might be having
second thoughts and decide not to go. I knew that if Kirby
didn't go they would find someone else to do the job.

The captain came on the intercom and announced we would be leaving shortly. There was a slight jerk and the plane began to roll out to begin taxiing towards the runway. In a way I breathed a sigh of relief. Kirby was sitting in row 8, seat A, which was a window seat. I sat two rows back in row 10, seat D, which was an aisle seat. Neither of us acknowledged we knew each other. Kirby was to say later his mind raced with thoughts about what he was doing. Here he was making a commitment to help the RCMP, yet they had neither supported nor financed him in the four months since he became an informant. He knew I was being honest with him and that I was trying my best. I was really his last and only alternative.

Apprehension ran amuck in my own mind as I reflected on the incompetence and lack of creative thinking back at my own office. I knew from my last contact with Sgt. Silverton that we were getting close to working out a deal for Kirby. I was convinced this new development would be the straw to break the camel's back. Now we just had to make it work.

At 12:00 PM when we hit the main runway and the captain threw the throttles forward on flight 351, I sat back and relaxed because I knew we had some very busy times ahead. At 12:05 PM the wheels of the jet touched down at LaGuardia. At 12:10 PM Kirby and I walked off the aircraft. Just inside the door of the terminal I smiled and was greeted by the warm, friendly smile and handshake of Peter Miceli. We exchanged a few words and began to walk with the flow of people towards the baggage claim area. Miceli was a bit surprised when I pointed Kirby out to him. Kirby was always meticulously clean and well-dressed. He just didn't fit the image of a biker and Mafia hit man. Miceli motioned to two other men who blended in with the crowd and the surveillance commenced. Miceli introduced them as Bill and John. We discreetly acknowledged the introduction with just a slight glance and continued toward the baggage claim area.

After claiming our luggage Kirby walked slowly towards the front entrance of LaGuardia as we had requested. There was no sign of anyone else following Kirby. He grabbed a cab, even though the hotel was just across the street. We all scrambled for the police cars and followed the cab to the hotel. We were certain now that no one else had trailed Kirby. He registered at the hotel under his code name of Jack Ryan and checked into room 205. When Kirby finished at the front desk, I also checked in under an assumed name. The clerk handed me the key to room 207, right next door to Kirby. One can appreciate that if this whole scenario was for the purpose of getting rid of Kirby, one very thin hotel room wall didn't exactly give me much security. None the less, I didn't want to draw any attention at the front desk, so I didn't protest. Although my trust in Kirby had increased, I didn't want him to know where I was staying and it wasn't until I returned to Canada that I told him I had stayed in the room next to his. His contact number for me was through Det. Miceli's office. Over the next couple of days I met Kirby several times in the hotel lobby. The other coppers and myself had several meetings in my room; when we were ready to leave we would go to the front entrance, call Kirby, and tell him to meet us in lobby. This arrangement seemed to work out fine.

At 5:15 PM that same day Det. Miceli, his partner and I were joined by agents Mickey Mott and Doug Fencel from the New York office of the FBI. Mott and Fencel were clean-cut young rookies, both farmboys from the American Mid-West. After introductions I briefed the two FBI agents on the investigation to date. We considered the two most likely possibilities: one that Kirby would actually be asked to do the hit, and the other, that Kirby had become a liability and would himself be the target. With the second option in mind, I told Mott and Fencel that I had a bodypack tape recorder. I intended to wear the bodypack when talking to Kirby so that if anything did happen to him, the recording would show we had no previous knowledge of it. I also wanted Kirby to wear the bodypack to potentially afford us some evidence against those who might be responsible in the event of an attack on Kirby.

Mott wanted nothing to do with that decision and stated agent John Schiman would be the senior agent and he would make the decision in Stamford, Connecticut. I was disappointed when Det. Miceli and his partner had to bow out of the investigation due to the fact that the main portion of the investigation would take place outside their jurisdiction. This seems to me a major drawback in American law that works to the criminals advantage. Even the FBI, which is a national force, requires at least two felonies before getting jurisdiction to act.

Before leaving the hotel I called Sgt. Norm Ross back in Toronto. He had done some fine research on Mr. Romeo. Norm found out that he actually lived at 19 Gravenhurst Avenue, Toronto. He learned that Romeo had organized crime connections in Stamford, Connecticut, and in fact had lived there for several years before coming to Canada. He also learned that his associates in Stamford were in turn connected to the Gambino Family in New York.

At 6:00 PM Mott, Fencel and I met Kirby in the lobby of the hotel. We drove to the Holiday Inn in Darien, Connecticut, located in a secluded, well-treed area just off Interstate Highway 95. I suddenly realized I had stayed overnight at this very same hotel in 1967 on the way to Florida for a vacation. At that time I was stationed in Corner Brook, Newfoundland. Little did I think I would be back under these circumstances.

We went to room 221 where Kirby and I were introduced to agent John Schiman, who was in charge of the operation at that juncture. We also met agents Don Brutnell and Bob Martineau. All three were senior investigators. Brutnell was Schiman's partner and Martineau, formally a Canadian, was in charge of surveillance. Kirby and I briefed the agents on what had transpired to date. Again I raised the issue of the bodypack. I asked Schiman if he felt Kirby should wear it. I remember vividly Schiman's reply as he sat on one of the beds with his back against the wall.

"In this country the Vice-President of the United States couldn't grant us permission to use the bodypack, even if he were right here."

I said, "Fine, you guys know the law."

Kirby, who had been party to all conversations, said he wouldn't feel comfortable wearing the bodypack anyway in case they patted him down. "Besides, Italians have a habit of putting their hands on you when they talk to you," he said.

Several months later, during the RCMP Internal Investigation, Schiman and Brutnell would deny they disallowed the use of the bodypack, saying that it was Murphy who would not allow Kirby to wear the bodypack. I could understand them protecting themselves if US internal investigators were after them, but there was no reason to be untruthful about a Canadian investigation. Agent Mott from New York also backed their story, but he had to confirm my offer to use the bodypack in New York because Det. Miceli and his partner had witnessed it. If I was lying, why would I offer to use the bodypack in New York and not in Darien, just three hours later? Why would I even bring the bodypack to the US?

As the 9:00 PM meeting grew nearer, Kirby quietly mentioned that he didn't have enough money for a cab back from the hotel. The FBI didn't volunteer any funds, so I gave Kirby another $20 out of my pocket for cab fare.

At 8:50 PM I called Sgt. Ross in Toronto for an update to see if Romeo had boarded the flight. Norm advised that he had just learned that Romeo was at the airport but the flight was delayed due to fog. Ross had also discovered a contact number for Romeo in New York, in case we needed it later.

Even though Romeo would not be at the hotel, we decided to have Kirby go anyway, in case someone else had been sent to the hotel to meet him. At precisely 9:00 PM Schiman and I dropped Kirby at the rear of the parking lot at the Marriott Hotel. Kirby, under the watchful eye of agent Martineau and his crew, entered the hotel. Every few minutes we were updated. Kirby was at the bar and had not met anyone. He also made several trips to the lobby, but no one had approached him. At 10:30 PM Kirby left the hotel and took a cab back to the Holiday Inn, Darien. We had a short debriefing and left with Mott and Fencel for the return trip to the Holiday Inn at LaGuardia. Kirby would contact Toronto for further instructions. He called from his room, touching base with an old friend of his, who would in turn contact Commisso for a message. What I didn't know until sometime later was that Kirby gave his number where he could be reached instead of calling back for the message. It was 2:00 AM when we finally turned in. It had been a long day.

At 8:00 AM on Saturday, the 21st of February, 1981, I got a message from Det. Miceli's office to call Kirby. Kirby had received word from his Toronto contact that Romeo's flight had been delayed due to fog. Kirby's instructions were to go to the Marriott Hotel for a 9:00 PM meeting Saturday night.

I was glad Kirby had given us an early start on Saturday, because we had a considerable amount of preparation prior to Romeo's arrival at LaGuardia, or so we thought. After contacting agent Schiman to arrange his surveillance crew, I called Cst. Terry Marks at the Airport Special Squad at Toronto International. Marks quickly advised there was a reservation for Mr. A. Romeo on American Airlines flight 237 leaving Toronto at 11:40 AM and arriving at LaGuardia at 12:50 PM. The weather cleared in Toronto and it looked as though the flight would get off the ground.

Agent Mickey Mott picked me up at the hotel and we hurried out to LaGuardia, where I was introduced to agent Chris Matteace, who made up part of the surveillance crew. Matteace was an ex-Viet Nam vet, quiet and unassuming, but gave the impression he was very capable. Matteace would prove to be worth his weight in gold when things started to happen later on. The FBI were no different than the RCMP when it came to cutting expenses on manpower. We only had Mott, Matteace, two other agents and myself to cover Romeo's arrival. Under normal circumstances it required twice that number.

Flight 237 was scheduled to arrive at gate 3 at 12:50 PM. Mott, Matteace and I had hustled through security and out to gate 3 to learn the flight would be late. Mott did some very quick checks and learned the flight had been diverted to Kennedy Airport because of the fog and was now on the ground. Passengers who requested ground transportation would be bussed over to LaGuardia, approximately one mile away. We were losing hope that Romeo would show at LaGuardia because it would be logical for him to grab a limo at Kennedy and go direct to Stamford. If that was the case he was long gone. We knew our target would show at 9:00 PM at the Marriott to meet Kirby, but we felt it important to keep him under surveillance during the day to try and identify his contacts and determine who was behind the intended hit.

Approximately twenty minutes passed and we had all but given up hope that Romeo would show at LaGuardia. Like Toronto International, LaGuardia has two levels with throngs of people in a rush to get to their destinations. Fleets of busses, limos and taxis are in constant motion. I had only seen Romeo for a brief moment back in Toronto; I thought to myself, "Even if he shows up, finding Romeo in this crowd would be next to impossible."

We were approaching the front entrance to LaGuardia, returning to our cars, when none other than Mr. Romeo caught my eye. He was meticulously dressed in a light green corduroy suit, white shirt and a bright red tie with a matching handkerchief in his chest pocket. His jet black hair and slightly protruding chin made him an easier target to identify than I had ever hoped for. Although he was walking with several other people who had apparently obtained ground transportation from Kennedy to LaGuardia, Romeo stood out from all the rest. By this time we were nose-to-nose with Romeo, so rather than draw attention, I simply allowed the FBI agents and myself to walk out the front doors without saying a word. While on foot, the FBI were not radio equipped, so it had to be a verbal communication. When the doors had safely closed between Romeo and ourselves, I mentioned to agent Mott that we had just met our target in the doorway. We quickly passed the message to the other agents and surveillance commenced.

Romeo spent the next two and a half hours inside the airport. For the first half hour or so he appeared to be trying to assist an elderly Italian lady who had obviously arrived on the same flight; she had missed her contact at the airport and now required transportation. The irony of a messenger for murder being a good Samaritan was not lost on me. With only agents Mott and Matteace to assist, we had a hell of a time to remain inconspicuous for that length of time. Romeo wandered from one bank of payphones to another making calls, always taking in his surroundings with his perceptive eyes. With no radio communication between the three of us, I still wonder how we managed to avoid Romeo's detection. I remember vividly how on one occasion Romeo entered a single phone booth with a seat and a glass door, located across the corridor from an airport bar. Mott and Matteace were unable to get an eyeball (term used when you have a visual contact on your target) so I entered the bar and found a convenient spot to watch our target. He made several calls and was in that one booth for more than half an hour. During that time, I was entertained by a group of airport employees, apparently on their break. They sang just like the Ray Charles singers and after each song were soundly applauded by every patron in the bar.

During the lengthy surveillance inside LaGuardia, I gained great admiration for Matteace. My stature of 6'-5", 230 lbs., doesn't exactly make me the ideal surveillance man. I can't allow myself to be seen too often by the target. But Matteace, at 5'-11", 165 lbs., blended well with other people in the airport. When Romeo withdrew to isolated areas, Matteace performed impressively by passing the locations virtually unnoticed by our target.

At 4:09 PM Romeo finally left LaGuardia by way of the front doors. We were so busy inside that we didn't have time to forewarn the remaining surveillance crew outside the terminal. Luckily Romeo spent several minutes negotiating with cab drivers about his intended trip to Stamford. In the meantime, agent Mott returned to his unmarked Ford and without cover had brought it to within seventy-five feet of our target. I walked out to the front of the terminal and got in the passenger side of Mott's vehicle. We were sitting right in Romeo's line of sight. He looked at us several times and I thought we would be burnt (noticed by target) to a crisp. We couldn't drive by because other than Mott and myself, only agent Matteace knew what he looked like. I told Mott to get out of the vehicle and start unloading suitcases from the trunk until Romeo got into his cab. Mott spent the next ten minutes loading and unloading briefcases and other material from the trunk of the FBI vehicle. Romeo suddenly got out of one cab and into cab number 5E96, which immediately started to drive away. We had taken so much heat we decided to stay put and call on other units to take the eyeball. That move didn't pan out and Romeo was immediately lost.

The lead surveillance vehicle had radioed that they had the target and he was circling back to the front of the airport. Based on this report Mott and I committed ourselves to also circling the airport in an effort to catch up with him. All hell broke loose when lead surveillance suddenly discovered they had followed the wrong cab. When we finally received confirmation that the target was nowhere in sight, several minutes had elapsed. After all our efforts at the terminal, our target was lost.

I asked Mott to beat it out to Interstate Highway 95 and see if we could locate the cab. Mott was a junior agent and didn't know his way around LaGuardia or the surrounding New York area that well. After several wrong turns, we managed to hit Highway 95 and headed towards Stamford, Connecticut. As we drove I longed for our Special "O" unit from Toronto. They rarely lose a target, and if they do they usually pick it up again in a matter of seconds. It was at this juncture that I confirmed previous misgivings that the FBI had not exactly put a high priority on our project by assigning two rookies (with the exception of Matteace) to the case. In a case of conspiracy to murder with lives at stake, the FBI showed up for a surveillance with no radios, lack of manpower, and rookie agents to boot.

We drove out Interstate Highway 95 for approximately twelve miles in a crush of traffic. About half-way to Stamford we approached one of the many tollbooths. I don't normally praise the toll booths or their attendants, but thank God for them because we suddenly noticed Romeo's taxi clearing the inside lane from one of the booths. We were so far out of New York that we had great difficulty advising the other vehicles we had located the target. After several miles of running bare (without cover or change of vehicles), a second and third surveillance vehicle caught up with us. By this time we were just entering Stamford's heavy traffic. Romeo got out of the cab at 4:41 PM in front of the Marriott Hotel. We saw him paying the cabbie and Matteace had learned that he had received four US dimes from the cabbie for phone calls. Romeo had gone inside the Marriott Hotel at 5:15 PM. Mott and I decided to terminate our part in the surveillance and go back to New York to pick up Kirby for the impending meeting.

After a short debriefing on what had transpired, agent Mickey Mott and I headed back to New York to pick up Kirby. Kirby had had a long day waiting at the hotel for us to return and was happy to see us. As we worked our way through the traffic to Stamford, Kirby related he had a call from a guy named Vince who said he was a friend of Romeo's. Vince wanted to confirm with Kirby that the meeting was set for that evening at 9:00 PM at the Marriott hotel. Kirby had assured him he would be there.

As we travelled along Interstate Highway 95, just leaving New York City, we came upon an old rusty clunker, travelling in the inside lane, with two black youths that I would estimate to be about nineteen years old. Mott was driving, I was in the passenger seat and Kirby was in the back. As we slowly overtook the old vehicle, I noticed the driver pass a roll of American money to the passenger. Without exaggeration, the roll of bills was approximately five inches in diameter. The passenger took possession of the money and both youths were laughing and joking until they noticed they were being observed. Their expressions immediately changed as the passenger tried to conceal the money. I asked Mott if he had noticed the two and he said yes. Kirby said they must have either just robbed a bank or did a big drug deal. I looked at my watch and, seeing that we had plenty of time, I asked agent Mott if he wanted to check them or have the state police check the vehicle. Mott didn't want to get involved so we continued on our way. In the RCMP Internal Investigation that followed, Mott told the investigator that I was trying to tell him how to do his job. Personally, I think he was inexperienced and afraid to get involved.

Arriving back in Stamford, we met agent Bob Martineau, an experienced copper and surveillance man. Martineau and his capable crew had continued surveillance on Romeo and gathered a considerable amount of new information. Martineau briefed us that Romeo had met an individual identified as Vincent Melia, 52 Appletree Drive, Stamford, Connecticut. Melia was driving a yellow 1975 Ford Squire station wagon with wood panelling on the sides, Connecticut licence plate number YH-5002. Martineau knew also that Vince Melia tied in with the Siderno Group and the Gambino Mob Family in New York and that his brother Nicky Melia ran a hairdressing business in Stamford. Nicky Melia was suspected of pumping five shots into some guy on the street; the guy had lived. Nicky's real Italian name was Aneillo Melia. Martineau also learned that a second individual and vehicle had shown up. He was Donald Russo, 34 Stephen Street, Stamford. He was driving a 1973 grey Caprice, Connecticut licence plate number WX-3134.

The time had slipped by. It was now 8:48 PM and we were still at the Holiday Inn in Darien. Kirby mentioned to me that he didn't have enough money for a cab after the meeting. I gave him another $10 of my own money. Despite the seriousness of the situation, I chuckled under my breath. The Mob, the RCMP, and the FBI all involved in a case of conspiracy to commit murder, and I had to help finance the operation.

It was precisely 9:00 PM when agent John Schiman and I dropped Kirby off at the outskirts of the parking lot at the front of the Marriott Hotel. I wished him luck and told him to take care, having already discussed in detail the inherent dangers that might lie ahead. I thought to myself that Kirby had more nerve than Dick Tracy as without hesitation he jumped from the car and strode toward the front of the Marriott. You could tell he enjoyed the challenge and welcomed the opportunity to finally prove himself. He was not a braggart or a showboat, but he exuded confidence. I had the feeling he had done this before, and there was no doubt in my mind that unless something really unexpected happened he would be able to take care of himself. Schiman later commented that Kirby was the most capable undercover agent he had ever met.

At 9:07 PM agent Martineau advised that the yellow station wagon belonging to Vince Melia was parked on the lot. Surveillance further advised that Kirby had met Romeo in the bar at the hotel and Romeo had introduced Kirby to Vincent Melia. They all sat in the bar having a short drink, but Melia was uncomfortable there because of possible surveillance. In fact he pointed out two men seated at the bar and said they looked like "heat" (cops). Kirby said he didn't think they were, then felt like adding that the real cops were seated over there, which in fact they were.

Kirby couldn't get over the amount of respect Romeo was showing for Vince Melia. Although the meeting inside the Marriott had only lasted a few short minutes, Melia told Kirby there was a female living with a member of his family and she was causing trouble. They wanted her out (murdered). Melia told Kirby he would give him more detail later. Melia was so uncomfortable talking inside the bar that he suggested they go outside to talk. He also told Kirby that there was another guy he wanted Kirby to meet. That was not part of the game plan and Kirby wondered why another party was involved. Usually in this type of deal the fewer people involved the better. Kirby remembered that Cosimo Commisso had not mentioned anyone else. Was this the guy that was to do a hit on Kirby? Romeo, Melia and Kirby, the gutsy guy that he was, got up and walked out to the parking lot.

At 9:08 PM Agent Martineau advised us that Melia, Romeo and Kirby were walking down the driveway at the front of the Marriott. He also advised they had just observed a black Cadillac with Connecticut licence plate number VJ-6591 driving slowly through the parking lot and headed towards the three men. Martineau felt it was being driven by Jerry Russo, who had showed up earlier with Melia. Schiman and I were sitting in his vehicle on the side street, adjacent to the parking lot of the motel. It was a tension-filled moment as we discussed what was happening. Schiman and I felt it was a very real possibility that they might take Kirby out. I started for the door handle with the intention of covering the distance of approximately fifty yards to where the meeting was taking place. I knew there were agents closer than I was, but then I wondered if they were as concerned as I was about Kirby's welfare. I had the door open when Schiman asked me to hang tight for one second to see what was going on. Just then Martineau came on the air to say that Kirby had gotten into the caddie with Russo. Melia and Romeo were leaving in Melia's car. I knew if Kirby was one on one with Russo he could take care of himself. Schiman and I, along with several other units, followed the Cadillac to 98 McMullen Avenue, Stamford. There the vehicle stopped for a few moments and then Russo drove Kirby back to the Marriott. Kirby got out of the Cadillac at 9:50 PM and walked inside the Marriott. I followed him inside, with neither of us exchanging a word. I saw Kirby pick up a direct cab line and place an order. Cab number 1463 picked Kirby up in front of the hotel and headed for the Holiday Inn in Darien.

Agents Schiman, Brutnell and Martineau, along with myself, anxiously followed Kirby back to room 221 of the Holiday Inn in Darien, arriving at 10:10 PM. We had all had some long days and short nights, but the flow of adrenaline motivated us to usher Kirby into the hotel room for a debriefing. Kirby described the meeting with Romeo and Melia at the Marriott. He mentioned that Melia had outlined that this unknown female was connected to a member of his family and was causing trouble and had to be taken out. Kirby confirmed his grave concern when he saw Jerry Russo showing up in the Caddie, but as it turned out, Russo had given Kirby the keys to the intended victim's house and car.

Kirby had been allowed to make some notes and he recorded details about the intended victim on a small piece of paper. She lived in Cummings Park, third house from the corner, 98 McMullen Avenue, second floor. She drove a white

Datsun, Connecticut licence plate number YZ-1852. Her first
name was Helen, she was a blonde and worked as a hairdresser. She was out of town at the moment, but would be
home Sunday night at 8:00 PM. Vince left a contact phone
number with Kirby. Vince also stated emphatically to Kirby
that Helen might well be with a male member of his family
and Kirby was to make certain this male was not present or to
be harmed.

Melia made arrangements to meet Kirby at 2:00 PM on
Sunday, February 22, 1981, on the parking lot of the Marriott.
At that time he would be supplied with a .38 revolver
equipped with a silencer and $5,000 cash in advance. Kirby
seized the opportunity to tell Melia he had already been there
two days and he was short of cash. Melia gave him $50 and
Russo gave him $250 in cash. Melia also told Kirby he had
been waiting two weeks for Kirby to arrive and that he had
been at the Marriott last night at 9:00 PM, but had not spotted
Kirby. Kirby told him he was there but hadn't seen Melia
either.

Agent Schiman seized the keys and the note from Kirby,
but allowed him to keep the money. At this time there was no
indication there would be any charges laid and our sole
objective was to identify the victim and remove her from
danger. Since the FBI could not supply the informants award
Kirby and I had requested, Schiman decided to let him keep
the money as his reward. It wasn't my duty to call the shot
and I didn't disagree. This would become a contentious issue
in the RCMP Internal Investigation. Schiman and his partner
Brutnell would later deny to internal investigators that they
had allowed Kirby to keep the money. They would say that I
failed to seize the money from Kirby, allowing him to keep it.

My concept of the investigation at that point was that if
there were to be any charges, they would take place in the US.
Since we were in the US and I had no authority to act as a
police officer, it was Schiman's duty to seize all the exhibits,

including the keys, the note made by Kirby and any monies he had received. Without question, it was Schiman and only Schiman who had the authority to seize the money. As a result of the Internal Investigation, it was decreed that it was my responsibility to seize the money. Although Kirby backed my version of the story, one can appreciate why I had wanted another RCMP officer to come along.

Agent Schiman picked up the phone and called his dispatcher. He asked for the registered owner of the Connecticut license plate number YZ-1852. After a few seconds, he repeated what the dispatcher was saying at the other end of the line: the registered owner was Helen Nafpliotis, 98 McMullen Avenue, Stamford, Connecticut, date of birth 26 Jul. 47.

The intended victim had been identified. Several theories were developed as to why the Mob wanted this woman eliminated. Schiman did some quick background checks on Helen Nafpliotis and found she was the girlfriend of Nicky Melia, Vince's brother. Nicky was seeing Helen on a regular basis, despite being a married man, and this had caused so much disruption in the family that we deduced this had to be the main reason for the hit. There were, however, more serious reasons to consider. Nicky Melia ran a hairdressing shop in Stamford and his girlfriend Helen Nafpliotis was working for him. Because Nicky would not leave his wife, Helen decided to play the field, and went out with another hairdresser, who mistreated her. She made the mistake of telling Nicky about the incident. Nicky's method of settling the score, allegedly, was to shoot the guy five times on the street. Helen had allegedly witnessed the attempted murder. Stamford Police failed to make a case, but the State filed charges against Nicky and was bringing the case to trial. Vince and Nicky Melia might well have felt Helen Nafpliotis was being a little too helpful to the police and was an expendable liability.

A third theory developed around the fact that Nicky Melia was facing possible jail time on possession of stolen jewelry in North Carolina. There was a suggestion that Helen Nafpliotis would not wait for him to be released and hinted at interest in another man. Perhaps Nicky was extremely jealous and couldn't bear to think of her with a rival. Regardless whether it was one of these reasons, or some combination of the three, the decision had been made to have her killed.

It was 1:00 AM on Sunday morning when the lights of the FBI car I was in swung across the parking lot of the Holiday Inn across from LaGuardia. Agent Mott dropped me off on his way home. Kirby decided to lie low in his room, mainly because neither he nor I wanted the Mob to know where he was staying. As I said before, knowing that only a very thin hotel wall stood between me and Kirby's room wasn't exactly reassuring. As lights panned the parking lot, I had noticed a 1975 yellow Ford station wagon parked on the far side of the hotel. It was identical to Melia's, the one we had followed during the surveillance. Not wanting to sound paranoid, I didn't mention it to Mott. He dropped me off at the front door, said goodnight, and left for home.

New York is a big city. For those of us who only visit, well, let's just say it's a little unnerving to be alone there, particularly at night. Once inside the hotel I felt a little more comfortable, but apprehensive none the less, particularly because of the yellow station wagon and the type of people we were involved with. I crossed the front lobby and took the elevator to the second floor. It was late and there were very few people around.

I put the key in the door of room 207, listening for any unusual sounds that might be coming from inside. Hearing nothing unusual, I opened the door and cautiously looked about the room before entering. I wondered to myself just how many people in New York had a key to my room. The bathroom was located behind the door, so after checking that out I noticed the message light was flashing brightly on my phone. I wasn't expecting any calls at this hour of the night.

After quickly checking the rest of the room I went over to the phone and dialed the operator. When I asked for the message for room 207, the operator answered by asking if this was Dr. Pulsar. I said, "No, you must have the wrong room." I had checked in under a name similar to Pulsar for my own safety and I could understand the mix-up. The operator asked again if I was Dr. Pulsar and I reassured her I was not. With that there was a very loud knock on my door. In a low voice I said to the operator, "Look, I'm not Dr. Pulsar nor am I expecting any company at this hour. I'm going to answer a knock at the door, but if you hear any strange noises please send security right up." She assured me she would. I walked to the door and peeped through. Standing outside was a gentleman of Italian descent, wearing a white turtleneck and dark navy blue sports coat. I took out my gun and asked who was there.

"Management," was the reply. I wasn't really reassured, since that's the line most used to gain quick access to hotel rooms.

I replied, "Oh yeah? What do you want?"

"You left your key in the door, sir."

I quickly checked my pockets and could not find my key. I thought, "Well, maybe I did." I held the revolver in my right hand and put it up by the side of the doorcasing out of sight. I opened the door with my left hand and sure enough my key was in the door. In the process of trying to remove the key from such an awkward position, I noticed the security guard was carrying a portable radio, and he must have noticed the butt of my .38 because he beat a hasty retreat towards the elevator. I returned to the phone, convincing the operator she had the wrong room, and hung up.

I collected my thoughts and started to get ready for bed, though I knew it would be futile to attempt to sleep without

checking out the yellow station wagon on the lot. Getting
dressed, I headed outside, and breathed a sigh of relief to see
the car had New York plates and was in no way associated
with the Connecticut people. On the way back through the
lobby I met the security guard. I had already decided to tell
him who I was. I didn't want New York's finest kicking in my
door because someone reported a man with a gun in room 207.
People got shot under those circumstances. When I identified
myself as a member of the RCMP from Canada, the security
guard was relieved and turned out to be quite friendly. He
explained that his dad was a member of the NYPD. That
made me feel a little better as well, though I'm not sure why. I
slept with one eye open for what remained of the night.

Sunday, February 22, 1981, proved to be a busy day as
well. I called Det. Miceli to brief him on what had transpired
to date. Mott and his partner picked me up at the hotel at
12:00 noon. As we drove towards Darien, the conversation
centered around the previous day's surveillance. The FBI
agents got a charge when I related my story of the previous
night. The only new development was they had obtained the
name of the registered owner of the Cadillac Russo was
driving. It came back registered to a Mr. Chippatti.

We went directly to the room at the Darien Holiday Inn.
Kirby and some other agents were already there. During the
pre-meeting discussions, with Kirby present, I again raised the
issue of his wearing the bodypack or any other technical
devices the FBI would see fit to use. Kirby was present during
the discussion. This time the FBI were in favour of Kirby
wearing the bodypack, but feeling it would be too dangerous,
Kirby declined. I was to take the heat later for this decision,
although it was not mine to make. I admit I supported Kirby's
decision not to wear the unit at this time, since it was his neck
that was on the line, not Schiman's or mine.

It was 1:35 PM when Kirby caught a cab outside the Darien
Holiday Inn and headed for the Marriott Hotel parking lot for

the 2:00 PM meeting. We all arrived at the hotel at 1:42 PM.
Kirby paid the cabbie and with a few minutes to spare entered
the hotel. At precisely 2:00 PM Vince Melia met Kirby in the
lobby of the hotel. They exchanged some small talk and then
walked out to the parking lot where Melia seemed to feel
much more at ease. Agent Martineau was back in position and
called the targets' movements over the police radio. Agent
Don Brutnell, who I was with, maneuvered our surveillance
vehicle to within approximately 100 yards of the targets,
allowing us to get a look at Mr. Melia. He was wearing a
camel colored coat and red sweater, looked approximately 50
years old, 5'7", 170 lbs., with black hair. I would later be
grateful for this peek at him because I would have to pick
Melia out in a large crowd at Toronto International Airport
several months later.

Kirby and Melia talked near Melia's station wagon for
several minutes. At 2:32 PM a small silver car joined the two
men. Jerry Russo had arrived.

All three got into Melia's station wagon. Brutnell and I
shared the same concerns. Kirby was sitting in the front
passenger side and Russo directly behind him. They only
talked for three minutes and Kirby got out of the vehicle and
walked into the Marriott. Russo and Melia drove away in the
station wagon and we followed. I finally got a good look at
Russo, who was around 28 years old, heavy set with a black
moustache, and wearing a white trench coat. It's funny how
some things catch your eye while performing police work in
this type of situation. These two gentlemen were plotting the
murder of a rather innocent lady on a Sunday afternoon and,
as we drove beside their yellow station wagon, I couldn't help
but notice a statue of the Blessed Virgin Mary on the dash. I
wondered if they had noticed it.

At 2:44 PM our two subjects parked in front of the Giardino
D'Italia Cafe, 829 Cove Road, Stamford.~I dearly wished we
had technical surveillance so we could have overheard what

was being said, but such was not the case. At 3:04 PM Melia and Russo returned to their car and drove to the Marriott to pick up Russo's car. We decided to discontinue the surveillance and return to the hotel and debrief Kirby.

It was 3:23 PM when Brutnell and I arrived back at room 221 in Darien. Schiman had just arrived as well. The notation in my book reads as follows:

"Kirby has photo of intended victim. Two girls, one blond with sunglasses sitting on top of head, white suit, kneeling on red carpet with left knee, gold locket and barbecue in foreground with chicken, white building in background. This is intended victim Helen Nafpliotis on left of photo. U.K.F. (unknown female) #2 in photo. White shirt and dark hair, kneeling on red carpet on right of photo. Photo Polaroid. Kirby had a .22 automatic sturm ruger, 9 shot. Serial number drilled off gun. Silencer on barrel. Kirby says the gun was wrapped in a cloth, in a bag, when Russo arrived at meeting. Russo put the cloth and bag back in his car. Vince said a friend lives with the broad, but when Kirby talked of killing both Vince said not the guy because he is related. That would be Nicky Melia. Vince says the guy will be leaving for North Carolina tomorrow (Nicky on way to court) and broad will leave for work at 10:30 am Monday 23 Feb. 81. Kirby got $1,000 off Vince and $4,000 off Russo. Kirby told to wait until tomorrow before doing the hit. Vince told Kirby to say in front of Russo after the broad is dead, "I want my $5,000 sent to me the next day (through the Commissos) and forget you ever saw me." Vince tells Kirby he has "more business for him down there, like burning factories and other things." Vince wants the broad's body to disappear and never be found, if possible. Kirby told Melia that would cost an extra $1,000, to which Melia said he'd make it more profitable than that."

When Kirby first entered the hotel room, he threw the gun and photo on one side of the bed and they were immediately seized by Schiman. He threw the $5,000 in cash on the other side of the bed, then picked it up and put it in his pocket. Schiman made no effort to seize the money. I would be later chastised for not seizing the money.

After the debriefing, Schiman asked Kirby to take us to 98 McMullen Avenue and point out the house. We left the hotel and Kirby had no difficulty directing the FBI agent and myself to the home of Helen Nafpliotis. The intended victim's vehicle, Connecticut licence plate number YZ-1852, was parked in the driveway. It was now 4:17 PM on Sunday and the FBI were ready to call it a day. After the FBI agents left, Kirby and I went to the restaurant where Kirby treated me to a nice fish dinner. The dinner was enjoyable, but I took the quiet moments to reflect that these people for whom he was working thought nothing of killing an innocent woman who had three small children. I could see that that thought had really hit home with Kirby. Kirby loved children. Thank God I decided to stay in Darien rather than return to New York. It gave Kirby and me the whole evening to talk.

When we finished the dinner, we returned to room 221. My day had not finished, and, in fact, it would be 2:00 AM Monday morning before I could turn in for the night. I couldn't escape the thought that had I and the other policemen not been involved, Kirby's next appointment would have been with murder at 10:30 AM Monday morning. I spent the next two hours recording every serial number on the US$5,000 that Kirby had received from his contacts. Since there had been a noticeable change in Kirby's attitude, I decided to ask him to allow me to take the top three bills from the three separate stacks of money Kirby had received from Melia and Russo. I wanted to have them checked for fingerprints should they ever be required in court, a possibility that had not even been considered prior to this.

Kirby and I continued to talk about his past, what had transpired on this trip and, more to the point, what the future would hold for him. Something had made a big impression on Kirby. As he put it, "I didn't really know there were coppers around that could act like gentlemen and cooperate the way this group had done." We had made Kirby party to all the conversation that had taken place during the operation. The FBI would even allow Kirby to take part in the surveillance the following day. I believe it was his first exposure to the other side of the police world, something different from having his club house door kicked in, guns pointed at his head and being thrown in the slammer.

It was exactly 12:00 midnight Sunday when I finally finished writing up my notes from the day's surveillance. Kirby was lying on the bed and I was sitting at the small table in the room. The time was right for some serious discussion. I started the conversation off by reviewing what had transpired over the previous week. The meeting in Toronto with Romeo and Commisso, the trip to the United States, and the meeting with Romeo, Melia and Russo. We discussed the kind of people that would have a woman like Nafpliotis killed. It appeared she was to be the victim of a jealous lover who could not bear to see her with another man while he was in jail. She had three small children, one of them the son of Nicky Melia, who we believed was behind the intended murder. If only Kirby would consider testifying, the evidence we had to corroborate his story in Toronto and the US, along with the evidence we could gather back in Toronto in future meetings between Kirby and Cosimo Commisso, would be phenomenal.

We considered two other very convincing arguments for testifying, which I knew Kirby could not put out of his mind. One was the fact that Kirby was owed a lot of money for contracts he had completed in the past. That made him a definite liability with the Mob. The other was that he knew far too much for comfort. We discussed Ian Rosenberg and his common-law wife Joan Lipson, who had been murdered by the Mob in Toronto. It seemed inevitable that Kirby was destined for the same fate. The time had come for me to be able to offer Kirby a solid proposal.

First we discussed money. Kirby suggested $100,000. I told him not to be so foolish; he should ask for at least $200,000. He would need $100,000 for relocation expenses and the other $100,000 to set up a small business for some type of security. The second issue was the relocation and protection of himself and his family after it became known he would testify. A third and very important issue was immunity to prosecution. During the trial, evidence would surface that would implicate Kirby in many crimes. Immunity to prosecution would be essential. He knew that if he went to prison he was a dead man. The fourth issue was raised by Kirby. He wanted me to remain as his police contact, particularly until an agreement could be signed, because he would not trust the other coppers. With the four essential elements of the agreement reached, we shook hands and I reassured Kirby there would be no double-cross. In fact, I told him that he and I had just agreed to travel a very rough road together. There would be times when he would have to have ultimate faith in me and I would have to put my full faith and trust in him. There was no room for compromise. As it turned out, truer words would never be spoken.

There was never any doubt that Kirby was heavily involved in organized crime activity, and that he had never really opened up as an informant. The time had finally arrived. It had taken several months to establish trust and rapport between us. Kirby was ready to talk.

I told Kirby I wanted to know about some of the things he could help us with, so that when I arrived back in Toronto I could make a proposal to my people on this conspiracy, which was labeled The Connecticut Caper, and any other incidents that might be of interest. Kirby began to talk, insisting I not take notes. He started out by saying he had inadvertently

supplied the gun used in the murder of Metro Toronto Police
Constable Michael Sweet. Kirby said he felt bad about what
had happened, because when he supplied the gun he thought
it would be used to settle a debt in a drug-related incident. He
disclosed a location in Madoc, Ontario where he could easily
obtain dynamite and blasting caps. He was responsible for the
bombing of a Chinese Restaurant at 111 Elizabeth Street,
Toronto in which a Chinese cook was accidentally killed.
Kirby stated he had bombed Napoleon's Restaurant, located
across the street from the Women's Hospital in Toronto, on
instruction from Cosimo Commisso because Cosimo's wife
had been insulted by the Mâitre d' at the restaurant. He had
bombed a guy in a car on Dixon Road, Toronto. He had
bombed a car in Montreal because the owner had refused to
pay his business partner the $100,000 he owed him. He had
attempted to bomb a witness for the prosecution in a large
drug deal in Toronto. He had bombed the car of an electrical
contractor in Hamilton who owed $200,000 and had refused to
pay. Kirby sat back and grinned. He then said the guy's name
was Jack Ryan .

No wonder he had turned white when I suggested the
same name for an alias for him back in November at our
meeting at the Casa Loma. He searched my face for further
information on just how much the police really knew about
him. We didn't know much, but I couldn't tell Kirby that. I
just grinned and said, "I'm not prepared to discuss that just
yet." Kirby continued on and mentioned he had bombed an
apartment building complex on two occasions and had thrown
a bomb on the owner's front lawn on another occasion. Kirby
talked about the murder of an individual at the Satan's Choice
Club House, where the victim was shot up with battery acid
and later dumped in Rice Lake near Peterborough, Ontario.
Kirby said he was responsible for all the bombings in Toronto
over the previous seven years and was willing to give full
details to investigators if an agreement could be reached. He

was willing to testify against the Commissos in the conspiracy to commit murder and could clear up as many as one hundred major criminal offences, mainly in Toronto, but also in Montreal and Vancouver. If the agreement could be reached, he would give total cooperation.

It was to be another sleepless night for me, even though it was 2:00 AM when we finally turned in. Needless to say, I was astounded by what Kirby had been involved in. I knew an agreement had to be reached, but how was I to deal with Inspectors Wylie and McIlvenna? I knew there had to be a solution, and it eventually came in the form of a very close friend of mine outside the RCMP, Assistant Crown Attorney Al Cooper.

I first met Mr. Al Cooper in 1979 during an investigation involving Donald Freeman, a victim of a Toronto loanshark operation. I had known Freeman previously. He was a former lawyer from Britain who was active in the stock market and real estate, and drank more than he should. One Sunday morning he called our office looking for me. I returned his call and he related the story that approximately two years earlier he had borrowed $600 from an individual by the name of— what else?—Jack Ryan. Ryan was fronting money for some organized crime types in Toronto. Freeman said he had paid $1,800 in interest on the $600 loan over a period of one year. He had stopped paying for approximately another year and now the Mob wanted $4,000 to settle the loan. Freeman stated he had a visit from Ryan and his associate Arthur Hunt and felt his life was in danger. Ryan and Hunt had threatened to put him "in the ground". They had also threatened his family. Freeman had arranged a meeting with these crooks that afternoon at the McDonald's Restaurant, Leslie and Cummer Street in North End Toronto at 2:00 PM.

Freeman came to our office at 12:30 PM that day to meet with me and Cst. Brian Reteff. We wired Freeman and covered his meeting with Hunt. By mid-afternoon we had sufficient evidence against Mr. Hunt for extortion, as he again threatened Freeman with murder and injury to himself and his family. Rather than arrest him, we decided to find out who was behind this scam. We obtained an authorization for a wiretap and eventually arrested five members of organized crime in connection with Extortion. Four were convicted, while the other, who played a very minor role, was acquitted. The prosecutor on that case was Mr. Al Cooper. It was his first trial involving wiretap evidence as well as his first trial involving organized crime. Mr. Cooper, Reteff and I had had long conversations where Reteff and I described the workings of organized crime in the Toronto Area. Mr. Cooper was in awe of what he was hearing, and from that point on, maintained a keen interest in anything related to organized crime.

Mr. Cooper was a relatively young Crown Attorney at that time. He turned out to be a prince of a guy, in addition to being quite clever. You could throw all kinds of names and facts at him and he just devoured them. I was impressed with him from the day we met. He had a keen interest in seeing justice done, and was fair and understanding with everyone he met. I had been in his office on several occasions when Metro coppers needed a decision on some case and he didn't hesitate in making one. He was a gentleman in every respect and I considered him a close friend. On the Kirby deal, I felt he was the man that could be trusted to rise above the petty politics that existed back in Toronto.

Before calling it a day, I told Kirby about Cooper. I told him Cooper was a man I would trust with my life, and that as soon as I returned to my office I would seek his help in getting a firm proposal.

It was 7:30 AM on Monday, February 23, 1981. I hadn't slept well, yet it didn't take much to awake me. Kirby and I went for breakfast. At 9:00 AM the FBI agents arrived at the hotel. With Schiman was a new agent by the name of Dave

Cotton, also out of the New Haven Office. He was pleasant enough, but I couldn't help but think that the FBI must operate like the RCMP in many respects. Cotton was senior to Schiman and now that things were looking favourable, senior officers were jumping on the bandwagon. It happened all the time in our office. The problem was you could never find these individuals if trouble developed.

At 10:08 AM Monday morning Agent Robert Martineau set up surveillance on 98 McMullen Avenue. Kirby rode with one of the surveillance units and in fact took one of the first photos of the intended victim. At 10:37 AM Martineau reported a female had just left the address and started her vehicle with Connecticut licence plate number YZ-1852. She then went back inside. At 10:41 AM the same female came out of 98 McMullen Avenue and got into the vehicle, this time accompanied by an unknown male. I was in a car with Don Brutnell. About three blocks from the house we pulled up beside the car at an intersection. For the first time I saw Helen Nafpliotis. Approximately 38 years old, she was wearing a red coat, had blond hair and gold rimmed glasses, and despite a rather flat nose was very attractive. Seated next to her was Nicky Melia. They carried on a conversation as if everything was normal. It was 10:40 AM when Nicky Melia kissed his lover for what he thought was the last time at the bus stop in downtown Stamford. He was on his way to court in North Carolina. Helen was supposed to be taking her last car ride. Kirby had his instructions to do his job after this individual had been dropped off at the bus stop. Surveillance advised they had taken a photo of Nicky.

Nafpliotis drove through traffic towards Interstate Highway 95 North. Just north of Exit 5, Agent Schiman pulled up beside her vehicle and with red light and his badge, signalled for her to pull over to the curb. About five other surveillance units stopped as well. Schiman had a short conversation with Nafpliotis by the side of the highway. After producing proper identification he got into her car and we all headed for room 221 at the Holiday Inn in Darien. At 11:05 AM agents Schiman, Cotton, and Brutnell and myself began to outline the circumstances of why we were there, information that left Helen Nafpliotis in utter shock. Schiman convinced her she was in grave danger. She asked if she could call Greenwich Furs where she worked and tell them she wouldn't be in that day.

Helen came from Greece and had been in the US for approximately ten years. She had worked as a hairdresser for Nicky at his shop Continental Coiffures, 111 Highridge Road, Stamford for three years, but no longer worked there because of the trouble with Nicky's wife. Helen at first felt Nicky's wife might be the one who would want to harm her, since she had found out about her husband's affair over two years ago. Helen loved Nicky and wanted to marry him, but he wouldn't leave his wife. Helen had then returned to Greece for six months to try and resolve her problems, but Nicky had asked her to return. Helen did return and was assaulted and beaten very badly with a stick by Nicky's wife on one occasion. She was in the hospital for several days. On another occasion, someone had slashed her tires while parked at Kennedy Airport to pick up her mother and daughter. On the return trip to Stamford a tire blew on the highway, almost causing the car to roll over. Another time Nicky's wife had threatened to kill her. She called the Stamford Police, but they said they couldn't do much.

Helen had then started to date Tony Innello. Nicky became extremely jealous. The next thing she knew Tony was shot five times, but lived. Nicky was now charged with attempted murder. When she told him she would be seeing another friend who was arriving in the US in the near future, Nicky had said, "I would prefer to have you dead rather than see you with another man."

Helen told us that Jerry Russo had dropped Nicky off at her house the day before. He had stayed the night and she'd dropped him at the bus stop this morning. She knew Nicky was also in some kind of trouble over stolen jewelry, but didn't know anything other than what she had read in the papers. Schiman asked if Nicky was involved in organized crime. Helen responded by saying, "I'd like to know the answer to that question myself."

I could tell that Helen was not sure whether to believe the FBI and was probably considering the possibility that this was some sort of sting operation. I showed her my RCMP badge and told her the plot to kill her was very real, that I had followed a guy from Canada who was to do the job. She hugged me and thanked me, then broke down and cried, finally convinced the information about her intended murder was correct.

It was an emotional moment for all of us, even a bunch of hard-nosed coppers who had dealt with loads of tragedy over the years. I'll be honest, I had a hell of a time holding back the tears. Here was this beautiful young woman who had out-lived her usefulness. Had it not been for the intervention of fate, instead of talking to us in this hotel room she would have had about five .22 bullets in her head and been dumped into some lake, never to be seen or heard from again.

When Helen regained her composure, Schiman continued with the interview. Helen related she knew something was wrong over the past couple of weeks. Nicky had taken her to the West Coast of the US for an enjoyable weekend and had taken her to dinner at the Astoria in Queens, New York last night. She had sensed a change in his behavior toward her. "He's been all kindness; he hasn't even yelled at me lately." Although Nicky was never charged, it seemed likely that he knew about the impending contract, and in fact may have even been instrumental in the arrangements.

Helen broke down for the second time and said, "I don't want to die! I'll have to hide for the rest of my life. If I go to God he will still find me. I don't know where to go." Helen reiterated that she knew nothing about Nicky's criminal activity. If he wanted her dead it was because of jealousy. Helen had not witnessed the shooting of Innello, but it was suggested she might have helped the police by allowing them to search her place for Nicky without a warrant. She was alone in the house at the time and knew Nicky was not there, so she saw no harm in allowing the police to search for him. She learned that Nicky was upset about that. Helen confided in us that Nicky was the father of one of her daughters, which made it more difficult to understand why he would want her killed.

We were satisfied Helen Nafpliotis was probably not targeted for murder because of her knowledge of organized crime. It was most likely she was causing family problems within the Mob Family. With that issue resolved, the conversation turned to her future and security. The FBI made those arrangements and the interview terminated at 1:52 PM.

As we left the Holiday Inn and walked towards the cars on the parking lot I spoke to Helen, knowing it would probably be the last time I would see her. I wished her all the best and that someday she could get her life back together, be reunited with her children and make a new life for herself. With tears streaming down her face, she again hugged and thanked me. This time I know a few tears rolled down my cheeks as I bid her good-bye. Kirby had been sitting in a nearby car and had witnessed what took place. He was even more determined than ever to testify against these people.

The FBI were fully apprised of Kirby's disclosure and willingness to testify. They took a calculated risk when they allowed Nafpliotis to return to her house and gather up her belongings and jewelry. Two agents accompanied her. Neighbors had spotted Helen getting into the car with two men and reported to police that she looked despondent; it appeared, when she was not heard from over the next three days, that she might have been kidnapped. Stamford Police were called in to investigate, but since there was no trust between the FBI and the Stamford Police, the FBI decided not to inform them of what had transpired. Since Kirby had decided to testify, provided an agreement could be reached that satisfied the four conditions we'd discussed, the story that Helen allegedly had been kidnapped would fit in with Kirby's explanation to the Commissos when we returned to Canada.

It was 2:00 PM on Monday when Kirby and I left the Darien Holiday Inn with our FBI driver. We made the trip to LaGuardia and headed for home. We had both been through some stressful days and late nights, and were looking forward to familiar surroundings and some well-deserved rest. Our flight was scheduled to leave LaGuardia at 6:00 PM, but due to very heavy fog, it would be 9:30 that evening before we got off the ground.

During our wait inside the secure area of LaGuardia, I picked up the phone and called Al Cooper at his office in Toronto. It was Monday afternoon and I knew he would be there. Although he was usually busy, he always made time for me and today was no exception. I briefly explained the circumstances with respect to Kirby's break, entry and theft charges, the fact that he had already given the police a substantial amount of information, and that because of Tavenor and Hall he was now looking at serving two years on Thursday of this week. I explained that I had gone to my Inspectors but had received no support. I had spoken to Sgt. Bob Silverton on several occasions and on the very last contact I'd had with him he had suggested it was Crown Attorney Frank Armstrong who would not give on the deal. I explained to Cooper that we now needed Kirby to do the follow-up investigation on this current conspiracy to commit murder, and that he would be no good to us in jail. I told him I felt we could implicate the main members of the Commisso Family and other organized crime figures in many crimes. I told him it was absolutely essential that we work hard to be able to offer Kirby a proposal.

Al Cooper understood completely and recognized the importance of these events. We arranged to meet at his office the first thing in the morning. Before hanging up I asked Cooper if I could mention his name to Kirby, because I wanted him to handle his case and perform the resulting prosecutions. He said he would love to, but that might be subject to some politics in his own department. I thanked him and told him I would see him in the morning.

Kirby was pleased when he heard I had talked to Al Cooper. There is no doubt in my mind that had it not been for the intervention and support of Al Cooper, it would have been impossible to further this investigation. When I couldn't get support from my own people, he was there. He deserves exceptional credit and I thank him from the bottom of my heart.

Kirby and I landed at Toronto International Airport at 10:15 PM Monday night. I had some concern that he would be challenged regarding his American money but he passed through customs without incident. With just a slight nod we parted company. Kirby knew I would do all I could, and I knew he trusted me and on my recommendation trusted Al Cooper. It was imperative now that I be able to pull together a firm proposal for Kirby.

5

The Canadian Contracts For Murder

It was 11:30 AM the following morning when I met with Crown Attorney Al Cooper. I had already briefed my office and Inspector Wylie on the US aspect of the investigation, and told them I had scheduled a meeting with Cooper. Although I detected some resentment, I was allowed to attend. Cooper and I discussed in detail what had already transpired on the case. Based on facts presented to him, he suggested we visit the Crown Attorney in charge of prosecutions in the Toronto Area.

We travelled to 1100 Finch Avenue West in Northwest Toronto, where we met Senior Crown Attorney Steve Legett. Cooper outlined the details to Legett and asked that he help with an offer for Kirby. Legett, who had heard of Cecil Kirby, was cool to the suggestion. He asked that we go back downtown and meet with Crown Attorney Frank Armstrong. We met with Armstrong and his bottom line was there was to be no deal, but he did agree to have a meeting the following morning with the Metro copper Sgt. Silverton present. Cooper and I realized we were receiving little support from his department. Cooper's immediate boss was Robert McGee, who turned out to be great to deal with. Cooper discussed the proposition with him and, unlike my experience with my superiors, received his total support.

That afternoon I couldn't be contacted because of a two-and-one-half hour lecture I had to give on NCIS and organized crime to a training session at our office. At 5:00 PM I had just arrived home, some twenty-five miles outside the city, when the phone rang. It was Al Cooper. He wanted me to return to Toronto for a 6:00 PM briefing with Rod McLeod, Assistant Deputy Attorney General of Ontario. Without question or hesitation I said I would be there. I called my superior, Staff Sgt. Don Kennedy, briefed him, and hurried out the door. It was a forty-minute drive and I wanted to pick up my file at the office.

I met Mr. Cooper at precisely 6:00 PM and he introduced me to Mr. McLeod. We had a congenial meeting which lasted an hour and a half. Mr. McLeod's assessment was simple: "We've spent millions of dollars trying to investigate the Commissos and have not been very successful. If a good chance of success means letting Kirby walk, then there is no question." I looked at Al Cooper and nodded, trying desperately not to grin. Without Cooper, I would never have heard those words. With an ally such as the Assistant Deputy Attorney General of Ontario, I knew Kirby would finally get a deal.

Kirby's end was looked after, but what would be the repercussions for me? I was interested only in putting some bad guys in jail and saving some lives. I wondered if there was something wrong with that, with not taking "No" for an answer. I had followed my conscience and sense of what was right, but I had stepped on quite a few toes along the way. God only knew where that would lead.

The following day Rod McLeod discussed the matter with the senior officers at the RCMP office, who were caught off guard. The word that a deal was in the making quickly filtered down to Inspector Wylie and McIlvenna. From that point onward I could do nothing right. If I thought I lacked support prior to finalizing a deal with Kirby, I was to find out how much worse it could get. It seemed to me as though McIlvenna and Wylie wanted my hide tacked to the wall. I have to confess it was rotten working under those circumstances.

It was 10:00 PM that night when I reached Kirby. I told him things had gone favourably and we had a meeting set for 9:00 AM the following morning with Leggett, Armstrong, Sgt. Silverton and Cooper to decide what was to be done at Kirby's next appearance in court. Kirby was happy with this news and told me he had arranged a meeting with Cosimo Commisso for 12:00 noon on Friday, February 27, 1981, at Faces Disco, Howard Johnson Hotel, Dixon Road, Toronto, to discuss what had happened in the US. I said that was beautiful and we would be there. I was quite confident Kirby would not be going to jail on Thursday.

At 8:20 AM the following day I met with my two immediate bosses, S/Sgt. Kennedy and Sgt. Ross, and Inspector Wylie, to brief them on the previous night's meeting with the Deputy Attorney General and the upcoming meeting with the Crown Attorneys. I'm not sure what their thoughts were at this time, but none of them offered to attend the meeting. I could tell Wylie was steaming over the fact I had gone around him and McIlvenna directly to the Deputy Attorney General, but I felt that they had had ample time to intercede. Since they chose to do nothing, I had absolutely no misgivings whatsoever.

Inspector Wylie may have had sound reasons for not interceding in the Kirby affair, but if so I never knew what they were. In general, I feel the RCMP is hampered to some degree by commissioned officers who spend their entire careers in administration, circumventing the real world of police work. These officers often find themselves in positions of power and decision-making that surpass their capabilities.

At 9:00 PM on Wednesday, the 25th of February, I attended a meeting with Steve Leggett, Frank Armstrong, Al Cooper and Sgt. Robert Cowan, who represented an ailing Sgt.

Silverton. No agreement could be reached on Kirby, and Leggett was insisting on time in jail; he would not compromise. To our surprise Leggett phoned Rod McLeod with Al Cooper and me still in his office. Leggett was then ordered directly by McLeod to put Kirby's case over for adjournment the following day. After that, neither he nor Armstrong were to have anything further to do with the Kirby charges. I couldn't believe my ears, but I knew we were making real progress. I knew that Al Cooper had stuck his neck out on my behalf and in the interest of justice.

A beleaguered Steve Leggett took me aside and told me that he preferred to be called Mr. Leggett and not by his first name. There was no love lost between us and I replied that I hadn't heard him calling me Corporal Murphy.

Later that day I again met with Inspector Wylie. He was even further upset with the direct approach from the Deputy Attorney General. He told me I should have come to him. A politician I am not, and I wasn't long in reminding him that I had come to him, several times in fact, and he had refused to take any action. By this time I was fired up and didn't mince words regarding my feelings about his handling of the Kirby affair, but I was careful not to say anything that would give him grounds for disciplinary action.

Kirby appeared in court on Thursday, the 26th of February, and the matter of sentencing was postponed until the 10th of April at the request of the Crown. With that problem out of the way, it gave us time to prepare for the meeting the following day between Kirby and Cosimo Commisso.

Friday, the 27th of February, was another busy day. At 8:00 AM we met with the RCMP surveillance unit to brief them on the impending meeting at the Howard Johnson Hotel. I then called Schiman in Connecticut and confirmed that Helen Nafpliotis had in fact disappeared from the scene in Stamford. Schiman reassured me she would not surface for some period of time, allowing us time to conduct a series of meetings with

the Commissos in Toronto without endangering Kirby.
Schiman further confirmed that the Stamford Police were
investigating a missing persons complaint. Someone had seen
two men forcing Nafpliotis into a red vehicle. She was crying
and they had taken her car. That report had been in the papers
and it fit with the story Kirby would tell the Commissos, now
that he intended to testify against them. Agent Schiman
reassured me he would let me know immediately if there were
any changes. This information was passed along to Kirby,
who exuded confidence, saying he was ready for the meeting.

Getting the paperwork done is always a pain. We obtained a licence for Kirby to carry technical equipment used in
surreptitious surveillance. He was also required to sign a one-
party consent form authorizing the police to record and utilize
in court any conversations that took place between the party
that gives the consent and any other conversations to which he
might become privy. There was considerable danger in this
unimpinged consent form. Some time earlier I had raised the
issue with Inspector Wylie on another operation. The scenario
I had put to Inspector Wylie was this: supposing a police
officer signs a consent form and goes to meet with an informant. During the meeting the informant shows the police
officer a gun or a small quantity of drugs and the policeman
does not seize it, because it might jeopardize his relationship
with the informant or another investigation he is working on.
The information on the tape could be used in any criminal
code charges or even RCMP service court proceedings against
that police officer. Wylie didn't think that was a problem and
refused to consider any changes in the form.

I had never raised the issue with Kirby, but when I met
him at 11:00 AM in the parking lot of the Skyline Hotel, just a
short distance from the Howard Johnson Hotel, he read the
consent form that I had asked him to sign and his first question was, "What protection do I have against them (the RCMP)
using that tape against me, since an agreement has not been

settled?" I didn't argue the point because I knew he was quite correct. I agreed to add a rider to the bottom of the consent form, and all the other consent forms he would sign, which would afford Kirby some protection. On the bottom of the form I added in pen, "Provided the evidence obtained as the result of this consent form shall not be used against Cecil Kirby, and further, that I be afforded the protection of the Canada Evidence Act in any testimony I might give respecting these matters."

This protection is now provided for in the new Constitution, but it wasn't in place back then. Inspectors Wylie and McIlvenna would later be incensed that I added that rider, and they would make it part of an extensive one-year RCMP Internal Investigation in what appeared to me to be an ever more determined effort to tack my hide to the wall. It seemed as though they were intent on using the tapes against the Commissos with or without his consent. If no agreement with Kirby was reached, they could have used the tapes to expose Kirby as an informant; his life would not have been worth a plug nickel. Kirby was street-wise, however, and it appeared as if Inspector Wylie and his associates would have to set their clocks just a little bit earlier if they were going to beat Kirby at his own game. This incident strengthened the trust between Kirby and me because he knew I would have no part of any double-cross, nor would I lie to him. That trust was a bond that kept us on track in the months to follow.

With the formalities out of the way, I hastily put a transmitter on Kirby so I could listen to the conversation live and render assistance if necessary. Kirby also wore a small Nagra tape recorder as a backup in case the transmitter malfunctioned. Sgt. Ross was in a separate car and the surveillance team circled nearby. When I found a suitable location for the surveillance vehicle on a parking lot near Faces Disco, I radioed Sgt. Ross and he gave Kirby the signal we were ready for the meeting.

My actual notes for that meeting were recorded as follows:

27 Feb. 81 (Friday)

12:01 PM Cecil Kirby arrives Howard Johnson, photo taken.

12:05 PM Overheard Cecil Kirby on phone.

12:34 PM Overheard Cecil Kirby call person named Cosimo. Cosimo will be over.

12:41 PM New tape on Uher. Tested and clean. Tape CC #1, 27 Feb. 81.

1:21 PM   Surveillance advised Cosimo Commisso inside Faces Disco.

1:27 PM   Cosimo Commisso and Cecil Kirby out to front of the Howard Johnson. Transmitter recording. Photos taken with two cameras, 55 and 400 mm lens. Both talk on sidewalk. Cosimo described as 5'9" approx., dark grey and brown sports jacket, brown pants (short) white shirt (open neck) approx. 180 lbs., black curly hair and black moustache, smoking cigarette, age approx. 35/36. Cecil Kirby wearing brown sports jacket, black patches on sleeves, blue jeans, blue shirt (I will delete any further description of Kirby for security reasons).

1:31 PM   Meeting breaks up and Cosimo walks east on lot to Howard Johnson Restaurant entrance and stops and looks all around. Then goes to vehicle out of my sight. Norm Ross advised vehicle orange in color, licence plate number MHW-387. I see orange vehicle leave on side road. Kirby returns to his car.

1:34 PM   Tape CC #1, 27 Feb. 81 removed.

1:38 PM   I return to Skyline parking lot and met Cecil Kirby. Norm Ross covering. I recover equipment and mark the tape from the Nagra CC #1A, 27 Feb. 81. Kirby advised us that the meeting had gone exceptionally well and that he will get paid an additional $6,000 at the next meeting on 10 Mar. 81 at 12:00 noon at the same location. Cosimo had asked Kirby if he had done it and said he was pleased with the results. Cosimo told Kirby he had lots more work for him.

2:00 PM   Surveillance and investigation finished and away.

The following is a summary of the transcript that was recorded on tape CC #1, 27 Feb. 81, between Cecil Kirby and Cosimo Commisso:

> C.K.: You told me fifteen thousand. He paid me five.
>
> C.C.: You did it?
>
> C.K.: Yeah.
>
> C.C.: It's done?
>
> C.K.: Yeah.
>
> C.C.: O.K., that's all you gonna get, O.K.? But you did it? When you did it, Tuesday?
>
> C.K.: Monday. Ah, I don't want to get into details, O.K.? He said to me, he'd pay me extra if she was a missing person. I took another guy down there, O.K.? They didn't see him. She's gone, never find her again. Listen, I'm going to Vegas Saturday, tomorrow. I'll be back March 10th and I want to get five thousand. I told him (Melia), I said, "You want her missing, I want an extra thousand." Six thousand.
>
> C.C.: Yeah?
>
> C.K.: I got remanded in court yesterday until April 10th.
>
> C.C.: Yeah?
>
> C.K.: Alright, March 10th, here at twelve o'clock. I don't want to go near your bakery, O.K.?
>
> C.C.: Alright.

I had heard this conversation coming over the transmitter/recorder, and when I met with Sgt. Ross on the Skyline Parking lot he asked me how things had gone. I had trouble containing my excitement. I struck him on the shoulder with my fist and said, "We just got Cosimo Commisso for conspiracy to commit murder."

Ross said, "Are you sure?"

I replied, "No, I'm not sure. I'm positive."

We headed south back to the RCMP office on Jarvis St. Later that night I reviewed the tape at home to confirm the conversation was there. I was not disappointed.

On Tuesday, March 3, 1981, an early morning meeting was attended by Staff Sergeant Kennedy, Sergeant Ross, and Inspectors Wylie and McIlvenna. Word had leaked out that things had gone exceptionally well. Now the police politics were becoming more intrusive. Wylie wanted a further meeting in the Commanding Officer's Board Room later that afternoon.

That same day I turned over the three US bills I had received from Kirby for fingerprinting to the RCMP Identification Section in Toronto. As it turned out, no fingerprints could be identified on the money.

At 1:30 PM that same day a meeting was convened in the Commanding Officer's Board Room. Not only were Kennedy, Ross, Wylie, McIlvenna, and I present, but several new faces were on the scene. Wylie and McIlvenna had invited Inspector Don Banks, Head of Metro Police Intelligence Unit, Inspector Tom O'Grady, Head of the Task Force on Bikers, for whom Constables Hall and Tavenor worked, Staff Sergeant Lyle McCharles from OPP, who worked for McIlvenna on the Special Enforcement Unit, and last but not least, the guy who I felt had compromised my safety by telling Kirby he knew he was talking with the Horsemen, Cst. Ron Tavenor, Metro Police.

Wylie asked me to brief the meeting on what had transpired to date. I emphasized the fact that Kirby was still a Confidential Informant and outlined his four proposals to be contained in an agreement, if one could be reached. I also mentioned the potential of clearing as many as 100 major criminal offences, particularly all the bombings over the past seven years in Toronto.

I had been through this scenario on many other occasions, and was actually somewhat surprised I had even been invited to the meeting. It wasn't unusual for an NCIS investigator to work diligently on a project, then find out that a meeting had been convened without his presence and his project handed over to someone else. Once a project started getting results, you had to beat the upper echelon off the bandwagon with a stick. Yet it often seemed as though the very ones eager to take over would typically sit around and do nothing for months. I could see the writing on the wall. This one looked exceptionally good and the buzzards were circling.

The essence of the meeting was that the police might be able to reach an agreement with Kirby. In return they would expect him to give total disclosure of past crimes and be willing to testify. I reassured them that that would not be a problem. Then Insp. Wylie dropped the second shoe, so to speak; he suggested that Insp. McIlvenna's SEU section would be taking over Kirby and the investigation. It was surprising how things could change so quickly. From Wylie's "We are not investigators and have no jurisdiction to do anything" and McIlvenna's "I wouldn't touch it with a 100-foot pole" to wanting to take full control of Kirby and the investigation. Absolutely amazing. I felt Wylie had an ulterior motive in wanting SEU to handle the investigation. In my opinion he wanted NCIS out of it so that his competence in decision-making would not be challenged. And I was certain McIlvenna and his crew welcomed this opportunity to make some easy arrests. To hell with the total problem. The stats were impressive until you looked from whence they came.

I kept my composure and listened to the proposed changes to the investigation being tabled. They were prepared to cut me totally out of the investigation, but they hadn't considered one important fact—Kirby's fourth demand. In Kirby's own words, "It's Murphy I trust and it's only Murphy I'll work through."

I knew that all police officers in the room should have been bound by a common goal, but as the meeting progressed I felt a growing sense of indifference to me and what I had to say, as if I was an outsider intruding on some secret fraternity. Glancing down the huge oak conference table I noted the prevalence of Masonic rings. I wondered if this was one of the keys to being an accepted member of the club.

Later that day I heard from Agent John Schiman. Stamford Police were assuming that Nafpliotis had been murdered. There was a suggestion that they had reason to believe that Nicky had knowledge of the murder. Schiman had decided that for security reasons they could not take the chance of letting Stamford Police in on what was actually taking place. He felt strongly that the Melia family had a connection in the upper echelon of the Stamford Police. Nafpliotis would be going into hiding on March 5, 1981.

Schiman was so impressed with Kirby's performance that he wanted him to consider his earlier offer to work undercover in the US. He also offered Kirby the US Witness Protection Program. We discussed new ID for Kirby, and he told me if there was any change in the Nafpliotis security status, he would get back to me.

Some progress was being made with respect to Kirby's request. Inspector Wylie, RCMP Inspector Banks of Metro Police, and Inspector O'Grady of OPP had approached the Attorney General's Department and had reached an informal agreement on protection for Kirby and his immunity to prosecution. They had not reached an agreement on his award money. Wylie also wanted Sergeant Al Cooke, Metro Police, introduced to Kirby. I discussed this with Kirby but he would not trust Cooke.

During the time of the previous meeting with the Commissos some eleven days earlier, I had requested payment in the amount of $1,000 for Kirby for the drug information he had supplied. This was denied because they maintained Kirby was under charges and it was contrary to RCMP policy to pay an informant who is under charge. I argued that the policy allowed for exceptional circumstances. I felt the exceptional circumstances were that Kirby had already pleaded guilty to the break, entry and theft charge and there was no way

payment would interfere with the outcome of the case. No
matter how I pleaded, there would be no change. I knew
Kirby was scheduled to get a further payment at the next
meeting on March 10th. Since I had been unable to get him
any money from the Police, I knew he would, out of necessity,
want to keep the money he would receive from the
Commissos. I explained this to Insp. McIlvenna and S/Sgt.
Lyle McCharles after the meeting on the February 27th, 1981.
They had both promised that they would have $2,000 ready
for me prior to the meeting on March 10th. Kirby had had no
means of income since he'd started to work for us in November of 1980. He owed Chargex $4,000, owed large lawyer fees
for his court appearances, owed his father a considerable sum,
and had absolutely no money for day-to-day expenses. I tried
in vain to explain that he was getting desperate. I had been
able to wrangle two $100 payments for expenses through
Sergeant Ross, but that was all I could come up with. My
pleading fell on deaf ears and when the March 10th meeting
rolled around, I had no money to offer Kirby.

On the 10th of March, the excitement was building around
upcoming meetings between Kirby and the Commissos. NCIS
was informed that Sgt. John Simpson of Metro Police, and Cst.
Danielle Bouchard of OPP, both attached to McIlvenna's SEU
squad, would be responsible for the rest of the investigation.
Kennedy, Ross, and myself met with Simpson and Bouchard
along with Lyle McCharles and gave them a complete briefing
on the investigation to date. It was at that meeting that
McCharles advised me there was no money for Kirby, and that
if he were paid any monies by the Commissos I was to be sure
and seize it for evidence. Wylie convened a second meeting
and insisted I introduce Sgt. Al Cooke to Kirby. I said I'd do
my best, but knew Kirby would have the last say and his
answer would probably still be negative. Later that day NCIS
received a copy of a memorandum from Insp. Wylie to Insp.
McIlvenna stating that McIlvenna's crew would now be in

charge of the investigation. This memo was issued without agreement by S/Sgt. Don Kennedy or myself, who up until that point had control of the investigation. Insp. Wylie had become part of a three-man "steering committee", along with Insp. Banks and Insp. O'Grady. It was a safe position for Insp. Wylie, removed from the responsibilities of decision-making. After the work and the dangers involved to date, it would have been a little more acceptable had we at least been consulted on this decision. It wasn't the first time this sort of thing had happened to me, and I didn't expect it to be the last.

I was rather surprised after our briefing of Simpson and Bouchard, the new investigators from SEU, when Sgt. Ross and I were asked to cover the meeting of March 10th between Kirby and Cosimo Commisso. The meeting was scheduled for 12:00 noon, but was fortunately changed to 1:00 PM as we were hard-pressed for time. When the surveillance squad was arranged, consent forms signed, licence obtained, and all the other necessities arranged, Sgt. Ross and I, along with the Surveillance Unit, headed to the North End of Toronto to cover the second meeting. Simpson and Bouchard headed North as well, but only to sit and monitor our conversations from a few blocks away. Their excuse for keeping their distance was that Cosimo Commisso might recognize them, yet I was by myself in a large surveillance unit. I couldn't keep the thought from entering my mind that Bouchard and Simpson would be several blocks away if anything went wrong.

My notes for Tuesday, March 10, 1981, read as follows:

11:25 AM Place new Nagra Tape on body pack. CC#1B

12:10 PM Meet Cecil Kirby on west parking lot of Skyline Hotel, Dixon Rd., Toronto. Signs consent form to have conversation recorded between himself and Cosimo Commisso. Puts on body transmitter and Nagra tape recorder. Subject searched for money but negative.

Although not contained in my actual notes, it was at this time that Kirby and I discussed the necessity of seizing whatever monies might be paid to him by Cosimo Commisso for evidence. Kirby asked if the SEU or Wylie had approved any money for him. I said, "No."

Kirby became very upset and said, "I've worked for those bastards for over four months on nothing but promises, Mark. I know it's not your fault, but I'm desperate for money. I have no money for even food. This whole deal is off. You can tell Wylie and McIlvenna to go fuck themselves. I'm finished. I'll meet Commisso tonight when you're not around and get the money. Take the equipment; the deal is finished."

I asked Kirby to calm down. I then went over to Sgt. Ross' car parked nearby and explained the dilemma. We both recognized the importance of another meeting with further photographs and further recorded conversations to strengthen our case. Not only that, we needed Kirby's cooperation and testimony. Wylie and McIlvenna didn't know about the rider I had put on the consent forms at that time, and probably thought they had Kirby in a compromising position, but such was not the case. Ross said we were instructed to seize the money and we really don't have a choice. We called Simpson and Bouchard on the police radio with no response. Ross even went into the Skyline and called. Still no response, even at the SEU office. This was all taking place less than ten minutes prior to the meeting. When Ross had no luck reaching anyone, I went back to talk to Kirby. I emphasized the importance of the meeting, what could be gained, and told him if necessary I would take the money out of my own account. He made his final offer.

"Mark, I'll only go through with the meeting if you give me your word you will not seize the money. I'll keep the money for a couple of days if they want to buy it back for evidence. They don't realize it, but I'm under a lot of pressure here, too."

I was caught between a rock and a hard place. The situation had to be evaluated and a decision made. I thought about the ramifications of me not seizing the money as directed. Was it a criminal offence? I wondered, "Where's the hell is the steering committee or the investigators from the SEU, now that I need them?" I looked at Kirby and said, "O.K., you can keep the money, provided you show it to me when you come out and you keep it in your possession until we have an opportunity to buy it back." Kirby agreed. I would later be severely reprimanded during the RCMP Internal Investigation for allowing that to happen.

Continuing with my recorded notes:

12:50 PM   I place new tape on Uher receiver CC#1A at Skyline Lot.

1:03 PM   Cecil Kirby arrives Faces Disco, Howard Johnson, Dixon Rd., and inside. Photos taken.

1:16 PM   Special/Constable Danny McCormack and Constable Earla-Kim Black, surveillance unit, inside Howard Johnson via front door. Photo taken.

1:47 PM   I overhear on receiver Kirby talking to someone. Sounds like Cosimo Commisso.

1:54 PM   I ask Danny McCormack to go and check. McCormack confirms it's Cosimo Commisso. McCormack advised he's wearing brown camel sports jacket and had black moustache and close to height of Kirby. He is the same person photographed on 27 Feb. 81 by me and shown to Dan before leaving office today.

1:59 PM   Conversation ends.

2:00 PM   Kirby out Faces Disco door and into vehicle and away. Photo taken.

2:01 PM   Surveillance discontinued.

2:20 PM   Meet Cecil Kirby at Skyline Hotel and recover equipment. Debrief Kirby. Kirby says Cosimo wants two more persons killed in Metro. On Tuesday, 17 Mar 81, Kirby is to go to

Cosimo's house pick him up and Cosimo will show him where unknown male lives and arrange for contract. Kirby agrees to have the conversation recorded and to have his car wired for the meeting. Will leave it at Shopper's Drug Mart, Yonge and Steeles Ave. on Monday morning. I will meet him at Red Panzers, Tuesday 10 AM, 17 Mar. 81, at Plaza at Steeles and Bathurst, Toronto. Cosimo also talked about Mr. Gallo of Vancouver, and said he felt they had him on the drug deal that went down in Vancouver recently. Cosimo had to appear out in Vancouver on the twenty-first of March or April, and if bail revoked, then Kirby could deal with Remo Commisso, Cosimo's brother, concerning the murders. Kirby had approximately $5,000 in cash. Offered to sell it back to Police, but no agreement reached. Approximately 48 $100 and 10 $20 bills. Monies retained by Kirby.

Kirby and I continued to talk that day and he began to really open up. He said he could clear up eighteen bombings and several extortions plus three or four fires. We made a list as follows:

Montreal	Two extortions, one bombing, and a murder that he was not responsible for.
Guelph	One bombing and one fire.
Hamilton	One bombing and one fire.
Brampton	One bombing.
Mississauga	Three bombings.
Toronto	Five bombings.

Kirby told me that of all the bombings in the city of Toronto over the last seven years only the 1980 bombing at Arvivi's Disco on Bloor St. and the 1969 bombing at the Holiday Inn were acts he was not responsible for. With Kirby's information, several people have since been arrested and convicted for the Disco explosion involving the owner. Kirby told me that Cosimo, Remo and Michael Commisso were all involved. He said Larry Commisso brought the

dynamite to him for the Mississauga job. Kirby said the guy in
Montreal they wanted murdered lived on Heath St., and that
his office was on a street with several fabric factories. Kirby
said he was unable to get this guy, but he was later killed with
a shotgun. Although never charged with the crime, Kirby felt
Remo Commisso was somehow involved.

This had been an eventful day to say the least, but it wasn't
over yet. After Kirby left the area, Sgt. Ross and I got together
and he asked how things had gone. I told him exceptionally
well. Cosimo had really committed himself on the US conspiracy to murder and wanted two other people in Metro
Toronto killed. Ross then asked if Kirby got the money. I
winked at Ross and said, "No, but leave that with me; I have to
straighten some things out." In actual fact I wanted to discuss
the matter with my good friend Al Cooper before I said too
much. I wondered if I also would have to testify under the
protection of the Canada Evidence Act for my own protection.

The following is the actual conversation recorded on
March 10, 1981 between Cecil Kirby and Cosimo Commisso:

C.K.: You got the money?

C.C.: You got it coming. Don't worry about it. I went and
borrow for you. I didn't count it.

C.K.: So how much is here?

C.C.: Five thousand.

C.K.: Have you been talking to him? (Vince Melia)

C.C.: He called that kid that come with you. (Antonio
Romeo)

C.K.: Alright, like, he got it his way, you know.

C.C.: Yeah, because you killed her, eh?

C.K.: Yeah.

C.C.: The car disappear too? Her car?

C.K.: Well yeah, in a roundabout way, they'll never find it.
She'll be a missing person sooner or later, that's it, which is better
for everyone. Oh, there's something that I forgot to talk to you

about. Who the fuck is this kid that they introduce me to, that showed me around? Who the fuck is that? I don't like talking to somebody I don't know.

C.C.: I introduce nobody. But he's O.K.. You don't have to worry about him, O.K.? Listen Cecil, there are still things to be done. (In Toronto)

C.K.: You said you had some guy here you wanted to get rid of. For yourself?

C.C.: Yeah.

C.K.: How much?

C.C.: Got to get everything settled together, we have to get his address and everything.

C.K.: Yeah, right. The little guy out in Vancouver, what happened to him, what did he get, did he get any time, that guy Gallo? (Gallo and Cosimo Commisso were facing extensive narcotics charges in Vancouver at this time.)

C.C.: Yeah, very stupid for Gallo, very stupid.

C.K.: He's still in jail?

C.C.: Yeah.

C.K.: So can we still do that thing out in Vancouver or what? (They had intended to do an armed robbery connected with the fishing industry.)

C.C.: No.

C.K.: No good, eh?

C.C.: But I still worry they're going to get me. (The police)

C.K.: Naw, if they haven't got you now they never will.

C.C.: O.K., by the Hall (the Commisso Banquet Hall and Bakery), you know, yesterday, a car parks in the driveway in front of the house, and this guy comes out and goes through, takes a camera and starts 'tac, tac, tac'. One of those little black books, he wrote something in it in the middle.

C.K.: They're not too obvious, are they?

C.C.: Yesterday was nobody there, just me and my brother, they want a picture of us.

C.K.: Oh, it was the CBC again? (The CBC Connections series showed the Commissos in 1977 and 1979 on national TV)

C.C.: No, they were cops for sure. See what I mean, because if they had to arrest me they don't come take a picture then arrest me, they arrest me first. (This sounded to me like McIlvenna's Raiders; they just forgot their invisible paint)

C.K.: Yeah.

C.C.: When it was an arrest they were never obvious.

C.K.: Look, it must be the CBC doing another series. You'll see your picture on TV again. Alright, I'll see you next Tuesday morning at your house.

C.C.: Yeah. Get hold of a couple of guns.

C.K.: Alright, I'll see.

The following day, after I had handed the tapes over to the SEU for transcribing, they gathered in our office for a debriefing. There was McCharles, Simpson, and Bouchard from SEU, Kennedy, Ross and myself. We gave them full details on what had transpired the previous day, but then the issue of money came up. I said to John Simpson, who had several years' service with Metro, "I don't want to discuss that just at the moment. Just leave that aspect with me and I will let you know the answer either later today or tomorrow. Don't be concerned, I'll handle that end in court. It will be looked after."

With that, Danielle Bouchard of the SEU fired up my Irish temper. It was the SEU that had promised they would have $2,000 for Kirby prior to this meeting, and they had reneged. Bouchard, a rookie OPP officer, piped up and said, "We're the investigators and we want to know everything."

I said, "Look, Bouchard, you figure out if he got the money. If you say he got the money, then he got the money. On the other hand, if you say he didn't get the money, then he didn't get the money." I told her again to leave it with me; I wanted to see a friend of mine, and I would talk to them later. In the subsequent RCMP Internal Investigation I was accused of lying to the investigators about the money. S/Sgt. Don

Kennedy, who was not only my boss but a close personal friend, sat there and said nothing. It would have helped if he had diffused the situation by saying, "Calm down, Murphy, let's just work this out." I was in a corner, needed some help, and didn't get any.

Kirby called and we made arrangements to pick up his car so that the technical equipment could be installed for the next meeting with Cosimo Commisso. He also advised that his ex-common-law wife would likely be dropping the extortion charges that had resulted from a dispute over furniture ownership during a quarrel. He said she might drop the charges as early as Monday. I was later accused of interfering in those charges, but that was a matter between Kirby and his ex-common-law wife and I had absolutely nothing to do with it. His ex-wife would take the stand of her own volition and ask to have the charges dropped.

I reached Crown Attorney Al Cooper and discussed the problem of the money with him. His advice was not to worry about being charged. He said, "If they charge you for doing what you had to do, I'll defend you personally." I thanked him for his vote of confidence, then met with the SEU and gave them the full story. They did not want to buy the money back from Kirby. Another Crown Attorney, Howard Morton, who would handle the future prosecution against the Commissos, later stated, "It doesn't matter a row of beans whether the money was seized or not. The fact that it was paid is the primary concern."

I thought to myself, "Why all the fuss?" Staff Sgt. Lyle McCharles appeared to be obsessed with the notion that they needed a hammer to Kirby's head to get him to testify. I tried to convince him that with truthfulness and fair treatment Kirby would come through with the testimony. McCharles, Simpson and Bouchard announced on the 12th of March that they had obtained a tape from the York Regional Police wherein they were convinced they had something on Kirby, alleging he might be involved on a rape charge. McCharles probably thought he really had the "hammer" now, but as it turned out there was absolutely nothing on the tape for which Kirby could be charged. My assessment was that their efforts along these lines were up the proverbial creek, and none of them knew how to paddle.

On Sunday, March 15, 1981, Kirby called me at home and advised that a biker from Toronto had travelled to New York on the 14th of February and then on to Chicago last week and was very likely involved in the shotgun slaying of two mobsters in those cities. He had been checked at LaGuardia carrying a hand gun. That information was immediately passed on to Detective Peter Meceli, New York Police.

On Monday, March 16th, Sergeant Ross and I picked up Kirby's car and brought it to our office, where it was handed over to the technicians for wiring. They installed a transmitter and a tape recorder. It was not until 10:52 PM that night that the car was finally ready to be dropped off to Kirby. We met outside a coffee shop at Sheppard and Dufferin Streets. Ironically, while Kirby and I were sitting in his car discussing the upcoming meeting the following day, an individual by the name of Rocco Masterangello came out of a nearby building and got in his car. I recognized him because he had surfaced in another project we had worked on. I had only seen a photo of him, but he usually wore a long leather coat as a cape, loosely flung over his shoulders. Tonight was no exception. I pointed him out to Kirby and he said he thought he knew him. Later Kirby would surface evidence that would lead to charges resulting from a bombing in Guelph, Ontario, some time earlier. Masterangello had acted as a middle-man for the Commissos. Masterangello was convicted for his part in the conspiracy.

St. Paddy's Day, Tuesday, March 17th, was to be another eventful day. We met Kirby at the Plaza on the southeast corner of Bathurst and Steeles, in the North End of Toronto. Their meeting had been put off until 11:30 AM. It took considerable time to convince Kirby to wear a hidden body pack. He eventually agreed. Although he had worn it for other meetings, this one was inside Commisso's home where we would not be able to give him the same protection. There was that inherent danger the body pack might be discovered.

For this meeting we had three systems in place to record the conversations: a transmitter in Kirby's car, which afforded us a running commentary on what was happening; a Nagra tape recorder in Kirby's vehicle as a back-up; and the body pack on Kirby to record any conversation that might take place outside the vehicle. There had been nothing to suggest an inordinate amount of heat on Kirby thus far, but we all lived in fear it could happen at a moment's notice.

At 11:26 AM, Kirby arrived at Cosimo Commisso's home on Ellerslie Ave., Toronto. Shortly afterwards Cosimo Commisso and Kirby left the home and travelled to the southwest end of the city where Commisso pointed out Kirby's next target. We experienced only a small amount of difficulty following Kirby's vehicle. We were able to monitor most of their conversation live and offer Kirby reasonably good protection in the event of a problem. At 1:07 PM, Kirby dropped Cosimo at the Casa Commisso on Lawrence Ave. and returned to the Plaza at Bathurst and Steeles.

The following conversation was recorded on the 17th of March, 1981, between Kirby and Cosimo Commisso:

C.C.: I believe he lives over here, that guy, my brother told me. He goes to (poker) games two nights a week.

C.K.: Remember to write it down. (Refers to the licence plate number on the intended victim's car.) You got it wrote down?

C.C.: What you gonna do?

C.K.: Oh, I'll come back and do this. I'll just keep watching this guy. There's no hurry for this eh?

C.C.: No, no. He gambles a lot.

C.K.: Just gambles, he's a gambler, fuck I bet you I know him. Have I seen this guy? Does he park his car outside or underground?

C.C.: He parks outside. (Cosimo spots the intended victim's car) Last three numbers are 747.

C.K.: What's his plate number? Here, open this damn page up and write it in. You got his first name?

C.C.: It's Peter.

C.K.: Peter?

C.C.: Scarcella.

C.K.: Alright, I'll remember it.

C.C.: Remember it. That kid to give a couple of slaps to, that kid, did you send somebody? (Meaning a man by the name of Lillo that Cosimo wanted roughed up)

C.K.: Not right now; it'll be a little tough. I'll see if I can get this guy, O.K.?

C.C.: He did something. Bastard.

C.K.: What is he, a stool pigeon?

C.C.: Looks that way.

C.K.: So my best bet might be just right over here where he lives, get him in the morning. Sit there and watch the car. Alright, I'll figure it out anyway. And you said there's no hurry, so I'll take my time. I got to be careful over here, a lot of people know me.

C.C.: Tomorrow we see the guy at one o'clock at the bakery.

C.K.: Alright, I'll get a look at him. I'll park across the street. I can follow him around.

C.C.: Our best bet, you know, two, three nights a week he comes home at three, four o'clock in the morning.

C.K.: O.K., leave it with me and I'll come over to your house next Wednesday.

C.C.: O.K.

In the debriefing of Kirby that followed the meeting, it was established that the intended victim was a young man by the name of Peter Scarcella. At one time Scarcella had been closely associated with the Commissos, but in recent months had become involved with another organized crime Family in Toronto headed by Paul Volpe. He was a very heavy gambler and owed a considerable sum of money to the Mob. The Commissos had a feeling that he had betrayed them and was probably giving information to the Volpe Family that was useful in controlling gambling in Toronto. Kirby did not have a pen in his car that day so I had supplied him with one of my Papermates. It was the pen that Cosimo used to write the partial licence number 747, along with the name P. Scarcella, on a newspaper. The newspaper and pen were seized for evidence and later handed over to Cst. Bouchard. It was more than a year before I finally got my pen back.

Kirby intended to do surveillance on the next day's meeting between Peter Scarcella and the Commissos at the Casa Commisso. I drove Kirby home and we took his car to Headquarters to remove the tapes.

The SEU arranged a surveillance on the Scarcella meeting for the next day. They also learned that Peter Scarcella's licence plate number was in fact NXH-747, his car was a 1979 blue Chevrolet, and he lived at 85 Emmett Avenue, Apt. 203, Toronto.

At this point Insp. McIlvenna and his investigators tried a new tactic. Sgt. Norm Ross and I had done our very best to monitor all conversations between Kirby and Commisso. SEU, for some reason, must have thought Ross and I were holding out by neglecting to get the entire conversation. I felt they had conjured up in their minds that somehow we were trying to protect Kirby. If so, there was absolutely no foundation to the theory. I found out that SEU had secretly signed out a second receiver to monitor Kirby and Commisso at their March 17th meeting. During our surveillance of Cosimo Commisso and Kirby, when Cosimo was giving Kirby details about the intended victim Peter Scarcella, I saw an SEU vehicle pulling up behind Ross and myself. In the vehicle were John Simpson and Al Cooke of Metro and Danielle Bouchard of the OPP. Although they thought they were being discreet, I could see them taking in the small gutter aerial used to pick up the transmissions as they approached. As it turned out, the tape Ross and I had obtained was far superior in detail than the tape SEU had obtained. McIlvenna and his crew eventually realized we were not holding out.

It had been another long day, and I was heading home near Oshawa, Ontario at about 4:15 PM. I had just reached the top of the Don Valley Parkway and was hitting some open traffic when the office called and asked if I could return for a meeting with the Steering Committee. That would be Inspectors Wylie, Banks, and O'Grady. As I've said before, I'm not psychic, but I knew there was something brewing. I turned around and headed back to the city.

I arrived back at RCMP Headquarters to find out that the Steering Committee wanted to meet with Kirby to work out an agreement and introduce him to other investigators. Kirby had refused to trust any other coppers, particularly those from Metro and OPP, which is why McIlvenna and his crew had been kept at arm's length until this point in the investigation. I was sure that McIlvenna desperately wanted control of Kirby and to cut me out of the investigation. After all, this investigation could be an illustrious plum in his career. After exhausting anything worthwhile from Project Oblong, the SEU had mainly concentrated on minor gambling offences, which gave them stats but little credibility. My take on the situation was that McIlvenna thought if he could gain control, it would give his section the shot in the arm it needed.

Insp. Wylie now informed me that they wanted to meet with Kirby tomorrow. The Steering Committee had agreed to all the conditions of the agreement except the $200,000 payment. They would provide immunity to prosecution, protection for Kirby and family, and allow him to continue to work through Corporal Murphy. The method and amount of payment was still being negotiated.

At this meeting Inspector Wylie gave me hell for passing information about the recent New York murders on to Detective Meceli of the NYPD without first advising the Steering Committee. I was told not to send any reports to Agent Schimanm because of the Freedom of Information Act in the US, which would potentially make this information available to others.

I was informed that the Steering Committee had approved payment of $1,000 for Kirby for day-to-day expenses. They also wanted Kirby introduced to Sgt. Simpson. I suggested that they get a room at the downtown Holiday Inn and I would meet them there tomorrow at 2 PM. Wylie countered that I was to get the room, make sure Kirby was comfortable and they would join us at 2 PM. I said fine, but my intuition told me otherwise. I smelled a double-cross in the making, and knew I would have to get up a little earlier in the morning to cope with it, even though the meeting wasn't scheduled until mid-afternoon.

The following day Inspector Wylie approved the first payment of $1,000 for Kirby. At 1:35 PM, Sergeant Norm Ross and I met Kirby in Room 2534 at the Holiday Inn on Chestnut Street in Toronto. We paid Kirby the money and Sergeant Ross left to return to the office. At 2:10 PM, there was a knock on the door. The Steering Committee had arrived. I should point out that Inspectors Banks and O'Grady were very experienced coppers who were quite reasonable to deal with. I respected them and their opinions. To me the problems centered around Inspector Wylie. He acted like a puppet on a string, and in my opinion those strings were being constantly pulled by Inspector Jim McIlvenna.

When the introductions had been completed, Inspector Wylie turned and asked me to wait down in the lobby; he said that they shouldn't be any more than an hour.

"Fine, no problem," I replied.

Kirby stood up and literally stunned Insp. Wylie by saying, "If Murphy goes, I go. I don't know you guys, I don't trust you, and I will only talk to you if Murphy is present."

Insp. Wylie almost choked and sputtered, "O.K., Cpl. Murphy, you can stay."

They discussed several points of the agreement that would be proposed to Kirby later. With that out of the way, Wylie asked Kirby if he was willing to work with Cpl. Murphy and Sgt. Simpson from SEU

Kirby said "I know Simpson and I don't trust him; in fact, it was Simpson who the Commissos used to help them get their Liquor Licences for the Casa Commisso when they had a problem. I don't want to meet him and I will not work with him."

Wylie asked, "What about Sergeant Al Cooke?"

"I'll only trust Murphy until the agreement is signed. When that is signed, I'll be willing to meet any investigators to brief them, provided Murphy is present."

The Steering Committee approved $4,000 per month for Kirby's expenses, thus ending the need for Kirby to keep monies received from the Commissos. Inspector Banks then spoke up and told Kirby that he would have to trust them and that they would not do him dirty on the money end of the deal. I couldn't help but chuckle out loud when Kirby replied with a very small grin, "Don't forget, I can easily find out where you fellows live, you know." The three looked at each other and left the room. I couldn't help but think that their attempt to reassure Kirby had somehow missed the mark."

Several days passed and it was now March 24, 1981. It seemed as though Wylie and McIlvenna had not given up their playground antics. They said that several questions had surfaced pertaining to the investigation and it was absolutely essential that Sgt. Simpson meet with Kirby to have them answered. I explained this to Kirby and we arranged to meet him at the Ponderosa Parking Lot at Yonge and Steeles at 2:30 PM. Kirby was on time as usual. I introduced him to Sergeant Simpson. Kirby told him that he had heard from the Commissos that Simpson had helped them obtain a liquor licence for their banquet hall when they had a problem. Simpson spent considerable time trying to defend that situation, but didn't deny it was true. Then Simpson spent the next several minutes discussing Kirby's history and downplaying the NCIS section of the RCMP. Kirby was not impressed and told Simpson so. Simpson then asked a question to which we knew he already had the answer. Simpson also supposedly had some concerns about the upcoming meetings with the Commissos, but could add absolutely nothing which could make them any more successful than they had been up until this point. I chalked that meeting up to about strike six for McIlvenna.

The ground rules were clearly defined now that Kirby had told Simpson in no uncertain terms that he would not be working with any other coppers until the agreement was signed. Inspector Wylie authorized me to travel with Kirby over a period of two days in Southern Ontario to gather all the information available on crimes he had committed while under the direction of the Commisso family. On the 25th of March, Cecil Kirby and I set out to identify some of the crime scenes. A full report would outline in detail the many crimes committed by Kirby, though in my notebook I made the following brief notations:

(1) Murray Kalen - attempted extortion with two sticks of dynamite in mailbox. 123 Heath St. and business Mr. Greenjeans.

(2) Chinese Restaurant, 111 Elizabeth St., Toronto. Bombing - Chinese cook killed by accident.

(3) Napoleon Restaurant, 79 Grenville St., Toronto. Bombing because Cosimo Commisso's wife and mother-in-law were insulted by the Maitre d'.

(4) Car bombing of Drug Witness - 33 Grove Park Crescent, Toronto.

(5) Wanted extortion on man on Courtsville Crescent, Toronto. Worked at 20 Nashville Ave., Toronto. No money so not done.

(6) Car bombing Corby Crescent, Toronto. Extortion - Remo and Michael Commisso involved.

(7) Car bombing, 41 Shenstone Rd. Wanted front or side door of house done, but did car rather than endanger innocent people. Cosimo Commisso did follow up calls on extortion.

(8) Restaurant Bombing, Niagara Falls, Ontario. Wanted blown up by owner and Cosimo Commisso but not done.

(9) Station Hotel, 123 Mill St., Acton, Ontario. Wanted burned but no money so not done. Done later by others unknown.

(10) Cook-O-Matic, Lawrence Ave. Extortion on owner. Broke jaw with black-jack.

(11) Abella Club, Eglinton Ave., Toronto. Arson for insurance fraud.

(12) Hi-jack tractor trailer truck loaded with cigarettes. Disposed of through Macri Catering Trucks, Toronto.

(13) Kingscross Estates, Lot 18, Blueberry Lane, King City, Ontario. Extortion by two sticks of dynamite in the mailbox. Guy owns business on Wildcat Road, Toronto.

(14) Car fire for insurance fraud, Bowes Rd., Toronto.

(15) Two bombings at Apartment buildings at 1400 Dixie Rd., Misissauga.

On the following day, Kirby identified the rest of his crimes:

(16) John Ryan bombing and black-jack attack Hamilton, Ontario. Extortion. Went to Montreal and did blackjack assault on Ryan's partner.

(17) Set house on fire for insurance fraud. Bradford Rd. and Middletown Road, Ontario.

(18) Guelph bombing and fire, 97 MacDonald St., Guelph, Ontario. Arson and insurance fraud requested by owner.

(19) Extortion by threats to guy on Milton Side Rd., Milton, Ontario. Guy involved in real estate.

(20) Attempt murder of Jewish man in Montreal. Bomb left in car but found and set off prematurely by security guard. Not killed.

I'm sure most people reading this list of crimes will wonder that the police would even consider making a deal with an individual like Kirby. Not to defend his actions, as I'm sure Kirby himself would not defend his criminal acts, but there are several things one must consider. The police didn't have one shred of evidence to link Kirby or anyone else to these crimes. In addition, while Kirby played a significant role in the crimes he committed, it was the organized crime figures behind the scenes who orchestrated the acts of criminal activity. By enabling Kirby to testify in many of the cases involving the aforementioned crimes, the SEU, OPP, Metro Police, Guelph & Hamilton Police, and other police departments were able to see organized crime figures and their associates sentenced to many years in jail. Kirby himself received a life sentence of sorts, in that he can never assume his true identity or become involved in crime again—if he does he's a dead man, and no one knows this better than Cecil Kirby.

At this time the Steering Committee put forth a dismal attempt at an agreement with Kirby. It read as follows:

We the undersigned agree to the following conditions to be undertaken with Jack Ryan during the period of debriefing, and cooperation in current investigations:

1. Jack Ryan agrees to provide detailed information concerning all pertinent activities, which will be taken down in writing and signed by him, in addition to being tape recorded. He will agree to testify at any subsequent judicial proceedings and give in evidence the statements that he supplies;

2. In return, Jack Ryan is given assurance that his statements will not be used against him in any criminal proceedings;

3. Jack Ryan and his family will be given full protection, if and when required, at the decision of the police forces involved;

4. Corporal Murphy will be available and will attend at all dealings with Jack Ryan;

5. In all future dealings with Jack Ryan, Corporal Murphy will be accompanied by Sergeant Al Cooke, MTPF, or a second policeman agreeable to Corporal Murphy; and

6. Jack Ryan will make himself available to investigating personnel as

    required.

S/Insp. D. Banks - MTPF

Insp. T. O'Grady - OPP

Insp. J. T. Wylie - RCMP

Agreed:

_____

Jack Ryan

Kirby read the proposed agreement and immediately refused to sign it. Whether the document was intended as a double-cross or not is debatable, but Kirby was not willing to sign without an Immunity To Prosecution clause and details of a financial settlement. I brought the unsigned agreement back to the Steering Committee, who still didn't seem to have a clue about the league they were playing in.

On the 27th of March, Kirby was to meet with Cosimo Commisso at Cosimo's home. After the routine of getting technical equipment in place, Kirby met Cosimo Commisso at 10:46 am. The following conversation was recorded:

C.K.: Listen ah, I got a few things to talk to you about, about this Scarcella. Let's go outside. I went over to the apartment about nine o'clock and I sat there. I saw him come out. I got the licence plate number of his car and everything, it's NZX-747. I followed him right down to the Four Season's Sheraton Hotel.

C.C.: Yeah.

C.K.: You know who he's talking to?

C.C.: Who?

C.K.: Paul Volpe.

C.C.: He's close to him. That's O.K., forget it for now.

C.K.: But who wants him killed? Is it Volpe who wants him killed, or you, or what?

C.C.: No. No. I'm wondering that he wants to do it to me. (Meaning Volpe wants Commisso killed)

C.K.: It's you that wants this done, or Volpe?

C.C.: It's me, not Volpe. They want to do me and my brother.

C.K.: They what?

C.C.: They want to do me and my brother, maybe I can't trust any one of them.

C.K.: You think Volpe wants to kill you and your brother?

C.C.: Yeah, it's the two of them.

C.K.: What's this Scarcella, playing both sides? He's telling Volpe everything about you and him?

C.C.: No, nothing about me and him, it just, I don't know what's going to happen next year, you know?

C.K.: So what do you want to do, you want to kill Volpe in the future?

C.C.: No, not for now. Like, wait for this guy (Scarcella) for another week or so, O.K.? I'm waiting for an answer. You are with me, eh? Because there's a lot of things will go on with this fucking town, you see what I mean? You sure you are with me?

C.K.: Yeah.

C.C.: O.K. Send somebody over here special, to give somebody a couple of smacks (Lillo). You should do this today or tomorrow.

C.K.: You want this done tomorrow?

C.C.: Today or tomorrow. Send somebody over here. The guy's at Villa Furniture. His name is Lillo. There's two guys working there, the younger guy is the one. Just give him, ah, you know. They close the store at nine o'clock tonight.

C.K.: I'll see, O.K.? Alright, so you want me to wait another week on Scarcella?

C.C.: Yeah.

C.K.: You want him left laying around, or buried or drowned, whatever? Do you want him disposed of?

C.C.: No, but before you go ahead on the hit with this guy, I want to talk to you before. What's easiest for you?

C.K.: It doesn't matter, whatever you prefer? Do you want him left laying around so everybody sees him, sees his head blown off, or do you want him buried and a missing person—nobody ever sees him again. It doesn't matter to me, whatever you want. Unless you want other people to say, "Well look, here's a stool pigeon that got a bullet in his head."

C.C.: You know what to do, find yourself a spot.

C.K.: I got a way of getting to him. If I walk up to him and show him a badge and say, "You're under arrest. Come with me," how can he be suspicious then? O.K., so we'll meet on the 25th. What about the rest of the money. (For the US contract on Helen Nafpliotas)

C.C.: The first of the month you gonna have it.

C.K.: Seven thousand, American?

C.C.: Yeah, alright. You won't betray me, eh? You wouldn't go against me?

C.K.: Never. I'll see you Tuesday.

The investigation had taken on greater importance and a new meaning. Now they were considering the contract killing of Paul Volpe, head of another large organized crime Family in Toronto. Cosimo Commisso was not certain that Peter Scarcella would have to be killed. Cosimo was of the belief that Paul Volpe wanted him and his brother Remo killed. If that was the case, then they would have Kirby take Paul Volpe out first. As an afterthought, Cosimo wanted a man by the name of Lillo roughed up a bit, but not killed. That sounded like some kind of extortion scam.

I had overheard on the transmitter Commisso's concern about Volpe and the suggestion that he might have to be killed. My first thought was that after all the work the police had put into trying to investigate and prosecute him, it would be the police that might ultimately be responsible for saving his life. The second thought that crossed my mind was that I probably knew Volpe as well as anyone else in police circles and this would afford an excellent opportunity to talk to him again. What would his reaction be if a contract were put out on him by his own people? I had thought of approaching Volpe many times in an effort to get information. Even though for some strange reason I had been ordered by my boss not to communicate with Volpe, this could be the perfect opportunity to do so. On March 31 we covered another meeting between Cecil Kirby and Cosimo Commisso at the Casa Commisso. During the meeting they decided to hold off on the Scarcella hit, and Remo would pay Kirby for his earlier work if no money was received from the US. The most significant part of a rather short meeting was the following:

C.K.:   What about Volpe?

C.C.:   I'm waiting for an answer, O.K.?

C.K.:   Alright.

C.C.:   And maybe we know next week. You see what I mean?

C.K.:   O.K.

C.C.:   See what I mean. It's not us.

C.K.:   Someone else.

C.C.:   Right. O.K., you see what I mean?

It was obvious from that conversation that Cosimo
Commisso had asked the permission of the Mob to hit Volpe
and he was still waiting for their reply before giving Kirby the
go ahead. In all their years of investigating organized crime
the Canadian police had rarely been privy to such information,
a mobster in the process of arranging the contract killing of
one of the most prominent leaders in organized crime in
Canada.

Life surrounding Cecil Kirby was never dull. He lived in
the fast lane. He was one of the finest undercover operators
that ever surfaced, but there was another side. He had been
living in common law with a woman for several years. Now
that relationship had deteriorated to the point where fighting
and quarrels were commonplace, and the break-up of the
relationship was inevitable. With the personal trauma involved, Kirby was unpredictable. On a daily basis we weren't
sure if he was going to testify or not, adding to the stress and
tension between the investigating officers. There were those
that felt it was useless to continue, believing Kirby would
never testify. I felt he would come through and testify, but
only if he could stabilize his personal life. Sgt. Ross and I took
a patrol up north and were able to rent a cottage that Kirby
and his woman could share, thus eliminating some of the
tension in their relationship and in the ongoing investigation.
A $5,000 payment for expenses had been approved, and that
also helped to relieve Kirby's mounting tension.

On April 3, 1981, Kirby and Cosimo Commisso had
another meeting. Kirby had not received his full payment for
the alleged murder of Helen Nafpliotis and he continued to

press Cosimo for the money due. For the first time since the investigation had begun, I was accompanied by Staff Sgt. Lyle McCharles in the surveillance unit. The following conversation was recorded:

C.C.:   Vince (Melia) gonna come in next Tuesday.

C.K.:   Next Tuesday he'll be here?

C.C.:   That's what I said. You'll be paid.

C.K.:   You know he promised me a bonus, eh? (For disposing of the body) I'd like that bonus.

C.C.:   Yeah, alright. You carry a piece with you?

C.K.:   Yeah, I got one on me today.

C.C.:   Why, eh? Cec, how come?

C.K.:   I always carry one. So I'll see you next Wednesday at one-thirty. See if you can have a lot of money for me O.K.?

C.C.:   Alright.

Kirby had received further instructions to hold off on the Peter Scarcella murder until he received a message through Michael Commisso to either go ahead with the hit or hold off entirely. The police were interested in knowing that they were expecting Vince Melia to come to Toronto. They would cover his arrival for evidential purposes.

Just prior to this meeting between Cosimo Commisso and Kirby, Inspector Wilf Stefureak, who had temporarily taken over from Insp. McIlvenna as Officer in Charge of SEU, approached me to ask if Sgt. John Simpson could talk to Kirby by himself after this meeting. I mentioned this to Kirby and he reluctantly agreed. I was not told the purpose of the meeting, though I knew Kirby was capable of looking after his own interests. By this time all policemen connected with the investigation were aware of the rider I had placed on the bottom of the consent forms, and most were extremely upset that they needed Kirby's consent to enter tapes as evidence against the Commissos and the other conspirators. Simpson met Kirby on the parking lot of the Skyline Hotel after Kirby's meeting with Cosimo. Simpson, unknown to me, had their conversation recorded by McCharles and Bouchard in a nearby surveillance vehicle. Their conversation centered around the admissibility of the tapes with or without Kirby's consent. After approximately twenty minutes of conversation, Simpson reached the same conclusion that had been reached some time before. The tapes were inadmissible without Kirby's cooperation, and his cooperation would only be forthcoming when an agreement with the police meeting his four conditions was completed. With each delay or stall tactic came the very real possibility that Kirby would simply forget the whole deal. Kirby asked me shortly after this latest episode, "When are these jokers going to quit?"

During this period of time another rather significant event took place. Corporal Robin Earmacora of NCIS, Toronto, assisted by the RCMP Surveillance team, photographed two individuals in Toronto believed to be from the Bruno organized crime family in Philadelphia. Raymond 'Long John' Mortonano and Beni Daidone were observed meeting with Paul Volpe and Peter Scarcella outside the Prince Hotel. This could very well have been the meeting that decided the fate of Paul Volpe and Peter Scarcella. It is also conceivable the Commissos looked upon this meeting as a decision of Volpe and the Philley Mob to do a hit on the Commissos. Scarcella may have conveyed that message to them.

On the 6th of April I called the Special Squad at Toronto International Airport and asked them to watch for any visitors from the US that might be of interest to police, especially either Vince or Nicky Melia.

Several months earlier, Bloors St. in Toronto was rocked by a huge explosion in an area just west of Yonge St. at approximately 3:30 am. The explosion and fire that resulted completely destroyed Arviv's Disco. It was nothing short of a miracle that no one was injured in the explosion. Bloor St. in

Toronto is usually very active, no matter what hour of the morning. I had done some investigative work on the owner, Harold Arviv, and knew he had links to organized crime. When the explosion occurred, I had some suspicions about its origin.

On the 7th of April I met with Kirby to recover some technical equipment and my suspicions were confirmed. Kirby related the story that he was approached by Harold Arviv to blow up the Disco about one month before it happened. Kirby said he would do the job for $10,000. Arviv told Kirby he wanted the place blown up because he was sick of the business and owed money to too many creditors. Arviv gave Kirby $200 to purchase the dynamite and, in fact, Kirby did a survey and decided the best place to put the bomb was in the furnace room. Arviv was to give Kirby $2,000 at their next meeting, but failed to do so; Kirby reneged on the contract. At their last meeting, Arviv stated he had commando training, knew how to handle explosives, and was considering doing the job himself. This information was handed over to the SEU investigators and Arviv, Chuck Yanover (who had ties to Paul Volpe), and an individual of Chinese descent were arrested and convicted of this offence. That investigation was completed by Sgt. Ron Sandelli (Metro Police) and Cpl. Ross Oak (RCMP), in my opinion two of the best investigators on the SEU Squad at that time.

The next meeting between Kirby and Cosimo Commisso took place on April 8th, 1981, at the Howard Johnson parking lot. Prior to the meeting, I met Kirby on the Skyline parking lot, next to the airport. With all the surrounding noise, we had some concerns about the quality of the tapes. Kirby's ingenuity would resolve that problem. After I had arranged all our technical equipment, Kirby slipped off his shoe and sock. I asked him what he was doing. With that, he removed an elastic bandage and wrapped his ankle and foot. Kirby grinned when he said, "Today's meeting will be nice and clear." Kirby could have won an Oscar for his performance that day, or any other day for that matter.

Claiming he had a foot injury, Kirby convinced Cosimo Commisso to join him in his vehicle. As a result, we managed to record one of the best quality tapes of the entire investigation. We also obtained excellent photographs.

Their conversation went as follows:

C.C.: What's wrong?

C.K.: Broke my ankle I think.

C.C.: How did you hurt yourself?

C.K.: I was running and I struck the fucking curb. I think I broke it.

C.C.: O.K. Try to grab more information on that guy Peter (Scarcella) if you can, because then...ah, Monday.

C.K.: Scarcella. I check his car all the time; every week.

C.C.: Ah, next week Michael (Commisso, Cosimo's youngest brother) gonna call you. And ah, without mention name, gonna say yes or no, O.K.? If it's yes, go ahead, O.K.?

C.K.: For Scarcella?

C.C.: Yeah.

C.K.: If he says yes, go ahead? Alright, what about Volpe?

C.C.: No, not for now. Forget about him for now.

C.K.: You're gonna have to get rid of him sooner or later, aren't you?

C.C.: They say there's going to be a war involved, a war over here in Toronto, you know?

C.K.: Is that right, eh?

C.C.: Cec, things gonna be for the betterment, because there's a few things to be done, and then we gonna be, things gonna be smooth in this town. But there's a lot of problems. We want to know if we can trust you a hundred percent. You with us?

C.K.:   Yeah. I have been all the time.

C.C.:   All the time you for us?

C.K.:   Yeah. This guy Vince (Melia), did he come up? (from the US)

C.C.:   No, he didn't come up, but you get your money. Yeah, there is other people (he wants hit) right away, you know?

C.K.:   Another guy? Here in the city?

C.C.:   Yeah, but I don't know about that. My brother want to do it himself, but I don't know.

C.K.:   Who, Remo? (Cosimo's second oldest brother)

C.C.:   Yeah. You gonna get your money. Don't do that thing (murder Scarcella). You don't have to worry about nothing anymore, the rest of your life. Cause you were the only guy we trust. (Kirby and I couldn't help but notice that Cosimo said "were".)

C.K.:   Um, O.K..

Kirby was due in court on the 10th of April, 1981, for sentencing. On this occasion Kirby appeared, but we were able to manufacture an excuse with one of the co-accused's lawyers and the case was put over until the 7th of May. People were becoming much more understanding at this point in time and seeking a remand wasn't quite so difficult as it had been in the beginning. The proposed agreement was in the works, but nothing had been signed and Kirby was still apprehensive. There was absolutely no doubt in my mind that an agreement was in the making and it was just a matter of time. That task had been taken on by the Steering Committee. In order to give Kirby immunity, protection, and money, the committee would have to bring together the three major Police forces in Southern Ontario, which included the OPP, Metro Toronto Police, and the RCMP It also needed the sanction of the Attorney General of Ontario. Considering the politics, I must give full marks to the Steering Committee for their persistence and efforts towards this goal. Without it, we had nothing.

During the time I dealt with Kirby he had his share of domestic problems. On many occasions I was called in the wee hours of the morning to hustle into Toronto and try to resolve some volatile situation. Kirby and I had been through a lot and developed a tremendous respect for each other, although more than once I looked into his fiery eyes and could feel the violence of his temper. Despite confrontations between Kirby and those who upset him, there was never a cross word spoken between us. I never lied to him and he gave me credit for that. That's something most commissioned officers refuse to understand, that trust and friendship between an informant and his handler is often the only thing that keeps the objectives of an investigation on track.

On April 14, 1981, Kirby and Cosimo Commisso met at the Howard Johnson restaurant and we covered the meeting. The following are excerpts from that conversation as it was recorded:

C.K.:   Well, what's going on, do you have my money?

C.C.:   O.K. Cec, the guy (Melia) has no money. I've been trying to get it for you.

C.K.:   You said, "Kill this fucking broad and we'll pay you the end of the month." O.K., it's way past the end of the month. Fuck, I'm broke!

C.C.:   I give you some money in two days and the rest the end of the month, you gonna have all the rest.

C.K.:   What's wrong with this fucking Vince guy? I should fucking call him. I've got his number. My friend wants to go back down and see this Vince guy. I put 20 years of my life on the line for killing a broad. I'm getting nothing. I might as well be working for a living. Tell this Vince friend of yours the next time he wants somebody killed, tell him to go kill them himself, O.K.?

C.C.:   No, no Cec. I didn't do it for me, I did something for them. You gonna get paid.

C.K.:   Like, I've got expenses, too. I went to court the other day and my lawyer wants another five hundred dollars. Anyway, what's happening with Scarcella?

C.C.:   We're waiting to be sure on two things.

C.K.:   Do you want me to forget about watching him?

C.C.:   No, no, I want you to go make sure of all his movements so when you're ready (Here Cosimo makes a snapping sound) you can just do it, you know.

C.K.:   I go there a couple of times a week.

C.C.:   You see him come out?

C.K.:   Yeah. Do you want him left laying around. It don't matter to me.

C.C.:   Which is best for you?

C.K.:   Just to do him right there. People are getting killed in the city every day now.

C.C.:   Yeah. In two, three days you could be able to do it?

C.K.:   Probably within a day, two days at the most.

C.C.:   He comes home late at night.

I communicated with Kirby by flashing the brake lights of the surveillance vehicle. After he dropped Cosimo off, we were to meet in downtown Toronto at a donut shop, not far from my office. Cosimo sent his nephew out to the parking lot with $100 in cash for Kirby, then Kirby drove away. After my communication with Kirby, Staff Sergeant McCharles became quite agitated. I don't know if he thought Kirby was going to leave the country with the five $20 bills he had just received, or whether he was concerned about the recording equipment, but whatever the reason he came on the air and ordered Kirby and me to meet back at the Skyline Hotel. By this time Kirby and I had had enough of SEU's bullshit. I told McCharles in a very clear voice that I was unable to copy him and would be meeting Kirby downtown. A short time later Kirby and I met downtown and I recovered the money and the technical equipment. McCharles was still annoyed, so I grinned and gave him my best sex-and-travel look. There was no love lost between us, and he knew I wasn't going to run scared when he barked. When McCharles first came into the investigation he gave me the impression that he knew it all and that Sgt. Ross and I were dirt under his feet. I felt he was only attempting to reinforce his own insecurity by putting us down. His comments quickly revealed that he was not the expert investigator he apparently wanted us to believe he was. He told us he had investigated eight murders. We did a quick check on his background and discovered that he had spent most of his time in the Identification Section of the OPP. That job entailed taking photographs and fingerprints. That was where he had investigated the eight murders. He actually had a very limited background in investigating. It seemed at the time that McCharles, Simpson, and Bouchard were all tarred with the same brush.

Cosimo Commisso had an appointment with his lawyer on April 21, 1981, so he was unable to attend a scheduled meeting with Kirby at the Howard Johnson Hotel. Instead, he sent his younger brother, Michael Commisso. We felt very strongly that what one brother knew, they all knew, and this meeting, although unexpected, would provide the evidence we needed to tie Michael Commisso into the supposed Nafpliotis murder and also the proposed Scarcella murder. At that meeting the following conversation was recorded:

> M.C.: Thursday I'll bring you the money.
>
> C.K.: How much?
>
> M.C.: A couple of thousand.
>
> C.K.: You know he owes me eight, eh?
>
> M.C.: Yeah. That guy (Vince Melia) is supposed to come this week, this Saturday. There's a wedding of a cousin of ours here in Toronto. I went there (to Connecticut) two weeks ago and he had no money. That's why we know he is coming.

C.K.: I should wait for him out in the parking lot. Like, he asked me to do extra, to make sure the broad is never seen again. She's dead, she's gone.

M.C.: Yeah. He gave me the run around. He says there was some money missing in the apartment, some jewelry.

C.K.: Yeah, well I made it look good.

M.C.: His brother is in some trouble down in Kentucky. He's out on a hundred and fifty thousand dollar bail. He's waiting for his brother to beat the charge and come up with the money.

C.K: Fuck, that could be another two years from now.

M.C.: No.

C.K.: You heard anymore about this Scarcella?

M.C.: Ah, it...well, there might be some changes.

C.K.: What do you mean changes? Should I forget about it, or what?

M.C.: No, no, I'll let you know Thursday.

C.K.: Well, let me know on Scarcella. I've been watching him, but I just passed so far away.

M.C.: Alright, Thursday I'll come up with the money and I'll let you know more about it. If he brings me six, I'll bring you six.

C.K.: O.K., good.

With each passing day, the danger increased that the Commissos would learn that Helen Nafpliotis had not really been murdered. That was of immense concern for Kirby and me. We knew that if it was discovered, there would be fire-works of the most dangerous kind. Now each time I covered a meeting, not only did I have the tape recorders and cameras, but I was wearing a bullet-proof vest and holding a fully loaded .12-gauge shotgun. It never ceases to amaze me how the SEU members found convenient reasons not to join me in the surveillance vehicle during these meetings. It was almost as if they were secretly hoping something would go wrong.

Kirby had demonstrated he could think on his feet. When Michael Commisso mentioned they had discovered that some of Nafpliotis' money and jewelry had been taken from the apartment, Kirby didn't panic and simply said that he took the money and jewelry to make it look good. Michael Commisso accepted that story and Kirby quickly changed the topic. The final decision to kill Scarcella hadn't been made, but of even more importance was the fact that Vince Melia would be attending a wedding in Toronto in the near future.

With Kirby, you never knew what to expect. Most people never get the opportunity to understand organized crime, its power, money and influence. On April 22, 1981, Kirby called to say he wanted to meet with me. I met him near the Donut Shop on McGill and Church St. Kirby said he had been approached by Chuck Yanover, mentioned earlier as an enforcer for Paul Volpe, and asked to go to South America with Yanover and several other associates to take part in an armed takeover of a small Island called Dominica. The purpose of the takeover was to establish a location for organized crime to build a gambling casino. To most people this would seem like a pretty far-fetched idea, but it proved to be true. I passed the information on to John Toews, RCMP Security Service. With the help of SEU and the FBI, several persons, including Yanover, were arrested, charged and convicted of the attempted takeover of Dominica. Of special significance was the fact that James McQuirter, Canadian head of the Klu Klux Klan at that time, was arrested with Yanover.

Kirby had arranged for a meeting with Cosimo Commisso at 1:30 PM on the 23rd of April, 1981. It was now 2:15 PM on that day and Commisso hadn't showed. We were set up to cover the meeting. Kirby advised over the transmitter that he was going outside to call. When he came back there was some excitement in his voice. He had spoken to Cosimo's younger brother, Remo, who many in police circles felt was the leader

of the Commisso Family. Remo told Kirby that either Cosimo
or himself would be there to meet him in twenty minutes. We
shared Kirby's excitement when we heard the news, hoping to
catch Remo in a compromising situation, but our elation was
cut short when Cosimo Commisso showed up for the meeting
at 2:45 PM. His driver had become involved in a car accident a
short distance down the street.

The following conversation took place at the meeting:

C.K.:   Michael told me you'd give me two thousand
today.

C.C.:   It's hard to find. You know what happened, we
bought the place next door.

C.K.:   Yeah, well, I'm broke and you can buy a business?

C.C.:   Once we buy the business we won't be broke. I
give you five hundred dollar a week every week. I put you on
the payroll every week.

C.K.:   Finally, I'm on a payroll.

C.C.:   And also instructions from Remo. He wants to talk
to you.

C.K.:   Remo wants to talk to me? (Kirby and I well
realized the potential danger of 'talking' to Remo.)

C.C.:   We gonna put you on the payroll and when things
are done you gonna get a bonus for it. Ah, Scarcella, forget about
it for now. Just don't worry about it for now.

C.K.:   For how long?

C.C.:   A month, two months, we don't know yet. There's
another guy.

C.K.:   What the fuck's going on?

C.C.:   There's another guy that I want you to take care of
instead of him (Scarcella). He (Remo) wants to do another guy.

C.K.:   You don't want to do him (Scarcella), you want to
do another guy?

C.C.:   Yes, not him for now, O.K.?

C.K.:   Well, who the fuck is this other guy?

C.C.:   Ah, I'll show you, next week you'll see.

C.K.:   Another guy?

C.C.:   Yeah.

C.K.:   Holy fuck. Make up your minds. What, a close friend of Scarcella's?

C.C.:   Yes.

C.K.:   Not Volpe?

C.C.:   I'll show him. Maybe you know the guy a little bit. But don't worry about his name, you see him, O.K.?

C.K.:   What is he, another gambler?

C.C.:   Ah, you know, next week. You gonna have two thousand.

C.K.:   Vince is coming in Saturday. I'd like to be there; I'd like to kick his ass.

C.C.:   (Reverting back to the talk about the intended hit) See, my brother (Remo) wanted to do this job. Cec, I don't ever expect you to go against me.

C.K.:   I don't listen to other people, you know that.

C.C.:   Remember the more powerful you are, the more jealous people there are.

C.K.:   I know that.

The decision had been made to hold off on the hit on Scarcella, though it was evident they had someone else in mind. That other person would be Paul Volpe. Cosimo indicated that Remo Commisso wanted to do the hit himself, but they hadn't made a final decision. Although the danger to Kirby's safety increased with each exposure, the evidence that was surfacing was so valuable it was difficult to call a halt to the investigation. Kirby and I had several discussions about the dangers involved, but he felt with the coverage we were supplying he could continue on and we would assess the inherent dangers with each meeting.

At 7:30 AM on Saturday morning, April 25, 1981, I was enjoying a much needed sleep when the phone rang. It was

Constable Ed McSherry calling from the Airport Special Squad at Toronto International. McSherry advised that Vince Melia of Stamford, Connecticut, was scheduled to arrive on American Airlines Flight 317 at 3:15 PM. I contacted Simpson and Bouchard and they arranged for Metro Toronto Police Surveillance Squad to cover the arrival. Simpson insisted on the Metro Surveillance Team because he felt they were much more capable than the RCMP team.

At Toronto International Airport the flight arrival area is quite isolated, and one must walk through long tunnels to get to Canada Customs. As it happened, a huge 747 jet aircraft had arrived on a direct flight from Italy, spewing hundreds of Italian passengers into the Canada Customs, at the same time Melia arrived from New York. Three months had passed since I had seen Melia, and even then it was not really close. Call it fate or good luck, but at 3:30 PM I spotted Vince Melia coming off an escalator and walking directly towards me. I described him in my notes as having jet black hair, approximately 50 years old, white male, approximately 5'7", approximately 175 lbs., wearing a dark suit and carrying a coat over his arm. He was also carrying a brown leather brief case. He didn't know it at the time, but he had walked right past several police officers. I had to wait until he had walked out the doors into the general area of the airport before I could point him out to the surveillance squad. They picked him up for a short period of time, then lost him. Investigation later revealed that he had travelled by cab to 1275 Lawrence Ave., West Toronto, the site of Casa Commisso.

Later that day, I took a photo of one of Metro Toronto Police Surveillance Units most embarrassing moments. They had set up a surveillance unit in front of the Casa Commisso to cover Melia and the wedding reception. There were several huge gravel trucks parked nearby and the Commissos arranged to have the trucks surround the surveillance unit so the officers inside could not get out. After a standoff which lasted a couple of hours, a uniformed police officer approached the Casa Commisso. The trucks were removed and the red-faced officers escaped unharmed.

Finally, on April 27, 1981, a new agreement had been prepared and was available to be signed by Kirby. The new agreement met the conditions Kirby and I had agreed to in Darien, Connecticut, several months earlier. The Steering Committee had apparently decided to stop playing games. They had involved Mr. Rod McLeod from the Ministry of the Attorney General of Ontario. The agreement was quite suitable and Kirby signed without hesitation. This agreement was a first in the history of Canadian Law Enforcement. The following is the content of that historic agreement:

MEMORANDUM OF AGREEMEMT
(Part I of two parts)

Between Cecil Murray Kirby, DOB: 17 Aug. 51, and the Ministry of the Attorney General of Ontario.

That Cecil Murray Kirby agrees to provide truthful and detailed information concerning the criminal activities, which will be taken down in writing and signed by him in addition to being tape recorded. He will agree to testify truthfully with respect to any judicial proceedings at which he may be a witness and give in evidence the statements he provides.

He consents to the admission of any of the recorded conversations between himself and any other person or persons which have taken or will take place.

The Ministry of the Attorney General of Ontario, in return, agrees:

That Cecil Murray Kirby will not be prosecuted by the Crown in Ontario in respect of any matter to which his statements relate, providing the police and Crown are satisfied his statements are true and complete, and providing he agrees to answer all questions of the police to these matters and any other criminal activity he is involved in, or has knowledge of, to date.

That the statements already given to date will not be used against Kirby in any event.

That it is therefore understood that even if independent evidence became available that would be admissible against Kirby he will not be prosecuted on the basis of that evidence as long as that evidence does not show his statements are untrue or incomplete.

AGREED:

Witness:

_____

R. M. McLeod, Ministry of the
Attorney General of Ontario

_____

Cecil Murray Kirby

The above agreement is subject to discussion and consent by the following parties:

_____

S/Insp. D. Banks
Metropolitan Toronto Police

_____

S/Insp. T. O'Grady
Ontario Provincial Police

_____

Insp. W. Stefureak
Royal Canadian Mounted Police

MEMORANDUM OF AGREEMENT
(Part II of two parts)

Between Cecil Murray Kirby, DOB: 17 Aug. 51, Ontario
Provincial Police, Metropolitan Toronto Police Force, and the
Royal Canadian Mounted Police.

That Cecil Murray Kirby agrees to provide truthful and
detailed information concerning criminal activities, which will be
taken down in writing and signed by him in addition to being
tape recorded. He will agree to testify truthfully with respect to
any judicial proceedings at which he may be a witness and give
in evidence the statements he provides.

He consents to the admission of any recorded conversations
between himself and any other person or persons which have
taken or will take place.

That Corporal M. Murphy will be available and will attend
during dealings with Cecil Murray Kirby, if required.

That Cecil Murray Kirby will make himself available and
cooperate with investigators who are investigating pertinent
cases, as required.

The Ontario Provincial Police, Metropolitan Toronto Police,
and Royal Canadian Mounted Police in return to the above
agrees:

That Cecil Murray Kirby will be provided physical protection for himself and his family prior, during, and after any
related criminal proceedings are instituted to the satisfaction of
the police involved; and, to provide adequate living expenses
throughout that period, and to financially and administratively
assist him in a reasonable manner in the development of a new
life style agreeable to the police and Kirby.

AGREED:
Witness:

_____

S/Insp. D. Banks
Metropolitan Toronto Police

D/Insp. T. O'Grady
Ontario Provincial Police

Insp./W. Stefureak
R.C.M..P.

Cecil Murray Kirby

The Ministry of the Attorney General of Ontario agrees with the above Memorandum of Agreement and will participate in an appropriate cost sharing arrangement to fulfill the requirements of the Memorandum stated therein.

R. M. McLeod, Ministry of the
Attorney General of Ontario

Date: April 27, 1981

There was very little by way of comparison between the first agreement the Steering Committee had asked Kirby to sign and this new agreement. Kirby had operated at great risk based only on good faith and trust, and now that the agreement was signed he could be certain that trust had not been betrayed. Sgt. Norm Ross and I signed the agreement, witnessing Kirby's signature. He gave that familiar Irish grin, shook our hands, thanked us and left. I was satisfied it was an excellent agreement for all concerned.

Two days after the agreement was signed, Kirby handed over a small semi-automatic Baynard Handgun. I took possession of the handgun and a few days later gave it to Mr. Robert

Monument, Forensic Science Laboratory, Toronto, for ballistic
tests to see if it might have been used in a murder or something similar. Mr. Monument did some tests and advised me
they were negative. He also advised that the gun was inoper-
able because the firing pin had been broken off and the gun
would not fire. When I received the gun back from the lab, I
was so busy with the ongoing investigations, that I just threw
it in my locker for approximately a month. When things
slowed down, I checked the gun through Police records and
found it had been stolen in Peel Regional Police area. I called a
good friend of mine on the Peel Police Force, Det. Noel Catney
(now Police Chief in Peel Region), and handed the gun over to
him and his partner, after an interview of Kirby pertaining to a
murder that had taken place in their area. I had been ordered
by Staff Sgt. Kennedy, my boss, to hand over all exhibits
directly to the investigating officers of the Kirby investigation.
Since the gun was part of the Kirby investigation, I did not do
an Exhibit Report because I felt it was not necessary. In the
Internal Investigation that followed, I was given an Official
Warning pertaining to the handling of this particular exhibit.
Literally hundreds of other exhibits had been handled in the
same fashion without any problem.

At a meeting on the 29th of April, the level of tension
increased in relation to the supposed hit on Helen Nafpliotis.
Concern was growing that the FBI might have allowed
Nafpliotis to make contact with some people who might in
turn have relayed the message that she was still alive to the
Mob in Connecticut. If that was the case, Kirby was in unprec-
edented danger with each exposure to the Commissos. Those
of us who were assigned to cover the meetings were also in
danger. Those thoughts were foremost in my mind. How far
should we push for evidence without risking people's lives? If
the Commissos knew Kirby was working undercover, they
would be enraged. But if they knew the police were only a

few feet away, they probably wouldn't try anything stupid. The problem was they did not know we were so close, and at any given moment they could strike out at Kirby. For his own protection, Kirby made every effort he could to stay close to the surveillance unit, the only backup he had. Kirby displayed a tremendous sense of bravado. The recorded transcript of the meeting that followed offered no reassurance that all had gone well. The following is an edited portion of the conversation:

C.C.:   Why you want my brother here for?

C.K.:   Well look, you told me last week that you were going to put me on the payroll. Now I just want to confirm it with him in case something happens to you. If you get picked up or get another charge.

C.C.:   You know, he said that they worry about that (Kirby's story of the Nafpliotis murder), they still don't believe that it's O.K.

C.K.:   They don't what?

C.C.:   Because, ah, even her suitcase is missing.

C.K.:   Yeah, well, I took care of all that, O.K.?

C.C.:   He said that all the jewelry is missing.

C.K.:   My partner took some jewelry and some stuff, O.K.? We took stuff out to make it look like she more or less went on a vacation.

C.C.:   Oh no, no. Just a minute. You know, the radio, American radio, said that she's living in Italy, in Greece or in Toronto.

C.K.:   Who said that?

C.C.:   The radio, the car they no find yet, where's the car, in the lake, too?

C.K.:   Yeah.

C.C.:   That's where she died?

C.K.:   Yes.

C.C.:   Far away or nearby?

C.K.:   About thirty miles from there, how fucking far do you want me to drive the car, back to Canada?

C.C.:   No, no that's good. They probably just made those stories up. I think excuses because the guy is broke, so he try to, you know.

C.K.:   Look it, she's dead, O.K.?

C.C.:   I know it.

C.K.   You got my guarantee on it, O.K.? Do you want me to go show you where she's dead?

C.C: No, no. What happened must be just excuses.

C.K.:   Well, what the fuck's wrong? Where's my fucking money?

C.C.:   It's O.K. What bothers me is we don't make no money.

C.K.:   What does he think, I got the broad shacked up here in Toronto or something?

C.C.:   Yes, that's what he said.

C.K.:   Is that right, eh?

C.C.:   You know they wanted her dead.

C.K.:   She is dead!

C.C.:   About the thing I do with the Chinese people. You tell anybody about that thing? (This is a reference to the bombing of a Chinese Restaurant at 111 Elizabeth St. in Toronto, in which a Chinese cook was killed by Kirby's bomb because Kirby was given erroneous information. Cosimo had told Kirby that the restaurant would be vacant in the early hours of the morning)

C.K.:   What?

C.C.:   That Chinese thing that you do for me.

C.K.:   No. You tell me, I tell you, and that's as far as it goes, you know that. What did you give me there, a thousand?

C.C.:   Yes. I trust you now.

C.K.:   So I can see them being a little suspicious, but I'll go back down there and show him were the fucking car is. He can go down there and swim down there, to see if it's there. Unless she can hold her breath for fifteen minutes, unless she's the best swimmer I've ever seen in my life.

C.C.:   Tell me one thing, was she dead when you . . . ?

C.K.:   I knocked her out, I didn't use the gun. I threw the gun away somewhere else. I don't know where this gun had been, O.K.? They hand me a fucking gun, and first of all it's supposed to be a .38.

C.C.:   I know, I understand what happened.

C.K.:   When I went down there things were different, which it shouldn't be. I was to see one guy; who the fuck is this other kid?

C.C.:   No, they said on the radio that she calls from over there.

C.K.:   Do you believe everything you hear on the radio and see in the paper? They never print anything right in the paper.

C.C.:   Why am I at fault, just to do a favor?

C.K.:   So what about the other guy you were going to show me?

C.C.:   We wait for a week or two, we have things all in order, you understand?

C.K.: You're in no rush to get rid of Scarcella?

C.K.: No, we gonna get him with us. But even tomorrow, if I say kill him, you understand what I mean?

C.K.: Yes, I understand. What about Volpe? You want me to do him?

C.C.: Yeah, O.K.

C.K.: Kill him? I know where he's at. I know where he lives. When do you want me to get him, kill him tonight?

C.C.: Alright.

C.K.: I'll see what I can do. I'll guarantee you he'll be dead in the next two weeks. You got to be careful, he's a very suspicious man you know. I'll see if I can get Volpe, that's why I don't want to see you in the next two weeks.

C.C.: Alright. Listen, I don't care if people fought with everyone, as long as they're not stool pigeons. That's what I care about. I'm sure you're not.

C.K.: Would I be here?

C.C.: That's what's important, O.K.?

C.K.: I know that.

After this meeting we all met back at room 420 at the Cara Inn on the airport strip. Cosimo had borrowed $20 out of the $1,000, so Kirby had $980 to hand over to John Simpson. Our concern that the Commissos had found out that Nafpliotis had not been killed was not unfounded. Commisso had brought the subject up, but Kirby was able to convince him the US people were only saying that because they did not want to pay the money now that the hit was complete. That thought had obviously entered Cosimo's mind and it was enough to convince him to drop the topic once he was convinced Kirby had not betrayed him.

The big news was that Volpe had definitely been targeted to be murdered. In terms of our investigation on the Commisso Family, the knowledge that they were putting out a murder contract on a major mobster right in our backyard was sensational, yet my first thoughts were for the inescapable fate that was rapidly enveloping Paul Volpe.

6

The Set-Up &
The Take-Down

Cosimo Commisso had decided that Peter Scarcella was now firmly on their side, meaning he no longer swore allegiance to the Paul Volpe Group. Kirby was therefore instructed not to do the hit. Commisso had decided to hold off on another hit as well, but the word was definitely out that Kirby was to go ahead with the hit on Volpe.

Later that same day I touched base with Kirby and advised him that the group headed by Chuck Yanover had been arrested for the attempted take-over bid of the Island of Dominica.

The information we were receiving about the hit on Volpe was phenomenal, although one thing bothered us. Remo Commisso was almost certainly involved in the conspiracies to commit murder, but up to this point in the investigation not one shred of evidence had surfaced that would implicate him. We had plenty of evidence on Cosimo and Michael Commisso, along with Antonio Romeo and the U.S. criminals Vince Melia and Jerry Russo. We knew if we were to do a take-down, however, Remo Commisso would walk and the Commisso Family business would continue to operate under his direction. The indication from Cosimo Commisso that his brother would take over if he was required to go to jail urged us to push farther to gather evidence against Remo, even though the dangers increased with each day that passed.

On April 30th, 1981, we convened a rather large gathering in Inspector McIlvenna's office to go over the investigation and assess just what we had so far. I don't know if it was fate or luck, but McIlvenna was away on leave and Inspector Wilf Stefureak was temporarily in charge of the SEU. The meeting was attended by the Steering Committee, Crown Counsel Howard Morton and his assistant Murray Segal, McCharles, Simpson, Al Cooke, Bouchard, Sgt. Ted Bean and Sgt. Bill Legga from the SEU, and Kennedy, Ross and myself from Toronto NCIS. Everyone was quite pleased with the investigation to date, the only real concern being the fact that Remo Commisso had not yet been implicated.

At the risk of sounding egotistical, I'd like to clarify once and for all who was responsible for a suggestion that would eventually implicate Remo Commisso in the murder conspiracies. Others have claimed responsibility in previous books such as *Mob Rule* and *Mafia Assassin*. In *Mob Rule* it was Crown Counsel Howard Morton, and in *Mafia Assassin* it was Staff Sgt. Lyle McCharles who took credit . The truth of the matter is that I was the one who suggested that we wait until Cosimo Commisso was in jail on a weekend (he was serving weekends for some minor offence) and Remo Commisso and Paul Volpe were both home under surveillance, at which time we would approach Volpe and ask him for his cooperation. If he cooperated, we could fake his murder by giving his wallet or other personal item to Kirby to show to Remo Commisso, who we would also have under surveillance. If Remo Commisso admitted knowledge of the conspiracy to murder Volpe, that would be sufficient evidence to charge him.

When I finished my proposal, most of those in the room broke up laughing, including Morton and McCharles. I can still see McCharles' eyes roll upward as he stood near the door. There were hoots and howls when I suggested Volpe would cooperate. I'll be eternally grateful that there was one person in that room besides myself who was not laughing—

Inspector Stefureak. You could see the group starting to wipe the smiles from their faces when he said, "As I see it, it's the only option we've got. It's worth a try." You could have heard a pin drop. The embarrassment on the faces of the old timers was quite evident.

It was decided that since I knew Volpe fairly well, Sgt. Al Cooke and I would be assigned to approach Volpe and make the proposal if everything else fell into place. As I walked out of the meeting I glanced upward and said, "Thanks."

Preparations were being made for the day the take-down would occur. Sgt. Ross and I had secured a cottage north of Toronto, through a Whitby lawyer, Mr. David Franklyn, who was a friend of mine. It would temporarily act as a secure area for Kirby, his common-law wife and the security detail that would be an integral part of his life for the next couple of years. Since the agreement had been signed, Kirby held to his part of the bargain and agreed to a debriefing by two Metro homicide detectives in relation to the bombing and murder of a Chinese cook and restaurant at 111 Elizabeth Street, Toronto in 1979. Sgt. Al Cooke and I picked up Kirby and took him to a room at the Holiday Inn in downtown Toronto to meet Detectives Dave Dicks and Tom Milne. With a reassuring glance from me, Kirby described the bombing in detail in a recorded interview. He even drew diagrams, at the request of the police, detailing the mechanism used to set up the timer and the detonator on the bomb. He drew a diagram of the inside and outside of the restaurant. He estimated he had used 100 sticks of dynamite, which he brought into the restaurant in a briefcase and a carrying bag. He ordered some take-out food, and while waiting for the order, he slipped into the bathroom and set up the bomb above the ceiling tiles, setting the timer for 4:00 a.m. when, according to his information , the restaurant would be vacant. (We would learn later that Cpl. Al McDonald, RCMP Drug Section, was in the restaurant talking to an informant when Kirby entered and set up the bomb.) Kirby stated the bombing was done at the request of Cosimo Commisso, who had paid $14,000 to do the job. Kirby told us he bought a white Corvette with some of the money.

When the debriefing ended, the Metro coppers had no doubts that they were talking to the person responsible for the bombing. Kirby was upset that the Chinese cook had been killed because he had been assured the restaurant would be vacant at the time. The unfortunate murder of the cook was accidental, although we must not forget the planned bombing, and the consequences that would result, were not. Over the next couple of days Sgt. Cooke and I continued the debriefing at the Holiday Inn, Eglinton Avenue, Toronto, and we covered the incidents that Kirby and I had already covered during our tour of Southern Ontario some time earlier. The conversations were recorded and passed on to the police agencies responsible for each investigation.

On the 12th of May, Kirby and I made a patrol up north to a cottage area. There he handed over some of the last remaining tools of his trade. Accompanied by OPP experts, Kirby handed over 43 electrical blasting caps and 61 sticks of dynamite. This particular incident reminded me of a poem that had come to mind so many times in dealing with Kirby. The poem was one we had all learned in high-school, entitled *A Road Not Taken* by Robert Frost. It struck me so many times that Kirby was that individual who had come to the division in the road and decided to take one route, only to learn it was not for him. He returned to that same division and decided to go the other way. That may sound naive, but if you knew Kirby as I did you could appreciate that thought. I'm convinced Kirby would have been a much better copper than a criminal, and he had been a good criminal.

On the 15th of May, Cecil Kirby would have his final meeting with Cosimo Commisso at the Howard Johnson Hotel, Dixon Road, Toronto. It was 1:53 PM when Cosimo arrived and met Kirby.

The following is an edited version of their conversation:

C.C.: Going out tonight?

C.K.: No. Been trying to watch Volpe for the last fuckin' two weeks. Ah, I've seen him a few times up there, eh? I got a good idea when I can get him. I'd say, ah, soon, very soon.

C.C.: Yeah.

C.K.: This thing with Volpe, I want to know how much you gonna give me for that. I want it all in one lump. I want to know how much you're gonna give me, and then how much you can give me after that, O.K.? Cause I want out, I want to fuck off out of the country. I've been out in the rain for the last two nights watching the guy's place for Christ's sake. I'll end up with pneumonia.

C.C.: Cec, how is . . . this car is still O.K.?

C.K.: This car is, I had it checked out, ah, two weeks ago.

C.C.: Listen, I don't want to promise any more to put up until I'm a hundred percent sure.

C.K.: All right. I just want enough money to get around in, and I want it after Volpe's killed. He'll be killed soon.

C.C.: No, no talk, O.K.? We know what we're talking about, O.K.?

C.K.: I got three options how to do this. Can we do it the same as before? Same as always?

C.C.: Yeah.

C.K.: It's out in the country, O.K.? I got a mile to go O.K. where I got a good spot to park. I got a mile to go through the bush. I tell you I've been fuckin' soaked the last three days.

C.C.: In the morning, Cec, how it look?

C.K.: He's got, ah, Foxhill on the mailbox, with TV towers and a tennis court back there. He drives a maroon Cadillac, burgundy, and he's got a station wagon, too.

C.C.: He drives one of those Audis, you know the car?

C.K.: Yeah, an Audi. I saw him come home one night in the Cadillac, and I didn't have anything with me at that time, I wasn't even expecting him, O.K.? When he comes home, eh? I have a very good idea, and it's beautiful. Nobody'd fuckin' hear it out there.

C.C.: There's no people.

C.K.: He won't be much of a problem. Just catching him at the right time.

C.C.: But you know him.

C.K.: I know him. Tall, but sorta bald, hair on the sides. He's had three-piece suits sometimes. I saw him down at the Four Seasons with Scarcella.

C.C.: I wanna make sure, you know, it's very important, you know what I mean, Cec? I want to make sure.

C.K.: There won't be no mistakes in this, O.K.?

C.C.: All right, I know.

C.K.: You know that if this guy gets knocked off I want twenty thousand?

C.C.: I couldn't give you it, I couldn't give it all at once, not that much money.

C.K.: All right, twenty thousand over periods of time.

C.C.: All right.

C.K.: All right. Soon after, the next day after it's done, I'm gonna come and see you, O.K.?

C.C.: Four days after.

C.K.: Four days after? All right. Make sure you have at least five thousand on you or somebody, O.K.? Either you or your brothers or somebody, make sure you have five thousand on you.

C.C.: All right, all right. And then I pay you after two months. We bought property, we mortgage ourselves over our heads. I have no cash, O.K., but we have a lot of property, we have maybe ten million dollars worth of property.

C.K.: Ten million. Is there property in King City?

C.C.: We have ten acres there. You know how much we paid for it?

C.K.: What?

C.C.: Half a million dollars.

C.K.: Those guys down in Dominica, they got pinched, they're looking at about fifty fuckin' years.

C.C.: You know that the first people that they talk to was us.

C.K.: From Dominica?

C.C.: Yeah. I was down there. The deal was twenty-five years casino, twenty-five years free of tax. Ah, for us to build them a runway and airport.

C.K.: An airport?

C.C.: Yeah. They will give the best side of land, five hundred acres of farm land. So much percent to the Prime Minister there.

C.K.: All right, what you gonna give me, another thousand next week, eh?

C.C.: Yeah.

C.K.: All right, a thousand. And right after I do Volpe, five thousand, O.K.? So make sure you got it in your pocket.

C.C.: Yeah, O.K..

C.K.: I'll catch him at the right time soon, I know I will.

C.C.: All right. O.K., take care.

C.K.: What if there's somebody with him? What if his wife's with him? I'm getting impatient, you know.

C.C.: I leave it to you.

C.K.: I'll do the wife?

C.C.: They hardly go out together.

C.K.: I got a licence plate number off the station wagon, eh? The last letters are VOLPE. Can't be any mistakes made now. Cause when you go up there, O.K., and, like, it's a bad area. I got a couple good spots up there to park, but it's so fuckin' far away, you know? When I go up there, I'm gonna be carrying a gun, and that's it. It'll be done. You know, I don't care if I got to sit there for fuckin' twenty four hours and wait. It's gonna be done.

C.C.: All right.

Kirby had been able to plant an important seed during this meeting. The final word had been given on the Volpe contract and Kirby was instructed to carry out the hit at the first opportunity. Cosimo Commisso had promised Kirby $20,000 for the murder of Volpe. Kirby told Cosimo that either he or his brother Remo should keep $5,000 in cash on hand so he could get out of the country for a couple of weeks immediately following the hit. This was in line with our plan to implicate Remo Commisso in the conspiracy.

The reference to Volpe's wife during Kirby's conversation with Cosimo would later infuriate Volpe. Volpe didn't mind them coming after him, but by involving his wife they had violated an unwritten law among mobsters not to involve the family. I knew this would encourage Volpe to cooperate with the police.

On Saturday, the 16th of May, everything was falling into place. Cosimo Commisso was in jail serving his weekend time, Remo Commisso was under surveillance at his home, and Paul Volpe was at his home in Nobletown, also under surveillance. At 9:36 AM Sgt. Al Cooke and I met Kirby at the Wycliff Plaza, at Bathurst and Steeles in Toronto's North End We gave Kirby his instructions and I went to the phone to call Volpe. We were ready, but would Volpe cooperate?

My phone conversation with Volpe went as follows:

> UKM: Hello.
>
> M.M.:   Is Paul there?
>
> P.V.:   Hello.
>
> M.M.:   Yeah, Paul. It's Mark Murphy from the RCMP. I met you some time ago.
>
> P.V.:   Yeah, you're the tall guy Natie and I met a few years ago. I remember you.
>
> M.M.:   Geez, you've got a good memory; that's seven years ago.
>
> P.V.:   Yeah, what's goin' on?

M.M.:   Well I don't want to discuss it here, but there is something really important that pertains to you. Myself and Al Cooke from Metro Police would like to drop up and see you, unless you want to come downtown.

P.V.:   Well I'm waiting for a guy to come by to fix my air conditioner. You can come up here if you like.

M.M.:   O.K. We'll be there in about a half hour.

P.V.:   Good, we'll see you.

It was 10:37 AM when Cooke and I met Volpe at his back door. He introduced us to his nephew, who acted as a body-guard, and his wife, Lisa. Both Cooke and I kept a close watch on the two dogs giving us a menacing look. Paul didn't want to talk in front of his wife; he invited us downstairs to his den.

Once downstairs we began to talk:

P.V.:   Would you like a coffee?

M.M.:   No, thanks.

P.V.:   What's going on?

M.M.:   There was supposed to be a hit done on you this morning by a guy I'm involved with.

P.V.:   Yeah, really? Who would want to do that?

Cooke: Well, we don't want to say just yet. But that's not bullshit. There is a contract out on you and we learned about it.

M.M.:   Now we've got a problem. These guys even gave the go ahead on your wife, if she was with you.

P.V.:   Your kidding. Murphy, tell me who they are and I'll bury them. What's the problem?

M.M.:   Well, we've been able to tie in two guys that are involved, but there is a third guy. He's involved, but we don't have any evidence on him at the moment. That's where we need your help.

P.V.:   What can I do to help you?

Cooke: Well, we intend to fake the hit on you. Then we plan to go to this guy and tell him it's done.

P.V.:   So what do you need?

M.M.:   Well, we need your wallet or your cap or something personal to show the guy.

P.V.:   (He laughs) Murphy, how do I know I can trust
you? How do I know you won't put it with 10 pounds of heroin
in the trunk of a car or something?

M.M.:   Paul, I give you my word on my life you can trust
me.

P.V.:   All right, I'll get the wallet. Don't mention anything in front of my wife.

With that Volpe went upstairs and got his wallet out of his
bedroom while Cooke and I went outside to wait. He brought
the wallet outside and handed it over to me. We joked about
leaving a few bucks in it for the police. He left his driver's
licence and a few credit cards, along with some other identification. We asked him if he would be willing to go downtown
to the RCMP office for a couple of hours until we finished with
our meeting. Volpe and his wife got ready and left for our
office. We arranged to block off his driveway with a couple of
marked police cars, just as if it had been a murder scene, in
case the Commissos decided to check Kirby's story.

At 11:08 AM I arrived back at the Wycliff Plaza and met
Kirby. We wired him up and he headed for Remo
Commisso's. At 11:18 AM Kirby entered Remo's home where
he was met by Michael Commisso. He asked to speak to Remo
and the two proceeded downstairs where Remo considered it
might be safer to talk.

The following conversation was recorded:

C.K.:   Hi, is Remo home?

UKF: Yeah.

C.K.:   Can I see him?

UKF.:   Yeah. Remo! Oh, Remo!

C.K.:   George.

UKF.:   (Not clear)

R.C.:   Hi George. How are you?

C.K.:   Were you sleepin'?

R.C.:   No, I've been up, but (unclear) to stay in the house. Where you going?

M.C.:   How are you?

C.K.:   I gotta talk to you. (Directed at Remo)

R.C.:   Why?

C.K.:   Can I talk to ya? Outside I got something in the car I wanna show you, too.

R.C.:   (Unclear)

C.K.:   All right (Radio playing in background, child's voice heard.)

R.C.:   What is it?

C.K.:   Eh?

R.C.:   What is it?

C.K.:   I got something in the car I gotta show you.

R.C.:   Have something in the car.

C.K.:   Yeah.

R.C.:   You want to take me to your car?

C.K.:   Yeah. Not in the house. (Unclear) something gotta show you in the car.

R.C.:   Take it downstairs to someplace. I don't trust a car.

C.K.:   All right. I'll get it. I don't trust houses.

R.C.:   No, we go in the washroom.

C.K.:   All right.

(No conversation for approximately 14 seconds)

C.K.:   (To the police) I gotta go in the house and show him the wallet. I'm gonna talk to him in the house, and everything seems all right.

(No conversation for approximately 23 seconds)

C.K.:   How ya doing? Haven't seen you in a long time. Jesus, whata you babysitting?

M.C.:   No, on Saturday and Sunday I don't really do too much. I stay around the home and play with the kids.

C.K.:   Volpe, he's dead.

R.C.:   How come?

C.K.:   I just killed him, an hour ago.

R.C.:   What happened?

C.K.:   I killed him.

R.C.:   Did you?

C.K.:   Yeah.

R.C.:   How come?

C.K.:   Well, Cosimo told me you and him wanted it.
Want to go outside or talk in here?

R.C.:   You should never come here.

C.K.:   Well, look it, he's dead and so's his wife, O.K.?
They're both dead, O.K., about an hour ago.

R.C.:   You should never come here.

C.K.:   Well, listen, I need some money, and I'm broke,
O.K.?

R.C.:   (Unclear)

C.K.:   I told Cosimo yesterday O.K., when I saw him, I
said I'm broke, I need some money and I wanna get the fuck out
of the country now. I want some money today.

R.C.:   Tell me when I'm gonna get it to you, George.

C.K.:   Well, a thousand or something just to get me out of
here, O.K.? Look, the reason I got this (the wallet), I took this
right out of his back pocket, O.K.?

R.C.:   You should have thrown it away.

C.K.:   Well, listen, you people have doubted me in the
past.

R.C.:   All right, don't worry, we'll take care of you. You
know we respect you like a brother, don't worry about it.

C.K.:   Yeah.

R.C.:   (Unclear)

C.K.:   Yeah, but look at before. Cosimo still owes me five
thousand (from before).

R.C.:   You know you'll get the money from him.

C.K.:   All right, but I want it now, O.K.? There's two
people dead now, O.K.?

R.C.:   I don't even want to talk about these things.

C.K.:   All right, you know, I got this thing off him, partly it's just to prove to ya, O.K.?

R.C.:   That's all right. Throw it away, don't leave it around.

C.K.:   No, I'll get rid of it. I'll drop it down the sewer when I go out, far away from here.

R.C.:   Where do you wanna meet? When, ah, maybe tomorrow up here or Monday?

C.K.:   I need some money now, I wanna leave today. I'll meet you down at the Hall.

R.C.:   Where I'm gonna get the fuckin' money today?

C.K.:   A thousand bucks.

R.C.:   All right, but it's not good to come by the Hall.

C.K.:   Then where? Ah, get Michael to meet me down at Howard Johnson's again, O.K.?

R.C.:   What time?

C.K.:   Five o'clock. O.K., a thousand dollars. All right?

R.C.:   All right.

C.K.:   All right, what else can I say? All right, I'll be taking off for a week or two O.K.. I'll be back in two weeks. I want the rest of the money. Cosimo, I told Cosimo yesterday twenty thousand bucks, eh? I want at least five thousand of it.

R.C.:   I know nothing about this. I didn't know that he told you to do it.

C.K.:   But he told me long time ago that you and him wanted this done.

R.C.:   Me?

C.K.:   Yeah.

R.C.:   I never said that. Oh, come on, George.

C.K.:   That's what he told me.

R.C.:   Did you ever talk to me about this thing?

C.K.:   No, but hey, you know what's going on. You didn't know this?

R.C.:   No.

C.K.:   Oh.

R.C.   But anyways, what's the difference, so what?

C.K.:   Yeah.

R.C.:   All right, Michael will meet you at five.

C.K.:   Five o'clock.

R.C.:   All right.

C.K.:   All right, when I come back in two weeks.

R.C.:   But don't talk on the phone, don't . . .

C.K.:   No I'm not. What do you think I come here for? I didn't want to go to the Hall, I didn't want to talk on the phone, I just came directly here.

R.C.:   O.K..

C.K.:   All right. I got to be back in two weeks. What about this other guy, this Scarcella?

R.C.:   Forget about him.

C.K.:   Forget about him?

R.C.:   This fella we don't want to do nothing to no more. No problem.

C.K.:   All right.

R.C.:   (Unclear)

C.K.:   Well, I'm going.

R.C.:   Well, you go, five o'clock you get a thousand dollars.

C.K.:   Five o'clock, at least a thousand dollars.

R.C.:   O.K..

C.K.:   O.K.. All right.

R.C.:   Take care.

Kirby had again come through with flying colors. We had monitored the conversation and I knew it was exactly what we had hoped for. We were not disappointed when the tape was transcribed later. Not only were we able to link Remo Commisso to the Volpe conspiracy, but to the Scarcella conspiracy as well. Kirby retained Volpe's wallet and handed it over to Bouchard. Cooke unnecessarily released to the press that Volpe had cooperated with the police by giving them his wallet. In my view that was unprofessional and unfair. It exposed Volpe to grave danger from the Mob.

We had expected Remo Commisso to give Kirby the $1,000 immediately, but it appeared he might have a problem locating that much cash on such short order on a Saturday. That necessitated putting the payment off until 5:00 PM that evening. (It was later determined Dominic Racco of the Siderno organized crime family supplied the $1,000 for Kirby) We had no problem with the payment coming later in the afternoon, but Volpe and his wife were at our office waiting for word. Sgt. Cooke and Cpl. William Armstrong, who had provided backup for Cooke and me at the Volpe residence, approached Volpe and explained our plight. Volpe agreed to stay at RCMP Headquarters until the payment was made at 5:00 PM. Volpe was cooperating to the best of his ability, despite the original skepticism shown by most of the policemen involved in the case.

In the meantime, Kirby had returned to the secure room at his hotel with his security team. We had anticipated the take-down would take place when Michael Commisso showed at the hotel with the $1,000, and that it would not be necessary for Kirby to attend. At the time we felt his contribution to the investigation had been completed.

While waiting for the time to pass, I returned to our office and spoke with Paul Volpe. I thanked him for his cooperation and told him we really appreciated his help. He told me that if any statements had to be taken when this thing was over, I was to come to his place by myself. He said, "I don't trust Cooke. He double-crossed me in court before and I don't trust him. You come by yourself." Volpe trusted me just as Kirby had done, and I could hardly wait to find out where that road might lead.

We had a short meeting at the SEU. I was surprised that they wanted Kirby to meet Michael Commisso at 5:00 PM at the hotel. I told them I would call Kirby and see what response I would get. When I called Kirby, he said he was expecting it. I asked him if he thought it might be too risky and he said he was willing to take that chance. I told him we had placed two cruisers in Volpe's driveway in case they had sent anyone to check. That gave him some reassurance.

By the time I was able to get the surveillance vehicle geared up, wire Kirby, and get to the Howard Johnson Hotel, it was 4:48 PM. Kirby arrived in front of the hotel at 4:58 PM. Someone advised that Michael Commisso was on his way with three other people in a vehicle. We had no idea why he would have three others along with him. Were they going to do their own take-down on Kirby? We decided to see what developed. I had told Kirby if anything went wrong he was to hit the deck and we would do all we could to resolve the situation. This was a very tense moment for all of us. As I sat in the surveillence vehicle with my loaded shotgun and bulletproof vest, it appeared increasingly likely that I would soon be needing them.

At 5:04 PM. Michael Commisso and three others arrived on the lot. They were all dressed in suits. Michael got out and went to Kirby's car and sat inside. I saw him hand Kirby a bundle of money. We were relieved to hear Michael say they were on their way to a wedding in Niagara Falls.

The following conversation was recorded:

> M.C.: I got to go to a fuckin' wedding in Niagara Falls.
>
> C.K.: In Niagara Falls?
>
> M.C.: Me and my kid cousins.
>
> C.K.: Who's that, Ernie?
>
> M.C.: Claudio.
>
> C.K.: Claudio?
>
> M.C.: Claudio and Remo and Johnny.
>
> C.K.: Yeah. Well I'm going to fuckin' Miami in about another hour.
>
> M.C.: Take care of yourself.

C.K.:   How much is there?

M.C.:   One.

C.K.:   A thousand? Good, good.

M.C.:   O.K., see you later.

C.K.:   All right listen, I'll see you in about two weeks, after I get back from Miami.

M.C.:   Yeah, take care of yourself.

C.K.:   I will for sure.

The money was turned over to Bouchard, and John Simpson put the take-down into effect. Arrested that day for conspiracy to commit murder were Remo and Michael Commisso. Cosimo Commisso was already in jail. Antonio Romeo was also arrested in Toronto. In the US, Vince Melia and Jerry Russo were simultaneously arrested by the FBI. Nicky Melia was not arrested, because there wasn't sufficient evidence to link him to the Nafpliotis murder conspiracy.

Since the arrest on the 16th of May, a tight security blanket was thrown around Cecil Kirby. It's difficult for most people to comprehend what it's like to live in that environment, having security people with you twenty-four hours a day. Kirby tensed up like a caged animal. His nerves became extremely bad. On several occasions he bolted from the security mode just to get away from it all. He had more quarrels with his girlfriend. On many occasions I was called in the middle of the night to go into Toronto and talk to Kirby, trying to calm him down for the sake of the security net that had been set up. I was also under a lot of pressure. I even had people come to my house and try to convince my wife and four kids to move out because of the dangers involved. Word had filtered down to the police that an attempt would be made to hit Kirby at his next court appearance. They were talking of using a sniper, and with security so tight this appeared to be their only option. Information like this didn't help to calm my nerves.

On the 15th of June, Kirby was due to appear in court. Now that the take-down had occurred, SEU was talking about placing Kirby in "protective custody"—in other words, jail time. What were these people thinking of? During the court appearance, S/Sgt. McCharles ordered me out of the court. I refused to go, but my boss Sgt. Ross told me I had to leave. I felt I was misled by McCharles, who told me the judge had ruled that only a certain number of people were allowed in the court for security reasons. I checked with Crown Attorney Howard Morton, who initially said there was no such order, but later changed his story and insisted there was. Apparently, they didn't want me to know about sentencing Kirby into protective custody. Kirby and I both got upset over that and were able to convince them it was certainly a breach of his agreement. The idea was dropped, but Kirby had had just about enough and considered walking away from the whole deal. If they had insisted on protective custody it surely would have meant the end of all prosecutions, because Kirby would not testify. I was incredulous, and thought, "Why would they try these antics at this stage of the game?"

At 2:30 PM Kirby appeared in court. For his part in the break, enter and theft he received a suspended sentence and two years' probation. Part of the conditions of his probation was that he be available to testify if subpoenaed. The judge had been made aware of the special circumstances surrounding the case and had no difficulty with the sentence, commenting that Kirby would be testifying in matters of grave concern against people involved in organized crime. It had been a long, hard struggle, but the passing of a suspended sentence was another important step in the right direction.

During the period that followed court, Cecil Kirby kept to his end of the deal, giving extensive interviews to the various investigators about his knowledge of criminal activities, particularly relative to the various bombings over the years. Almost daily, Kirby and I met investigators and travelled throughout Southern Ontario identifying in minute detail the particulars of each criminal offence. Kirby had an excellent memory and would make a convincing witness in the court cases that were to follow.

It's still difficult to for me to comprehend, but on the 2nd of July, 1981, Inspector McIlvenna and his crew set up a highly suspect episode. Honest to God, at the time I didn't think they had enough brains between the whole crew to make one good policeman. At 8:10 AM Ted Bean, OPP officer attached to the SEU, called me to his office. Bean and Sgt. Bill Legga told me Sgt. Al Cooke wanted Kirby's girlfriend's new address for safety reasons in the event Metro Toronto Police got a call to her new address. The reason they gave for the request was to ensure the police would not be injured in an incident of violence that might occur. It was a logical request, even though his girlfriend's address was supposed to be on a 'need-to-know' basis. I discussed it with Sgt. Ross and he agreed that Metro should be aware of the address. I sent the address to Sgt. Cooke, who was at his Metro headquarters, by way of Cst. Vern Seacord, one of our team who happened to be on his way over. I had called Cooke and he reassured me he needed it for the reasons already given.

Fifteen minutes later I went back to the SEU office and on Bill Legga's desk I noticed the name and address I had just sent over to Cooke. I started to churn up inside but thought it better to wait until I cooled down before mentioning it to Bean. When confronted by me a few days later, Bean would avoid the truth as Cooke did about the reason for the request.

Several days passed before Ted Bean advised that Sgt. Bill Kerns of the SEU wanted to spend a day with Kirby, getting some information clarified. We met at 11:00 AM at the Ramada Inn where Kirby was staying. After a short discussion we left and drove through the city. As the day passed I mentioned to Kirby that there was something unusual going on, since we had not yet discussed anything of significance. Usually he would be asked to point out locations where he had set off a bomb or did an act of extortion. Today we did none of that. I began to smell a rat.

When we arrived back at the hotel that evening, it wasn't difficult to figure out what had happened. I should mention that earlier in the week McCharles had bragged that he had arrested Kirby's girlfriend for being party to a rape and insisted she testify against Kirby. Kirby now made a routine call to his girlfriend, and she told him that while Kirby, Kerns, his partner, and I wandered aimlessly around the Metro area, S/Sgt. McCharles and Ted Bean had approached her and suggested she testify against Kirby. Apparently, McCharles in his wisdom was, at that late hour, still trying to 'get a hammer to Kirby's head'.

Kirby was furious, more so than I had ever seen him. When Kirby's girlfriend told him of the police interview—though the police asked her not to—you could see pure rage in his eyes. He took off from the hotel without his security people, saying the deal was off and he was going after McCharles and Bean. As angry as I was at them, I felt obligated to let them know their lives were very much in danger. When I called her later in the evening, Kirby's girlfriend said Kirby had gone to the Beverly Hills Hotel with a knife looking for some people to even an old score. Kirby had picked up a gun and said he wouldn't be coming back, he would go down shooting before he would be back. It took me three days of negotiating before Kirby agreed to return to the security detail. SEU promised not to bother his girlfriend again.

SEU's actions described above were totally inappropriate. I could understand if Kirby had not been cooperating, but he had given one hundred percent and was more than willing to testify. What more did they want? During this period of time I had received information from different sources that there were plots being hatched by bikers and others to kill Kirby. There was a $500,000 bounty on his head. That was enough to keep me occupied without worrying about my fellow police officers. Kirby finally demanded a meeting with the Steering Committee and outlined his problems with McCharles and Bean. The Steering Committee would do nothing to help the situation, which made me think they were, in all probability, behind the ridiculous scheme of getting Kirby's girlfriend to testify against him.

7

Good-bye To You, My Trusted Friend

On July 29, 1981, I had an unexpected call at my office. The man on the other end merely said, "How are you."

"Fine, Paul," I replied, "How are you?" I had listened to Volpe's voice so many times it was easily recognizable.

"Can you meet me for a coffee?" he asked.

I agreed and we arranged to meet at the intersection of Bloor and Bay streets. Although I trusted Volpe, I called my brother, Ray, who was with the RCMP Security Service in Toronto and advised him of the meeting. My brother was concerned and wondered if I should meet with Volpe without a back-up. I told him there shouldn't be a problem, but if he didn't hear from me in an hour or two he would know where to start looking.

It was 12:00 noon when I walked up to the intersection of Bloor and Bay. Volpe had spotted me approaching, and greeted me with a smile and a handshake. From the very first time I met Paul Volpe, I liked the guy. He was one of the most personable and interesting individuals I have ever met, with a certain charisma that very few men possess. Like Kirby, Volpe had little in the way of formal education, although he was intelligent and seemed to know everything that happened on the streets of Toronto. No matter what subject I broached during our meetings that followed, he was never caught off guard. I admit that his network for gathering intelligence seemed to surpass any network utilized by the police.

Volpe was charming and intelligent, but he was also a Mafia boss. I had been exposed to the other side of Paul Volpe during covert technical surveillance. I had heard him screaming obscenities and demanding payment from individuals who allegedly owed him money.

No matter what he was and what he stood for, I couldn't help but like the man. I thought to myself as we stood on that street corner how strange life can be. After all the time I had spent investigating this S.O.B., I was now about to befriend him.

Volpe led the way to a lunch area inside the Manual Life Building in the same complex as Creed's, where Volpe's wife worked. We ordered coffee. During our series of meetings I made sure that if Volpe paid for coffee one day, I paid for it the next time. I didn't want to owe him anything, and feel I earned some respect from Volpe by not accepting or expecting things for nothing.

Volpe started the conversation by saying he had found out some information which would assist us in our investigation. He told me there was a piece of property that was jointly owned by him and his business partner, Angelo Pucci. It was located at 111 Queen Street, the building formerly occupied by City TV in Toronto. The property was sold to a man named Lou Cocomile for 2.5 million dollars approximately six months prior to my present meeting with Volpe. Volpe put what is known as a lien penance, or a hold, on the property because he found out that Pucci had plans to pull a scam by reselling the building to a second buyer. Pucci probably figured that Volpe would back him in the scam by threatening the second buyer, and that they'd walk away with another 2.5 million dollars. Volpe had most likely been involved in scams such as this before, but this time he was concerned they would both be held responsible, and he didn't want to entertain the thought of serving a long jail sentence.

Volpe had had to do thirty days in jail on some minor charge and missed by one day a chance to pay off the mortgage on the property he owned with Pucci. According to Volpe, Pucci and Cocomile conspired to take Volpe's share of the profits on that property. Volpe was certain it was Angelo Pucci who had instigated the murder contract on him, since the time of the contract was very close to the time of the property sale on Queen Street. Volpe felt it was also Pucci who had approached the Commissos, and that Pucci would spill his guts if he were picked up by the police and threatened with jail. In return I asked Volpe if he would use some of his influence to get the bikers to back off Kirby. He promised me he would do what he could.

Later investigation revealed that the date the murder contract on Volpe was issued did coincide with the time of the dispute over the property at 111 Queen Street. I didn't tell them my source, but this information was immediately passed over to Inspector McIlvenna, John Simpson and Danielle Bouchard at SEU for follow-up investigation. As far as I can tell, they did nothing with the information. They didn't even bother to talk to Angelo Pucci.

Several days later I had another call from Paul Volpe. He confirmed he had talked to "that guy" (Chuck Yanover) and everything had been taken care of, meaning he had contacted the bikers and asked them to back off with respect to Kirby. Prior to this, I had been picking up information from street sources that the heat was off in the biker world to murder Kirby prior to court. Volpe had used his influence and had accomplished what the police were unable to do. From that time on, the biker threat was drastically reduced, thanks to the most unlikely source in the world.

On the 12th of August, Volpe called again, saying that he wanted to meet me at 10:00 AM the following morning. Again I called my brother and advised him of the meeting. I had told Volpe during our very first meeting that I would never come to meet him without telling a very good friend of mine where I was going and, if anything happened to me, Paul Volpe would be held personally responsible. He grinned, saying he knew exactly what I meant, and that there would never be a problem from his people. I'm not sure just how comforting that was, but I really never worried about a double-cross from Volpe.

At 10:00 AM the next day I again went to the area of Bloor and Bay Streets to meet Volpe. He always stood in a small alcove where he could get a full view of the street. Like the others involved in criminal activity he never stopped looking, and this guy didn't miss a trick. Volpe told me he had more information on the contract on his life. He said, "Around the end of March Angelo Pucci and two other guys went to the US border on their way to Buffalo, New York to arrange a contract on me."

He believed the second guy was Frank Pucci, Angelo's brother, and the third guy was Michael Commisso. At the border, Angelo Pucci was turned back for drinking, and Frank Pucci was denied entry for having a criminal record. Michael Commisso got through. Volpe went on to say that in Buffalo Michael Commisso met with people who agreed to do the Volpe contract. I would later surmise that these people were in the old Stefano Magaddino Family. Volpe had one more important bit of information—the Commissos would be copping a plea to the conspiracy charges so the matter would not go to trial. By pleading guilty they eliminated a long, involved trial and the need for Kirby and me to testify. It's an unwritten part of the Mob code, to plead guilty when the prosecution obviously had a good case against you. This usually resulted in a lighter sentence and eliminated the exposure of other criminal activities that might come to light during a trial.

I wondered how accurate this information was, especially the trip to the US to arrange the contract. During a conversation Kirby had with Michael Commisso on April 21, 1981, Michael mentioned he had been to the US two weeks earlier to see Melia, which would have placed him in the US at about the right time.

Later that day I called Special Agent Jim Buile of the US border patrol, a friend and a good contact. I gave him the information about the Puccis and Michael Commisso and asked him to verify it if possible. Special Agent Buile called back on the 17th of August to confirm that Frank and Angelo Pucci had tried to cross the US border at Fort Erie on March 25, 1981, in a 1979 Lincoln Continental, licence plate number MY0-762. Frank Pucci was locked up due to a criminal record and Angelo Pucci was turned back. There was nothing on Michael Commisso and he was allowed to proceed into the US

I requested to be allowed to do a follow-up investigation on this information, but inspector Wylie forbid it. The information was passed over to Simpson and Bouchard for further investigation; to the best of my knowledge they didn't do much with it. Here was a golden opportunity for these investigators to get their teeth into something worthwhile and they didn't seem interested, perhaps because the information pertained to Paul Volpe and they felt it wasn't worth pursuing. I asked several times how the investigation was progressing, with no response from Wylie, McIlvenna, Simpson or Bouchard. They insisted I tell them who my source was, but I refused. I simply told them it was from an extremely reliable source and the information was good. They wondered what made me think the Commissos would be copping a plea. I just told them that was reliable as well. I was churning up inside to think they would not pursue this information and forbade me to do so.

Kirby called me from North Bay complaining his nerves were shot and he was leaving security. Returning to Toronto, he met with the Steering Committee. After requesting and getting the security dropped, he insisted he would touch base with me daily and still be willing to testify. SEU and the crown were justifiably concerned about Kirby being on his own. Someone had told Kirby the crown was plea-bargaining with the Commissos for a guilty plea and a lesser sentence, and this upset him. No one knew better than Kirby that if the Commissos hit the streets, his life would be in grave danger.

The security detail was being handled by Sgt. Ross and they were doing an excellent job under the circumstances. Our system sadly lacks a good witness protection program. I'm not advocating a system like the US Marshal's, where witnesses spend a great deal of time in protective custody (jail), unable to see family. However, we need safe houses where a witness can be relocated under an assumed name with a proper identification that would stand a security screening check. This would enable them to seek employment, become part of a community and start life for themselves and their family. Unfortunately, that type of system was not in place then, and to the best of my knowledge still does not exist. The lack of a good witness-protection program caused big problems for everyone concerned with the Kirby situation. I still can't believe how close we came to losing Kirby as a witness.

To help keep a lid on the situation, Sgt. Ross chose good men such as Fred Dane and Paul Lennerton of the RCMP, and others from Metro Police and the OPP These men were able to identify with Kirby. They ran, played cards, golfed and pursued other sports activities. Through their devotion and perseverance, they enabled us to get Kirby to return to the security mode and to the protection he so desperately needed.

Soon after, the tension of twenty-four hour protection, with at least three police officers with him at all times, brought Kirby once again to the boiling-point. His nerves shattered, Kirby bolted once again from security, saying he needed to get away but would still testify.

McIlvenna called me to his office around 7:30 PM the evening Kirby left. He asked if I knew where Kirby was staying and I said, "Yes." He ordered me to call Kirby and have him come to the office—he was going to arrest him for breach of conditions attached to a summons served on Kirby by John Simpson, with respect to his upcoming testimony against the Commissos.

I told McIlvenna that since Kirby had not refused to testify, there were no grounds for his arrest. He told me again to get him to come to the office, at which time he would be arrested. Tired of McIlvenna's nonsense, I said, "If you want him arrested, you fucking well call him and tell him to come in. I will not be party to a false arrest." McIlvenna backed down and the following day Kirby voluntarily came back to the security mode.

On the 21st of August Cosimo and Remo Commisso went to court and pleaded guilty to two counts of conspiracy to commit murder. They received eight years in prison on each count. Michael Commisso and Antonio Romeo also pleaded guilty to two counts of conspiracy to commit murder and were sentenced to two and one half years in prison. Volpe's information was bang on the money. That made SEU investigators even more curious about who I had obtained the information from.

Immediately upon the conviction of the Commissos and Romeo I began to hear rumors that Wylie and McIlvenna had asked for an internal investigation of me, and that I would no longer be allowed to work with Kirby. Those rumors were partly confirmed in a memorandum I received from Insp. Wylie on September 22, 1981. Wylie, on directions from McIlvenna, put out an order which read, "Cpl. Murphy is to have no further contact with Cecil Kirby, effective immediately." McIlvenna was finally able to get the control of Kirby he had so desperately desired since the beginning of the investigation.

I had been under tremendous pressure for a long time, and welcomed the thought of terminating my involvement with Kirby. He knew it was not by choice that I was leaving, and he understood. He called me to say he was finished with the investigation as well. He said he would not testify against Vince Melia or Jerry Russo, or in any other investigation relating to the bombings and extortion. I told him to watch out for his own interests. He still needed the protection and he needed money. He certainly couldn't go back out on the street.

"Look, I'm a survivor," I said. "I'll be all right. You and I have been to hell and back. You can't let these people walk after all we've been through. I told you in Darien, Connecticut, it would be a rough and bumpy road; this is just one of those bumps."

Kirby reluctantly agreed to continue with his role in the investigations.

On October 6, 1981, I received another call at home from Paul Volpe. Kirby had saved Volpe's life and now it was time for him to reciprocate. Kirby and his security detail of three police officers per shift were staying at a hotel in the Richmond Hill area, north of Toronto. Volpe had learned that some bikers had spotted Kirby and his bodyguards in a bar in the area during the afternoon. Volpe asked me if I was involved in guarding Kirby. I told him I wasn't personally, but that some police officers were providing a security detail. Volpe told me the bikers knew where Kirby was staying and we had better move him quickly to a new location. I immediately called the detail and in very short order they were on the road to a new location. There is no doubt in my mind that the tip from Volpe saved Kirby's life, and quite possibly the lives of the three young officers who were guarding him.

I felt the time had come to have Paul Volpe, as they say in police jargon, coded as an informant. Let me say that contrary to what most people would believe, Paul Volpe was not really an informant for the RCMP at this stage. As most critics will agree, the information given up to this point was about the contract on his life and he did not give it to the police for profit or gain. I realized the information he was supplying was of limited scope, but then Kirby started out much the same way. It was more his potential I was thinking of, and the fact that it was getting more and more difficult to protect his identity without coding him or giving him a number by which I could refer to him in any reports submitted.

To initiate the coding process, I filled out a sheet listing his name and other particulars required and brought them to Sgt. Gerry Gilfoy, the CIB officer's assistant. He was the one in the office responsible for all coded informants. I handed him the form saying I wanted to code this guy and needed a number.

"Sure," said Gilfoy. "No problem." Then he began to read my request. He looked up and said, "Volpe. Paul Volpe. You want to code Paul Volpe?" When I replied, "Yes, I do," his eyes were popping out of his head. He jumped to his feet and ran into the office of the CIB Officer. They had a hurried conversation and Gilfoy came back. He said the CIB Officer would look into it and he'd get back to me with the number.

Volpe was probably the best known organized crime figure in Ontario at that time, but I hadn't really expected such an extreme reaction to my request. Before leaving I asked that Volpe's name be put on a restricted list so McIlvenna and his crew would not be hounding him for information. Gilfoy agreed, but that was no guarantee it would be done. Simpson had already approached Volpe, and been told to get lost. I thought there was a message here. Volpe did not trust Simpson, McIlvenna or any of the SEU members. He felt they had double-crossed him before, and Volpe was probably astute to realize they might do it again if given the chance. Although he was assigned a coded number, I would learn one year later that the CIB Officer and senior management would not accept Volpe as an RCMP informant. Most people would probably agree with their decision, but to me this will always be truly astonishing. Yes, he was a senior Mafia boss and the subject of many police operations over the years. But in my view his role as an informant represented a golden opportunity: for the police to gain valuable information against organized crime, and for Paul Volpe to begin a new life away from crime.

On October 26, 1982, I was transferred to a desk job in the Toronto Commercial Crime Unit doing administrative work. An opportunity soon presented itself for me to have a man-to-man talk with Insp. Wylie. When we were alone, I told him in no uncertain terms what my feelings were toward him and Insp. McIlvenna regarding the entire Kirby affair. He made no reply. What I had to say I said to his face, not behind his back. When I finished I walked out the door. I don't think it was one of Wylie's better days, and I know it wasn't one of mine.

Kirby called me on January 29, 1982. Although under orders not to talk to him, Kirby took time to advise me that John Simpson and Danielle Bouchard got letters of commendation from the Attorney General's Department for their part in the Commisso investigation. Kirby and I laughed because we knew their contribution was limited to looking after the exhibits (that Kirby and I had taken the risk of obtaining) and filing the court brief. Crown Attorney Murray Segal hit the nail on the head when he went over the twenty-three pages of evidence I had amassed during the investigation. He was slightly confused, having been under the impression that Simpson and Bouchard had done the major part of the investigation. When he asked where Simpson and Bouchard were during all the meetings, I told him straight out that they used to sit several blocks away, moving in only afterwards for the tapes and the money that was to be used as evidence. Apart from that, they had little to do with the whole thing. I later learned that the Attorney General's Department intended to give me a letter of commendation as well, but apparently Insp.

McIlvenna shot that idea down saying I was under investigation and that it wouldn't be proper for me to receive such an award. My reward was to follow a short time later.

On February 24, 1982, I was called to S/Sgt. Mike Prisk's office. He was in charge of internal investigations for the RCMP in Toronto, and was less than pleasant to deal with. At any rate, McIlvenna wanted his pound of flesh and he was determined to get it by having Internal Affairs hound me for more than a year. Although I had done nothing criminal, they tried hard to find a chink in my armour.

The following is an outline of the parameters of the investigation:

Cpl. Murphy, I am and have been over the past three months, conducting an internal investigation concerning your conduct during your involvement in handling an informant, Cecil Kirby. You were advised of this on 12 Apr. 81 and the four specific concerns to my investigation were outlined to you, namely:

(a) Prior to 29 Apr. 81 you had knowledge and permitted Cecil Kirby to possess an unregistered handgun and subsequent to having same turned over to you by Cecil Kirby on 20 Apr. 81, you failed to comply with instructions relative to handling of exhibits and failed to appraise your supervisor of having received an exhibit from Mr. Kirby;

(b) Allegations are suggestive that you induced Linda Cadwell to have or arrange to have criminal charges against Cecil Kirby withdrawn. These charges having been preferred by the York Regional Police in the fall of 1980. The charges were in fact withdrawn on 19 Mar. 81;

(c) You are alleged to have given a verbal commitment to your informant Cecil Kirby, that he would never be required to give testimony in court unless he consented to do so. Having given this commitment you arranged for "one party consent authorizations" to be signed by Cecil Kirby knowing full well that the prior commitment rendered such consent forms null and void. All investigation on the cases dealt with under the consent forms was done without the knowledge of your verbal commitment to Cecil Kirby; and

(d) While in the company of Mr. Kirby in the USA., you allowed Mr. Kirby to retain monies he received in payment for the intended commission of a serious offence and you refused permission in allowing tape recording equipment to be carried by Mr. Kirby. Your statements on Form C 237 dated 7 Apr. 81 are a claim on your part that the FBI allowed Kirby to retain the monies and they refused permission for Mr. Kirby to carry tape recording equipment. The FBI state otherwise and the concern here is a false statement by you on Form C 237 dated 7 Apr. 81.

Cpl. Murphy, a further concern has surfaced respecting an apparent payment of monies to Mr. Cecil Kirby on 10 Mar. 81, a sum of approximately $5,000 which you stated to C.F.SEU investigators that such payment was not made. Investigation indicates you had knowledge that payment was made to Mr. Kirby on 10 Mar. 81, and your advice to the contrary as given to CFSEU investigators is of concern as being a false statement. Plus the following two allegations:

That Cpl. Murphy took his gun to the USA in February, 1981, without asking for permission from the Force;

That Cpl. Murphy took a Nagra tape recorder to the USA. in February, 1981, without the permission of the Force.

I was verbally ordered to cease all contact with the few informants I presently had on the go. On March 1, 1982, one of those informants called and advised that the contract to kill Paul Volpe had been given to the Luppino organized crime family in Hamilton. Apparently, my informant didn't realize he wasn't supposed to call. However, since the information was considered reliable, I decided to write a report asking that

I be allowed to approach Volpe with this new information. I felt strongly that if I could convince Volpe that the information was reliable, and if certain conditions were met, he would be prepared to take the same route Cecil Kirby had taken. Volpe's potential for information was immense. He had connections in New York, Buffalo, Philadelphia, Atlantic City, and other locations in the US, as well as Toronto, Hamilton, Montreal, Ottawa, Quebec City and Vancouver in Canada. There was no doubt in my mind that Paul Volpe was living on borrowed time. When organized crime decides your time has come, there is no tomorrow.

My enthusiasm for approaching Volpe was short-lived. The following day I received a direct order on paper that I was to cease all contact with the informant that had supplied the information and, above all, I was not to have any further contact with Paul Volpe. That order was signed by superintendent M.T. Kerchuk, Officer In Charge Criminal Operations. This was incredible. There was something drastically wrong with this situation, and it took me some time to discover just where the problem lay.

Some time later, Sgt. Lou Nave, attached to Insp. McIlvenna's crew, called and asked me to introduce him to the informant that had supplied the latest information on the Volpe contract. I called my informant in the presence of Lou Naive and the answer was really quite simple. He said, "Tell him to go fuck himself."

A short time later I talked to Volpe. He told me that Simpson of SEU had called wanting to talk to him, but that he wanted nothing to do with Simpson because he felt Simpson couldn't be trusted. I was never one to take no for an answer when the opportunity arose for putting bad guys in jail. I met Volpe secretly several times afterwards. The first time I met him after I had been ordered not to talk to him was in an alleyway in the basement of the Four Seasons Hotel. He laughed when I told him I wasn't allowed to talk to him. I honestly believe that the departmental nonsense only served to develop a deeper trust between the two of us. He grinned when he reassured me he would certainly not mention our meetings to anyone. Volpe joked about his bad reputation, and perhaps I should have been more careful about the company I was keeping. I would later learn that although Volpe had been assigned a coded informant's number for reference purposes, he had not been accepted as an informant of the RCMP because they thought he might cause the Force some embarrassment.

I mentioned to Volpe the new information that had surfaced. He said he knew something was in the wind, but had not been able to figure out just what it was. He said for years Jimmy Luppino, son of the late Mafia Boss Giacomo Luppino of Hamilton, had visited him almost on a daily basis, but during the last year Luppino had not come near his house; Volpe had been unable to find out why.

Now he knew.

I told Volpe straight out that they would not miss a second time and he should think about getting out the same as Kirby had done. I know he was giving it serious consideration because he talked about his wife's position with Creed's and how difficult it would be for her if he had to move. He told me he would give it some thought and get back to me. Volpe would often say to me, "Let the bastards come. I'm ready for them," but deep down in his heart he knew it was just a matter of time before they got to him. He knew it and I knew it. I felt strongly that the right moment to turn Volpe as an informant had arrived. If I had been legally permitted to meet with Volpe and had received even a small amount of support from my superior officers, the outcome of this story might be quite different.

Vince Melia had been extradited from the US to stand trial in Canada for the Helen Nafpliotis conspiracy to murder charge. On June 14, 1982 he entered a plea of guilty to that charge . The following is a complete run-down of the persons, charges and the sentences that were handed down as a result of the information received from Cecil Kirby, RCMP confidential source 01901:

Cosimo Commisso:

1981 - Conspiracy to commit murder, three counts including Helen Nafpliotis, Peter Scarcella and Paul Volpe; eight years on each count, concurrent. Counsel to commit murder, two years concurrent.

1984 - Conspiracy to set fires (Guelph Sporting Goods Store); sixteen months consecutive. Conspiracy to possess stolen cigarettes; six months concurrent. Counsel to commit murder conspiracy, two counts; eight years each count but consecutive to the time already being served. On other charges, including extortion, explosion with intent, arson, counsel to extortion, aggravated assault and wilfully setting fires, he received sentences of three to eight years. In total he received more than twenty years.

Remo Commisso:

1981 - Conspiracy to murder, two counts (Scarcella and Volpe); eight years concurrent.

1984 - Conspiracy to possess stolen cigarettes, six months consecutive. Counsel to murder conspiracy, six years consecutive for offences that included extortion, arson, explosion with intent and aggravated assault, he received sentences from three to six years concurrent. In total, he received fourteen years.

Michael Commisso:

1981 - Conspiracy to commit murder, three counts (Nafpliotis, Scarcella and Volpe); two and one half years each count, concurrent.

1984 - Arson; sentence suspended plus two years probation.

Antonio Romeo:
1981 - Conspiracy to murder (Nafpliotis); two and one half years.

Jerry Russo:
1981 - Conspiracy to murder (Nafpliotis); two years and ten months.

Vince Melia:
Conspiracy to murder (Nafpliotis); nine years.

Cosimo Mercuri:
1982 - Second degree murder and arson (Dominion Hotel, Acton); life imprisonment with no parole for ten years.

Mike McCrystal:
1982 - Manslaughter (Dominion Hotel, Acton); two years less a day.

Armando Dicapua:
1983 - Arson conspiracy (Guelph Sporting Goods Store); two years.

Rocco Mastrangelo:
1984 - Arson conspiracy (Guelph Sporting Goods Store); one year.

Bruno Spizzichino:
1984 - Arson conspiracy (Guelph Sporting Goods Store); two years.

Nick Pallotta:
1982 - Robbery (Dolly's Credit Jewellers); two years.

Richard Cucman:
1982 - Robbery (Dolly's Credit Jewellers); three years.

Antonio Triumboli:
1983 - Charge unknown; three years.

Istvan Szocs:
1983 - Attempted extortion; six months.

Richard Corbett:
1983 - Possession of stolen cigarettes; three months.

Armand Sanguigni:
1983 - Possession of stolen cigarettes; three months.

Kirby supplied information that led to the arrest of twenty
more people, including Harold Arviv for the bombing of
Arviv's Disco in Toronto; Yvo Sajet for mischief in relation to
staged robbery at the Hippopotamus Club; and Chuck
Yanover for a plot to overthrow the Government of Dominica,
possession of forty-two pounds of hash, conspiracy to smuggle
gold out of British Guiana, five robberies, two shootings and
information on six unsolved homicides. Kirby was responsible
for saving the lives of Helen Nafpliotis, Peter Scarcella, Paul
Volpe, Lisa Volpe, along with another unknown male—all
within a period of four months. That doesn't include the lives
that might have been snuffed out had the Commissos not been
arrested.

Cosimo Commisso received the most severe sentence of
the entire group, much heavier than I had anticipated. To be
quite honest, I couldn't help but feel some sympathy for the
man. He committed violent crimes and deserved to be pun-
ished, but he also had young children and I know how
important real family means to most Italians. I'm realistic
enough to know it doesn't often happen, but I always hope

that when their sentence is over people such as Cosimo will get out of the violence and tension of criminal activity and rebuild what remains of their life with their wife and family.

My stay at my new posting in Toronto Commercial Crime didn't turn out as bad as I first thought it would be. I never had much of an aptitude for administration work, but I performed my new job as efficiently as I possibly could. I was replacing Cst. Brian Winters as Admin. NCO, and Brian became a valuable friend and trusted confidante who helped me through some bad times during the internal investigation. I will always be indebted to him. My new boss was Insp. Brockbank. Brockbank sincerely believed in getting the job of police work done. He didn't worry as much as other officers over the course his career was taking. He had the respect of his men and encouraged good, honest investigative police work.

I was in the administration job approximately eight months when Brockbank moved me to the Income Tax Section of the squad. Getting back to working on organized crime, I started a project on Walter Chomski, a loan shark from Oakville. Working closely with Detective Noel Catney, Peel Regional Police, we put together a successful investigation, completed on January 29, 1987, that resulted in the conviction and sentencing of Walter Chomski and his associates to huge fines. When all was said and done, they owed almost a half a million dollars in income tax.

On September 20, 1982, I received my final message of 'thanks' from the Commissioner of the RCMP through Insp. Brockbank. He called me to his office and told me he had been instructed to give me an Official Warning. When there is no evidence for a charge, the RCMP usually justifies an internal investigation by giving an Official Warning. Of course, I believed the whole internal investigation to be utter nonsense from the beginning. I wanted my day in court, but never got it. Insp. Brockbank appeared to have no love for Insp.

McIlvenna and was highly embarrassed to deliver the warning, so much so that he didn't even bother to read it to me. I signed it, thanked him for his consideration and left. The following is a copy of that Official Warning:

OFFICIAL WARNING

REG. NO. 23803, M.G. MURPHY
Toronto Commercial Crime section.

Cpl. MURPHY, you are before me today in order that an Official Warning may be administered in accordance with Administration Manual 11.13.1.3.

As a result of the following violations of our Code of Conduct. your actions are being considered as conduct unbecoming a member of the Royal Canadian Mounted Police.

1) As a result of your lack of action between 29 Apr. 81 and 16 Jun. 81, after having received a hand gun from Cecil KIRBY on 29 Apr. 81, you failed to comply with Operational Manual sub-paragraph IV.1.F.1.a. This was compounded by your failure to comply with the direct order of S/Sgt. D.J. KENNEDY relative to the turning over of exhibits to members of the Combined Forces Special Enforcement Unit.

2) By your actions between 1 Nov 80 and 1 Apr. 81, you neglected to inform the N.C.O. i/c Toronto National Crime Intelligence Section and Combined Forces Special Enforcement Unit of the commitment you made to Cecil KIRBY not to allow any Privacy Act tapes to be used against anyone without first obtaining KIRBY'S permission. These commitments may well have rendered subsequent "consents" signed by KIRBY to be null and void knowing full well the tapes were the basis of the evidential material to be used against COMMISSO.

3) By your report of 7 Apr. 81, you misled the NCO i/c Toronto NCIS and investigators within the Combined Forces

Special Enforcement Unit with the following statements, "Source 0-1843 was allowed to retain possession of $5,000 received on 22 Feb. 81 in Stamford, Connecticut. This decision was reached by the FBI and the source," and "I also offered to approach the source to see if he would be willing to wear a body pack, however, the FBI did not feel that it could be legally covered under their laws with which I am not familiar. The decision was therefore reached by the FBI, and not me, nor the source that no body pack would be worn during the meetings which took place," well knowing these items of information were incorrect.

4) Between 10 Mar. 81 and 11 Mar. 81 you misled Sgt. N. ROSS, Sgt. J. SIMPSON, Metro Toronto Police Department, and the Provincial Cst. D.M. BOUCHARD by advising them that Cecil KIRBY had not received any money during his contact with Cosimo COMMISSO on 10 Mar. 81, well knowing that Cecil KIRBY had received $5,000.

5) By failing to obtain permission prior to transporting your service revolver to New York City, USA. on 20 Jan. 81, you were in violation of our Operational Manual instruction II.1.F.4.a.1.

I would like to impress upon you at this time the need for absolute honesty in accounting for your activities at all times while a member of this organization, as well as the need to recognize your true position as a Junior non-Commissioned Officer in a large Force with heavy responsibilities where team-work and following all procedures is most essential. Your conduct in this case, due to your failure to observe the proper procedure in investigative standards, has resulted in consider-able discredit to yourself and to the Royal Canadian Mounted Police, not only within the confines of 'O' Division, but also internationally.

Your actions could clearly have led to Service Court pro-ceedings, but because of your past service and continuing potential, the Commissioner has ordered the lessor form of discipline in order that you may have a continuing career.

You are officially Warned that any future incidents of this nature will be dealt with swiftly and most severely.

Should you feel aggrieved by the administration of this Warning, you are directed to the contents of Administration Manual II.13.M.1. governing appeals.

Acknowledged: Administered by:
M.G. Murphy, Cpl.   R.T. Brockbank, Insp.

On November 2, 1982 I wrote a stinging appeal to the Official Warning and submitted it to the Commissioner of the RCMP. In the appeal I outlined in detail my version of what had taken place, including the lack of support I received, and justification for all of my actions in the Kirby affair.

Soon after, Insp. McIlvenna became laison officer, London, England. Insp. Wylie became officer in charge of customs and excise. Simpson and Bouchard were discreetly sent back to their respective offices. Ironically, McCharles and Ted Bean were put in charge of Kirby and his security. During my tenure with Kirby I had been given a rough time over the smallest of indiscretions I felt were necessary to keep the investigation and my informant on track. Yet while Kirby was under the direction of McIlvenna and in the care of McCharles and Bean, he was reportedly allowed full access to shotguns, a sub-machine gun—even allowed to drive police cars at times—with no reprimands given to the security detail. While these actions would be completely irresponsible, I must admit that, all things considered, I acquired some measure of respect for McCharles and Bean for their handling of Kirby during this time. They helped and supported him, often at their own expense, through some very difficult times.

While I was writing my appeal to the Official Warning, someone passed on to a newspaper reporter—one day prior to our take-down—a press release relating Cecil Kirby's exploits as a police informant. This type of action could have gravely endangered Kirby and ourselves, for, had the reporter printed the story, Remo Commisso could well have been reading about it in the morning paper when Kirby walked through the door on the final day of the undercover operation. Insp. McIlvenna was furious, and so were the rest of us who might have been endangered. McIlvenna apparently became convinced that I was the one who gave out the press release, and he called for a full investigation of the incident. As it turned out, the investigating committee found that it was a Metro Police Sergeant who had previously worked under the direction of McIlvenna, who passed on the release. The Sergeant, who worked directly for McIlvenna, was never disciplined and, in fact, later received a promotion and a transfer to a comfortable position. Fortunately, at the same time I was issued a letter complimenting my handling of Kirby. The letter was signed by an officer from all three forces involved in the investigation (see pages 196-197).

I was further exonerated from unprofessional behavior during my investigations of organized crime by Staff Inspector Bill McCormack, who later became Chief of Metro Toronto Police. He summed up my feelings when he said, "It appears to me, Mark, that petty jealousy was the motive behind the actions of the SEU. You were doing the actual work with the informants, getting all that good information. It seems as though they were simply jealous."

But the Force was not willing to admit that a mistake had been made in giving me an Official Warning. On November 10, 1983, more than one year later, I received a reply to my appeal from the Commissioner of the RCMP, R.H. Simmons. That the force never makes a mistake was clearly pointed out to me in the type of form letter I received (see pages 198-199).

So many times I've thanked God that the RCMP do not police Siberia. On September 24, 1982, I was called to the staffing office and informed that I was being transferred at the direction of the Commissioner into exile, so to speak, and uniform duties in the Province of Nova Scotia. At the very beginning of the Kirby investigation, when we first learned that he was tied in with organized crime, I had told a close friend of mine that I predicted two things would result from my part in the investigation: one day I would be transferred back East where I am originally from, and that I would eventually write a book on the investigation. But I thought that the transfer would be ordered to protect me from threats by organized crime. I didn't realize at the time that a greater danger might exist from fellow police officers.

I would be less than honest if I didn't say that I loved the work on organized crime and miss it desperately. I also miss some of my very close friends from those ten years I spent in Ontario. There are two things that I often wish for. One is that someday someone in the Attorney General's office will see fit to send that letter of commendation that was denied me by Insp. McIlvenna. The second one is only a dream, but someday I would like to return to Toronto as Staff Sergeant in charge of NCIS and conduct some other interesting projects on organized crime.

In the ten years I worked in Toronto, my partners and I started every successful investigation that was conducted by NCIS, and those investigations resulted in the arrest of more criminals than all those arrested previously since the inception of NCIS. People must realize the devastating effect organized crime has on our society. Metro Toronto Police have so much local crime that most of their resources and money must be directed to combat local problems. And I feel the OPP are too affected by politics and a lack of resources to combat organized crime. I honestly believe that the RCMP should be leading the way, not because they are better than other police forces, but simply because they are a national force with the proper resources.

February 16, 1982

The Commanding Officer
"O" Division
Royal Canadian Mounted Police
Toronto, Ontario

Dear Sir:

RE: Unauthorized Release of Confidential Information
     to the News Media - Cecil Kirby (Informant)

As you are now aware the tri-force investigation into this
rather complex matter is complete, and the report has been
submitted.

During the course of the investigation, many policemen were
interviewed. Varying views were expressed on the Informant
KIRBY, as to how he should have been handled. Criticism in
some cases was leveled at various police departments and, indeed,
at various policemen. One message that did come through,
however, was that were it not for the actions of Cpl. M.G. Murphy
in his handling of the Informant KIRBY, this matter may well
not have been successful. For us to comment on the actions of
Cpl. Murphy while handling the Source, would be inappropriate.
We well appreciate the narrow time frame that existed and the
immediate decisions that had to be made by Cpl. Murphy.

We wish to state that Cpl. Murphy was professional in his
approach to the Committee and recalled events in detail.

C.A.M. Cousens
Superintendent
Ontario Provincial Police

W.J. McCormack
Staff Inspector
Metropolitan Toronto Police Force

R.G. Fischer
Inspector
Royal Canadian Mounted Police

81-0-7659

O. I/C "O" DIV. C.C.B.

        FORWARDED for your information. Would you
please ensure that Cpl. MURPHY receives a copy of this
memorandum.

TORONTO   D.H. Heaton, Supt.
82-02-24   Officer i/c Criminal Operations

c.c.: O. i/c C.F.S.E.U.

o/i/c Tor. CCS

Please provide Cpl. Murphy
With a copy, expressing the
Views of the investigating
Committee and their observation
on her handling of the
source in a professional manner

1)   Supt
O/I/C Tor CCB
82/02/25

(O/I/C TOR. CCS)
(Please provide Cpl.
Murphy with a copy,
expressing the views
of the investigating
committee and their
observations on his
handling of the source
in a professional manner.

K.Supt.
O/I/C TOR CCB
82/02/25)

CONFIDENTIAL

1983.04.15.

C.O. "O" - TORONTO

Re: 23803, Cpl. MURPHY, M.G.
____Appeal of Warning_____

Reference is made to Cpl. MURPHY's appeal against the warning
administered to him on 82.09.20. I have carefully read and
considered his submission of the 82.11.02, together with all
other relevant correspondence. Having given this matter
careful consideration I find no reason to support his arguments
and I am, therefore, denying his appeal.

I would like to point out that when this matter first came
to my attention it had been recommended that his conduct was
such that Service Court action was appropriate. At that time,
and after careful consideration, I did not authorize Service
Court action but rather instructed that an official warning
be administered. I did that simply because he has a good
past record of service and a demonstrated potential for a
continuing and worthwhile career in the Force. I am therefore
rather surprised to find an indication on Cpl. MURPHY's part
that he considers the issues in question to be to some degree
frivolous. I would have thought that his attitude would have
been one of relief for not having been dealt with more severely.

In my review of Cpl. MURPHY's appeal I found nothing which would
mitigate or show that any element of the warning was in error.
My review has confirmed that Cpl. MURPHY contravened policy on
more than one occasion and, by his own admission, supplied false
or misleading information to his supervisor. As was pointed out
in the warning, Cpl. MURPHY is a junior NCO in a large and
complex organization where compliance with instructions and
policy is imperative. In addition, members of the Force must
work as a team and when dealing with Sources there can be no
doubt about where the member's loyalty must lie. There is

CONFIDENTIAL   - 2 -

certainly nothing frivolous in giving false or misleading information to superiors and the Force cannot tolerate this type of conduct on the part of its members.

I will not go into detail with respect to the various aspects of policy that were violated as that is already well known to Cpl. MURPHY. I will however remind him that the instructions contained in our policy manuals are there for very good reasons and as a result of long experience in the handling of major cases and dealing with informants. These instructions are to be accepted and practiced by members of the Force if they wish to have a continuing career. Nor can we have our relationship with organizations of other countries marred by members of the Force because they fail to follow our policies, or they engage in otherwise unacceptable practices.

In his appeal Cpl. MURPHY has pointed out that he did a great deal of valuable work in these difficult areas of investigation. That is acknowledged as being a fact and it is exactly what we expect of him and other members in a similar position. It does not however serve as an excuse for conduct that is less than that standard. It is because Cpl. MURPHY showed consider-able promise in the conduct of these cases that more serious discipline was not ordered, however I wish to make it clear to him that he should take this warning seriously rather than regard it as being trivial and unimportant.

Cpl. MURPHY is to be provided with a copy of this decision.

R.H. Simmonds,
Commissioner

C.O., "H" DIVISION, HALIFAX

          FORWARDED for your information and attention as indicated
in final paragraph above, please.

TORONTO   F.A. Howe, A/Commr.,
83-04-26   Commanding "O" Division

Before leaving Toronto, I had several more meetings with Paul Volpe. On several occasions I went to his home at night after work, while other times I met him during the day in downtown Toronto. Under the circumstances, we both watched very closely for surveillance. I would have incurred the wrath of God, himself, had I been caught meeting with Volpe. No matter what my instructions were, I knew that in the interest of justice and the lives that would have been affected, I had no alternative but to pursue the matter in hopes that some day Volpe would decide to become an informant. With each meeting the trust and intangible bond between a copper and an informant, which is hard to describe but so much a part of good police work, was enhanced. I went to his home in Nobleton one evening and he related the following information. He told me there was a Korean international terrorist network operating out of Toronto. In total there were approximately 20 terrorists involved with this group world-wide. Volpe had access to a package that contained a videocassette, several photographs and sixteen tape recordings identifying several of the terrorists in Toronto. In these recordings, the terrorists were discussing plans for terrorist strikes throughout the world. This group had already paid Chuck Yanover, one of Volpe's enforcers, two payments of $120,000 and $160,000, and had offered $1,000,000 to have Yanover assassinate the President of South Korea.

In return for the information on the Korean terrorists, Volpe initially requested that Yanover not receive more than 18 months on his involvement in the Arviv Disco bombing. Volpe even offered to have an undercover copper introduced to the Koreans for whatever follow-up investigation we wished to pursue. Volpe and Nate Klegerman had been on trial the previous year on a charge of possession of stolen diamonds. They had tried to make a deal at that time with Insp. McIlvenna, offering the terrorist package in exchange for beating the charge, but nothing could be worked out. Volpe and Klegerman ended up walking on the charge anyway, and now Volpe was using the package to try to help Yanover.

On another matter, Volpe said that there was talk that Cosimo and Remo Commisso might be deported back to Italy. He said that Remo had returned to Italy looking for the guy that had murdered his father several years ago. When the Mob found out he was there, they began looking for him. They eventually found him, and an innocent guy that was driving Remo around Italy was killed by a shotgun blast, though Remo himself escaped. Volpe felt that Cosimo had too big a mouth for his own good, and that if Cosimo and Remo were returned to Italy they would both be killed.

I now had yet another problem. How could I surface this new information from Volpe? According to my brother in RCMP Security Service, the information was extremely valuable because his branch had a great interest in the activities of the Koreans. I approached my immediate boss, Sgt. Ron Hartlen, and together we briefed Inspector Brockbank. Thank God I was supported by both men. The information was passed over to Security Service for follow-up.

On March 23, 1983, I called Volpe with the blessing of Inspector Brockbank. Cst. Ron Reid was with me at the time. By this time, Volpe just wanted to hand over the terrorist package, apparently with nothing in return. Remember that the Koreans had already paid Volpe, through Yanover, $280,000. It was to his advantage to have the Koreans deported back to their own country, thus alleviating Volpe's and Yanover's responsibility and possible recriminations by the terrorists. Whatever the motives, I'm certain the package would have proved valuable in the fight against terrorism. For reasons that are still not clear to me, I was told that I was not to accept any package from Paul Volpe under any circumstances.

The following is a transcript of the conversation I had with Paul Volpe pertaining to handing over that package:

P.V.:   Hello?

M.M.:   How are ya?

P.V.:   Good.

M.M.:   I'm a little while getting back to you.

P.V.:   Yeah, I been trying to make connections, you know, for you. But I tell you something, there's such a distrust for that McIlvenna, but they don't trust nobody.

M.M.:   Is that right?

P.V.:   Yeah. I gotta build their confidence in this thing all over again.

M.M.:   Is that right?

P.V.:   Yeah, so I'm just waiting, and the crazy part about it, I've gotta go out of town on Friday.

M.M.:   Oh, yeah?

P.V.:   And I don't know when the hell this thing is going to finish. (At the time, Volpe was building a tourist resort in the Cayman Islands.)

M.M.:   Yeah?

P.V.:   And I don't know what the hell . . .

M.M.:   How's it going, do you know?

P.V.:   I have no idea.

M.M.:   Is that right?

P.V.:   Ya know, I'm afraid to even ask about it.

M.M.:   There was something in the paper the other day.

P.V.:   I didn't even take notice.

M.M.:   Didn't you?

P.V.:   No, but, ah, now I may not go away.

M.M.:   Yeah?

P.V.:   Now if I don't go away, I'd like to be in a position so if they do contact me I can call you right away.

M.M.:   Oh, yeah?

P.V.:   You know, because I told you, if they hand that material to me, I don't want to carry it.

M.M.:   No, I realize that. Although, I mean, I don't think there is anything illegal about (carrying) it.

P.V.:   Yeah, I know. What was illegal before?

M.M.:   As long as you don't have any of the equipment that's used to get it.

P.V.:   No, I know that, but in the meantime just because Earl Levy spoke about him he got subpoenaed.

M.M.:   Yeah, I know what you mean.

P.V.:   You understand, so I mean that's why it's such a heavy distrust here . . . that I gotta build the confidence back again.

M.M.:   Yeah.

P.V.:   And I gotta go away to take care of my own affairs.

M.M.:   Yeah.

P.V.:   And if I don't go away and I'm going to continue on with it . . .

M.M.:   Yeah?

P.V.:   So you gotta tell me, can I reach you at the numbers that you gave me?

M.M.:   The numbers I gave you? Oh yeah. Quite some time ago. I think you have my home number, don't you?

P.V.:   Yeah. So supposing I try to give you a call if I don't go away. Maybe I'll call Saturday or Sunday.

M.M.:   Yeah, O.K. Well Saturday and Sunday I'll probably be at home, but, um, that may create a problem.

P.V.:   But I can let you know what the hell is going on. That's all.

M.M.:   Yeah, I guess that'll be O.K. I suppose as long as it pertains to this, that's fine.

P.V.:   That's all it pertains to.

M.M.:   O.K.

P.V.:   No, I'm not phoning to see how the weather is.

M.M.:   Now, I mean, it's just that our people downtown don't want to get into arrangements of any kind until they see what's there. You know.

P.V.:   Well, that's exactly what I say.

M.M.:   And they wanted me to introduce you to one of the SEU guys, eh?

P.V.:   You're not going to introduce me to nobody. I'm going to make arrangements for you to meet them and you do what you want.

M.M.:   Yeah, well...

P.V.:   Listen to me, buddy, what the hell have I got to do with it?

M.M.:   Eh?

P.V.:   I said, I've got nothing to do with it, so what do I want to meet nobody for?

M.M.:   No, I realize that . . . well, as long as you give them the word to go ahead and talk to me.

P.V.:   I'm going to give you the word . . . you do what you want after that.

M.M.:   All right, but all I'm saying is that I don't want to get involved in it either, O.K.? All I'm saying . . .

P.V.:   I know, but I told you that's the only way I could do it. But I gotta tell them that I trust this fellow here (Murphy) and you gotta go along with me, never mind him, it's me.

M.M.:   Yeah.

P.V.:   And you do what you want after that.

M.M.:   Yeah, all right, well . . . I'm thinking about it.

P.V.:   I'm trying to get you that much first. Let me get you all the material, then you go from there.

M.M.:   All right. But I'll have to give it over to somebody, because I don't want to get involved in it, O.K.?

P.V.:   I don't care what you do with it.

M.M.:   And what I'm thinking about is, ah, if you don't want to deal with anybody in McIlvenna's crew there . . .

P.V.:   No, no, forget it. That's the one thing that they are petrified about.

M.M.:   Are they?

P.V.:   Well, that's the whole thing.

M.M.:   Yeah?

P.V.:   I'm trying to tell ya.

M.M.:   I understand you made an offer on it before, and you got . . .

P.V.:   Yeah, they are petrified of this mess.

M.M.:   Yeah, anyway . . . O.K.

P.V.:   Cause they figure it's another double-cross. Guys, listen, please, if you don't want to trust me then let's forget about it. I mean, if you want to go along with me, I'm trying to help you.

M.M.:   Yeah, well all right. I've got a good guy that's involved, a fellow by the name Roach (Sgt. Jerry Roach, RCMP Security Service, a personal friend and trusted police officer).

P.V.:   Oh, yeah?

M.M.:   He's a good friend of mine and I trust him one hundred percent.

P.V.:   I told you that's the only way I'm going to do it.

M.M.:   And I'd like to, you know, let him look after it, eh?

P.V.:   Whatever you want to do with it.

M.M.:   I'll vouch for him, he's one hundred percent, I give you my word.

P.V.:   Well, that's fine as long as you're the one that's doing it and no one else.

M.M.:   Yeah.

P.V.:   You told me you'd do what you want from there.

M.M.:   Yeah, but I don't know whether they'll allow you to take me to him. You know, I don't know whether they'll go...

P.V.:   I told you the first meeting, you're gonna go. There's nobody else gonna go. You can forget about it, I'm not gonna vouch for nobody else.

M.M.:   Yeah, I know what you're saying. Well, I don't know whether they'll go along with that, but I'll put it to them. I'll put that back to them and see what they say.

P.V.:   Well, listen, you better put it to 'em because there is no other way I'm going to do it.

M.M.:   Well, you're not threatening anybody, are ya?

P.V.:   You can forget about it, I'm not going any further.

M.M.:   No, well, I'd like to see the thing come out, because I think it's worthwhile.

P.V.:   So would I, but I'm not bringing no stranger to these fellows here. I mean, it's bad enough that I gotta turn around and say that I trust this man one hundred percent, which is you. I'm not taking no stranger, because they're gonna ask me, "Do you know him?," and I'll have to say, "No."

M.M.:   Yeah, I know what you're saying, but some people have difficulty understanding that, you know what I mean?

P.V.:   Well, I'm telling ya, we can't do it any other way, because you are the only one I'm speaking for.

M.M.:   Yeah?

P.V.:   Who you bring . . . I don't care who you bring.

M.M.:   Well, what I'm saying to you is, if I bring a guy—this fellow Roach that I mentioned to you—if I bring him, he'll be one hundred percent and there'll be no double-cross.

P.V.:   No problem.

M.M.:   He'll just take the stuff, analyze it to see what's there, and determine if it's worthwhile.

P.V.:   That's right.

M.M.:   And if not, we'll forget about it.

P.V.:   Good enough.

M.M.:   You know, it's as simple as that.

P.V.:   Good enough. You'll probably hear from me over the weekend. Now, if you don't hear from me that means I'm gone out of town.

M.M.:   All right, but for how long? Are you going for a couple of days?

P.V.:   Yeah, two or three days.

M.M.:   Is that other thing going to be over with, do you know? (Volpe's going to court on the stolen diamonds charge)

P.V.:   Yeah.

M.M.:   Well, this is it. We would like to get a chance to look at it.

P.V.:   Oh, I know that.

M.M.:   Before you go.

P.V.:   It's been arranged already.

M.M.:   Oh, I see.

P.V.:   If that happens.

M.M.:   O.K.

P.V.:   Somebody's going to hand it to me.

M.M.:   O.K., well as long as we get a chance to look at it before you go. So that way, you know, we'll know what's there.

P.V.:   Oh yeah, don't worry, I'm right on top of it for you.

M.M.:   All right, so I'll talk to you in a few days whenever you get a chance. Let me know when it's ready and I'll try to make arrangements to grab it and have a look at it.

P.V.:   O.K., that's fine.

M.M.:   All right, take care.

P.V.:   All right.

M.M.:   Bye.

Although I tried every angle in the book to cooperate with Security Service and SEU, I was never given the green light to simply pick up this package from Paul Volpe. I could have understood if Volpe had demanded a reward or insisted on a deal, but that was not the case. He had even offered to drop the package in a box at the local train station with no strings attached, but even that was not acceptable to the senior officers of the RCMP. At the time I couldn't for the life of me understand why.

Then I remembered something Paul Volpe had said to me when I mentioned that I had been transferred out of the province. Volpe said, "Maybe you're just getting too close to too many people." I practically begged him to expand on that, but he never would. When he made that comment, a cold chill ran up my spine. I thought back to rumors that had circulated about possible links between polititians and organized crime. Were they just rumors? If not, was it conceivable that I was "getting too close" to the wrong people? Could this have something to do with not accepting Paul Volpe as a police informant?

Before I left Toronto, Paul Volpe asked me and my wife to join him and his wife, Lisa, at the Royal York Hotel for dinner, just to say thanks. I said, "Paul, I know your offer comes from the heart, but I cannot accept, as much as I would like to. Can you imagine what my superiors would say if I was seen having dinner with you? I deeply apologize, but I must say no thanks." I now regret making that decision. He made two other offers to me at this time. One was a fur coat for my wife from Creeds of Toronto, and the other to serve as his manager of the new hotel and casino he was building in the Grand Caymans. I respectfully declined both offers, telling him that though my wife did not have a fur coat and would appreciate it, I could not accept. The position of manager of his hotel and casino didn't interest me in the least. Even though Volpe could conceivably have used my acceptance of a gift to his advantage somehow, I knew from his voice and body language that these offers were sincere and not attempts to bribe. Besides, he knew I could not be bribed.

When I arrived at my new posting, I spoke to Volpe several times, still trying to work something out that would allow us to take possession of the terrorist package. It never materialized and to this day that information lies dormant. I'm convinced acts of terrorism are being committed throughout the world by those Volpe sought to have investigated and imprisoned. His motives were totally irrelevant. It's true that his offer to give us information was somewhat self-serving, but for reasons that still elude me Paul Volpe was never accepted as an informant. I felt at the time, and still feel, that organized crime would have been reeling in fear had the RCMP not missed the boat.

I had been at my new posting in Dartmouth, Nova Scotia approximately eight months. By prior arrangement, Paul Volpe had agreed to call me at a payphone at Fong's Restaurant at 7:00 PM on Sunday, November 13, 1983, in a last ditch effort to arrange the transfer of the terrorist package into the hands of the police. I waited patiently for the call that never came. I knew there had to be a problem, because he always kept his word.

The following day, Monday, November 14, 1983, at 9:00 AM, the phone rang at my office. It was a good buddy of mine, Cst. Brian Reteff, calling from Toronto.

"Have you heard the news?" he asked in an excited voice.

"No, I haven't."

"They just found Paul Volpe's body," said Reteff, "in the trunk of his wife's car at Toronto International Airport, with several shots to the head."

I closed my eyes, not wanting to accept the message I had hoped would never come, yet knew deep down must come some day. It was time to put Paul Volpe to rest, along with the demons that had haunted me since my transfer. I felt somehow Volpe could hear my thoughts, so I passed on a final, silent farewell, "Good-bye to you, my trusted friend."

8

Post-Mortem

I t has been fifteen years since the death of Paul Volpe, and the time has come for me to write the final chapter. Two major events have recently taken place. O.J. Simpson was acquitted of murdering his wife, Nicole Brown, in criminal court, but in a civil suit he was found guilty. The second event was the tragic death of Princess Diana, who was killed in a car crash in Paris, France. O.J.'s case reaffirms my belief that there is a law for the rich and powerful and another law for the poor. Princess Diana's death makes me realize that, unlikely as it may seem, she and Cecil Kirby had two things in common. One is the experience of being under 24-hour security protection. Unless one has experienced this, it's difficult to fully appreciate the stress and tension brought on by being under the watchful eye of security, day in and day out. In Kirby's case, just a few months of the unrelenting pressure of the security net almost drove him crazy. The prolonged effect on a famous personality such as Princess Diana is unimaginable. Their second common thread is analogous to the fox and the hounds. They were both pursued in an unrelenting fashion, one by the paparazzi and the other by the Mafia. If only the fox could speak.

Recently there have been cases where some members of the military have been harassed to such an extent they have committed suicide. Perhaps these tragic incidents have made

some of the commanding officers happy in some sick way. I'm
certain that some officers of the RCMP would have been
delighted had I chosen to exit the Force in the same manner.

The Mafia has long been known as the Secret Society and,
of course, is infamous for its crime and acts of terrorism. There
is another Secret Society, not quite so well known, but in my
opinion not without a detrimental effect on our society. They
are called Freemasons, or simply Masons. Their true origin is
uncertain, though they claim it all began twenty-seven hundred years ago with the building of King Solomon's temple,
and that originally members of the 'brotherhood' were actually
stone masons who worked on many of the great buildings and
cathedrals. Masonry has existed as a fraternity in the British
Isles and continental Europe for many centuries. Masons
would have you believe they are a benevolent organization
much like the Rotary or Lions who promote goodwill, charity
and fair play, but I disagree. I feel their motto "We help kids"
should go on to say "After we help ourselves". The Masons
do support charitable activities such as the Shriner's Hospital
in Montreal, but I feel this doesn't compensate for the negative
impact they have on society. I feel most Masons join solely to
further their worldly ambitions. In other words, like the Mob,
they join to become 'connected'. For those who are interested,
The Brotherhood by author Stephen Knight is an excellent
exposé of the secret world of the Freemasons.

Why include this information about Masons in a story
about the RCMP? I and many others feel that the Masons
cloak their self-serving ambitions with a subterfuge of secret
rituals and a few charitable works. In my opinion the network
of Masons placed in positions of power throughout the RCMP
and other organizations is a breach of the public trust, and
perhaps partially to blame for the premature end to my career.

On my boss's desk I once saw a list of officers in Toronto
who were attending a Masonic Lodge meeting. Of the RCMP
commissioned officers in Toronto at that time, only one or two

were not on that list. When I trained in Regina, most instructors were Masons. Once, a fellow officer in Toronto was called in and told to join the Masons or his career would go nowhere. He chose not to and ended up a Sergeant in Security Service. When I was in the Force almost every Division and many detachments had a Mason in charge. There was once a Heads of Section meeting in Ottawa, and of the approximately one hundred who attended only one French Staff Sergeant, representing his officer who was sick, did not wear the Masonic ring.

I feel that many police officers who rise within the ranks of the RCMP do so because of their Masonic connection, not their performance as a police officer. In my opinion some lack the ability to fight crime, especially organized and drug-related crime. Many commissioned officers that I know never made an arrest, never conducted an investigation, and never had an informant. I can only think they went to the top because they were well connected.

In recent times, it appears many members of the RCMP who are Masons are successful in having their sons and daughters join the RCMP, while other equally or better qualified candidates are refused admission because they are not 'sponsored'. I firmly believe that a federal government enquiry under the Human Rights Act is required to determine the extent of Masonic control of such organizations and agencies as the RCMP, the Justice Department, the Armed Forces, and the Coast Guard.

I should mention that I had an informant in Toronto who was a very good friend and also a Mason. We had some discussions about the Masons and he offered me an application and agreed to sponsor me into his lodge. Needless to say, I gracefully declined. I do not regret my decision, but I often wonder what effect it might have had on my career in what has sometimes been fondly referred to as the 'Royal Canadian Masonic Police'.

One of several commissioned officers in the RCMP that I respected greatly was Inspector Harry Murphy. I don't know his religion or whether or not he was a Mason, and he is in no way related to me that I am aware of, but Harry Murphy was a good copper. He came up through the ranks in Newfoundland and was a tremendous policeman. In my view he was one officer who deserved his commission. When I was exiled to Nova Scotia he was the Asst. CIB Officer. He called me into his office and we had a long talk about what had transpired in Toronto. He read my 23-page appeal to the Official Warning I had received, which had been denied, and wrote a very complementary A5 (memo) to me stating that had he been my Officer in Charge in Toronto, I would have received a commission instead of a warning. He felt that my downfall within the RCMP was an absolute disgrace.

Insp. Ralph Brockbank, ex-officer in charge of Commercial Crime Section, Toronto, where I was put in an administrative position for a few months during the internal investigation, called me into his office one day and told me that he wanted to get me out of the administrative position and back out on the street where I belonged. He's the one who moved me to the Income Tax Section of Commercial Crime, where I immediately started the lengthy joint forces investigation with Peel Regional, headed by a super copper and good friend Det. Noel Catney. I would later be transferred to Nova Scotia while this investigation was still in progress.

A transfer party was held for me in the Sergeant's mess. It was attended by the rank and file of various police forces, Crown Attorneys, and friends who knew the truth of my circumstance. They showed their support in such numbers that they had to move the party from the Sgt.'s mess out to the cafeteria to accommodate the crowd. Insp. McIlvenna had two of his officers attend the party to listen to my departure speech, in the event that I might have made some disparaging remarks about him. Recognizing the purpose of their presence, I took the opportunity to thank Insp. McIlvenna for his intervention in instigating the transfer, a transfer that under different circumstances would have been immensely appreciated by many members from the East Coast serving in Toronto. I learned shortly thereafter that Insp. McIlvenna didn't appreciate the thanks. Anyway, that's better than chasing ducks on Jarvis Street (an inside joke to members of 'O' Division).

In 1983 I was transferred to Cole Harbour Detachment, Dartmouth, Nova Scotia after receiving my Official Warning. It would have been Official Charges had the RCMP been able to resurrect any evidence against me. However, as an honest copper doing an honest job, not unlike hundreds of other members of the Force who would have done the same job, there was not a shred of evidence they could use. I did make some mistakes and perhaps some errors in judgement, but I did nothing criminally wrong.

On January 22, 1985, I wrote then newly elected Solicitor General Elmer M. McKay, outlining serious allegations of political corruption within the Federal Government and grave concerns about possible RCMP corruption pertaining to the Volpe matters. I requested a full investigation. In April of 1985 I received a call from one of MacKay's assistants saying they were concerned. The Minister had read the correspondence and they intended to take some steps to correct the situation. In the assistant's words, "The report is burning a hole in his briefcase." I haven't heard another word since, so I can only imagine his whole damn office is on fire by now.

For the next seven years I was harassed at Cole Harbour. My assessments went from the low nineties to sixty five. One year I handled 125 investigations and I was criticized for working too much. One year I was criticized for coaching juvenile hockey, the next year I was criticized for not coaching. Comments I made in the coffee room showed up on my assessment. When that happened, I stayed out of the coffee room for a year and they criticized me for being antisocial. My assessments turned from bad to abysmal. Some contained obvious untruths, necessitating appeals which, of course, were rejected. When I received my final assessment by a Sgt. Gary House on my birthday, January 29, 1990, it was so horrific that I decided to walk away. I had my twenty-five years in and my pension almost equalled my take home pay, so it was time to go before someone got hurt. After telling Sgt. House what I thought of him and offering to make a new door for his office, I walked out. I handed in my radio and keys, took my regular holidays and some stress leave for a few months, and never went back. One evening I returned to the office and said good-bye to some of the guys. I told them that I was sorry I could not attend a planned retirement party and left a note for the boss. It read, "Staff, I quit, Mark." So ended my career in the RCMP.

After I retired, I taught Law at Holland College for three years. I loved the job and enjoyed the students, who on several occasions invited me to be their guest speaker at graduation ceremonies. Yet I was dumped from the staff immediately after a major change of administration. I'm told my dismissal originated in Ontario. The harassment still continues, but so does life and I have much to be thankful for. I shall always remember a statement made at Princess Diana's funeral, "General goodness is threatening to those at the opposite end of the moral spectrum."

I hope the reader can now understand how I came to respect and trust the likes of Paul Volpe and Cecil Kirby. They were criminals, but they did not do me dirty.

On February 25, 1995, I finally received my 'letter of commendation', not from the RCMP or the Crown Attorney, but from a fellow RCMP officer, which makes it even more meaningful. It reads in part as follows:

Dear Mark,

Thanks for lending me your copy of *Mafia Assassin*. I was impressed with Cecil's understanding of you. I guess he survived so long because of his ability to read people properly. Every comment he made of you is along the lines of everything I and others who know you well enough would believe and appreciate. It is unfortunate supervisors are so often blinded by politics and a lack of common sense. How anyone could treat you the way they did is beyond me.

You were one of a kind, with a rare natural ability as a policeman. I only saw that special talent in a few members of the Force. It is so sad that they didn't appreciate it and treat you the way you deserved. Myself and many others in the Force have a great respect and admiration for you and the great job you did while you were in the RCMP Personally, I expected you to become a senior ranking officer before you retired. Unfortunately, real natural policemen don't always or often make it to the top because of the job they have to do.

My newest RCMP friend is a C/Supt., 26 years service, a sharp, nice fellow, but he was never a real policeman. He has a chance of going near the top, but because of a different, inside career path. I met him through business connections. I'm happy to be on my own now, where you advance by who you are, what you are, and who you help. He is learning from me, and I never call him Sir. It is a great feeling, being independent.

Whatever you do from here on in, your natural ability will be admired and appreciated more than it was in the Force. If you had gone into business instead of the Force, you'd probably be a millionaire by now.

Greetings to the family. I'm willing to bet that the students at the college really admire and respect you more than you'll ever realize.

All the best from Steady Brook,

Cpl. Ken Huxter, Corner Brook, NFLD

You may be wondering what happened to Cecil Kirby, Helen Nafpliotis, and the Volpe murder case. I'll give a brief update, but first let me tell you a little story of interest. Soon after serving as a police informant, Kirby was walking down a street in Vancouver. As he walked by a Salvation Army Hostel, he looked in the window and then crossed to the far side of the street. Suddenly he heard someone yell, "Hey, Cec." He looked back only to see a man by the name of Kenny Goobie standing in front of the hostel. Goobie was a fellow Satan's Choice biker who ran with Kirby a few years earlier in Toronto. You already know the type of activities they would have been involved in, and these guys had done it all. Kirby had two choices; he could run or go back and face Goobie. Kirby figured if Goobie had a gun he would be dead either way, but if not he could physically handle him. Kirby started across the street. As he approached, Goobie extended his hand. They shook hands. Goobie asked Kirby what he was doing in Vancouver and Kirby told him he was just passing through.

Kirby returned the question to Goobie and, to Kirby's amazement, Goobie said, "You're not going to believe this, but I became a Christian two years ago and I am working as a counsellor at this Salvation Army Hostel. I hope to get back to Toronto later."

Kirby said, "That's good. I became a Christian seven years ago. What do you say we go for a coffee?" They did just that, talked about old times and parted company.

In his new identity Kirby would later settle down somewhere unknown even to me. He eventually married and had some children. I believe he operates a small business of some sort. The trust and support we shared during the investigation will never be forgotten.

On the following page is a reprint of a letter sent by Cecil Kirby to RCMP Commissioner Simmonds.

To:
Commissioner Simmonds, RCMP
c/o Cpl. Ted Bean
SEU Section
RCMP Headquarters
Toronto, Ontario

January 25, 1983

Dear Sir,

It has come to my attention lately that Cpl. Mark Murphy has been discredited by the RCMP as to the investigation into the Commisso case, which turned out to be so successful. He has been highly criticized by other officers, who could not possibly measure up to the man or police officer that Cpl. Murphy is. I could not have gone through all of the stress and problems that happened during that investigation without the support and understanding of such a man as Cpl. Murphy. He is the most honest person and police officer that I have ever met. He has not received the recognition he deserves for his part in the most important, successful case against organized crime in Ontario.

I would appreciate your reply to this letter. Thank you.

Yours very truly,

Cecil M. Kirby

To my knowledge Cecil Kirby never received a reply to this letter.

Helen Nafpliotis is alive and well and living somewhere with a new identity. I will always remember how close she came to being snuffed out like a candle on the whim of the Mob.

The Paul Volpe murder case is still officially unsolved after 15 years. No one has ever been charged with this crime.